Praise f

English as a Seco

"I laughed out loud at the exploits of Megan Crane's delectably drawn characters."

—MEG CABOT,
New York Times bestselling author of
The Princess Diaries and *Boy Meets Girl*

"Alex Brennan's British grad school experience is fueled by too many pints, bad pop music, a crush on her teacher, and a wild assortment of friends. Our reading experience is fueled by Megan Crane's wry humor and sharp observations."

—ELLEN SUSSMAN, author of
On a Night Like This

"A rollicking good time with enough pints, pubs, and hilarious personalities to keep you turning the pages. . . . Cheers to Megan Crane."

—JENNIFER O'CONNELL, author of
Bachelorette #1

"Crane's novel is as funny as it is endearing. I couldn't put the book down!"

—SUZANNE SCHLOSBERG, author of
The Curse of the Singles Table

English as a Second Language

MEGAN CRANE

NEW YORK BOSTON

Warner Books

Time Warner Book Group
1271 Avenue of the Americas, New York, NY 10020
Visit our Web site at www.twbookmark.com.

Printed in the United States of America
First Printing: August 2004
10 9 8 7 6 5 4

Library of Congress Cataloging-in-Publication Data

Crane, Megan.
English as a second language / Megan Crane.
p. cm.
ISBN 0-446-69286-7
1. Americans—England—Fiction. 2. Teacher-student relationships—Fiction.
3. Women graduate students—Fiction. 4. Manchester (England)—Fiction.
I. Title.
PS3603.R385E54 2004
813'.6—dc22

2003024368

Cover design by Brigid Pearson
Book design and text composition by L&G McRee

This book is dedicated to the Fabulous Fabula and everyone else that year. You know who you are.

Acknowledgments

To Julie Barer, the greatest agent in the world, Sandra Bark for starting me off, Karen Kosztolnyik for her insightful editing, Michele Bidelspach, and everyone at Warner.

I would never have had the courage to finish a book without the support and example of Kimberly McCreight, and I would never have done anything with *this* book without the encouragement and input of Josie Torielli. I can't thank either of you enough.

Thanks especially to Tanya Jane Patmore, Alison Kilburn, Moyeen Islam, Angela Bate, Adam Hansen, Marta Vizcaya, Maria Sofia Mourtzini, Charmaine DeGrate, Emily Barnhart, Catherine Bennett, Louise Austin, Amanda Lower, Adrianne Crane, and the rest of my family. Also to Elena Thomatos, Cara Cragan, and Jon Reinish. Thanks also to everyone who read the manuscript in its various forms, and anyone I accidentally forgot!

English as a Second Language

One

I decided to go to England because of a guy. Pathetic but true. Not just any guy, but an ex-boyfriend. An ex-boyfriend I had, on more than one occasion, vowed never to think of again.

It's amazing what jet lag can do.

I spent my first night as a graduate student in England not engaged in intellectual pursuits but whacking my elbows into the wall. Repeatedly. I was used to sprawling across the queen-size bed, which had taken up most of the space in my New York apartment, an apartment that seemed vast and extravagant in comparison to my new home. New York seemed very far away. New York *was* very far away.

Somewhere over the Atlantic, after finally giving up on a laughable attempt to sleep in my economy seat, I had had a flash of inspiration. Graduate school, I decided, was an excellent opportunity for a social experiment. No one in England knew me, and I could therefore be the easygoing, happy-go-lucky creature I'd always assumed I would have been without the disruption of a hideous adolescence and a claustrophobic collegiate environment. I could just relax and be Happy Graduate School Me, or at least that was my plan.

The plane landed and the rest of my first day as an expat went by in a blur. I lugged my baggage through customs and immigration, and then onto various trains, which sped through a rain-soaked country I was too exhausted to properly appreciate. I did get the impression of many, many fields in more shades of green than I'd known existed. The university campus, which was to be my new home, sat a good mile or two outside the walls of an enchanting medieval city filled with twisting little cobbled streets and buildings dating from the Middle Ages and before. From the enclosing walls to the towering cathedral, it was a charming, delightful place.

My university accommodation, in contrast, was in a squat little block of concrete housing even farther out than the sprawling concrete main campus. It was, I was informed upon my arrival, about a thirty-minute walk to the city from my house. So much for that whole "located in the dynamic and ancient city" thing in the brochure. Happy Graduate School Me was looking more like Aesthetically Traumatized Me, but I tried to rally. What this meant was that I hid in my room until dark, and then fell asleep.

I sat up in my tiny cot and looked around my tiny room. It was just slightly bigger than a jail cell. Not that I had any firsthand experience with jail cells. The gray morning light from the single window only highlighted the fact that the room was a perfect square. One wall had a built-in desk space with two shelves, a woefully inadequate wardrobe, and a sink. I was overly impressed with the sink, as if having only part of a private bathroom made the whole place somehow luxurious. I had one surprisingly comfortable chair and one less comfortable desk chair, a telephone, which didn't allow for outgoing calls without a telephone account, a small cubby, which could function as a bedside table, and the reasonably comfortable if frighteningly small single bed.

The day outside was rainy and cold. *Welcome to England,* I thought. I was still exhausted, my elbows were bruised, and I was stranded in a foreign country, away from everyone I had ever known. I sank back into my little cot and pulled my comforter up around my ears. Happy Graduate School Me seemed like a fantasy, one right up there with International Rock Star Me. Why had I thought this was a good idea?

Stupid Evan.

This is what happened.

Evan was a nice, cheerful midwesterner who had looked around after graduating from some tiny Michigan college and decided just like that to move to the Big Apple. He made it sound like he'd endured an epic journey, which I imagine it would be, but that's only because my geography gets fuzzy between Philadelphia and L.A.

When I met Evan he was cheerfully working in his marketing job—not a sentence you often read. But it was true. He was a happy guy. Evan was like some kind of big, brawny breath of fresh air.

"Does he speak?" Michael asked archly the first time I paraded him in front of my friends, while Evan and I were in our strange almost-dating phase, which involved nightly phone calls but as yet no kissing.

"He doesn't feel the need to try and impress people with his rapier wit," I retorted defensively. "If that's what you mean." We both looked down the bar to where Evan was leaning, smiling that calm, genial smile of his and not even attempting to intrude on the conversations swirling around him.

"Alex, sweetheart," Michael said gently, "he's not really your type."

But I knew better. Evan was a *real man*, I thought.

My first clue to the contrary was his troubling virginity, at twenty-six years of age. Evan was not just a virgin, he was essentially *untouched*. Think about the ramifications of *that*. He was in love by the second date and rarely out of my studio apartment thereafter.

My second, more alarming clue was the discovery that he cribbed entire lines of conversation from sitcoms. It turned out Evan didn't actually have a sense of humor, he borrowed other people's.

Not that it was all his fault. It just got to the point where the very thought of him made me physically sick to my stomach. This was about two months into the relationship, which had included a terrible Valentine's Day I was still too embarrassed to discuss. (Here's a hint: what happens if those racy suggestions in magazines fail?) So I dumped him. This was a new experience for me, having spent most of my romantic life as the dumpee, on those occasions when the men in my life actually bothered to dump me before (a) disappearing or (b) taking up publicly with someone else. Since there was no way to really bust out and tell someone they made you cringe and you found them revolting, I opted for the fail-safe "it's me" explanation with Evan.

I should have just gone with the basics. *It's not you, it's me.* Let him work out the details. Most Top 40 songs exist to help with this very situation. But, naturally, I had to give it my own special spin. I put on quite a performance. I confessed that I was fucked in the head over my tragic past (about which he knew nothing, of course, because it's not like we talked outside of sitcom re-creations), I was insane, I required therapy, I needed to be alone. It seemed the best way. Until I kept running into him that whole spring and summer and he would ask me in an overly solicitous voice how I was.

Not, "How are you, Alex?" like a normal person upon encountering someone you didn't really wish to see, and speaking to them just to establish that you were not avoiding them.

Evan went with:

"How are *you*—"

Pause. Deep, meaningful look, scanning my expression for signs of the internal struggle.

"—*feeling*, Alex?"

Jerk.

Evan had gotten decidedly less cheerful after two months with me and could therefore infuse that simple question with whole paragraphs of resentment and hurt. He looked at me like I'd just escaped from the nearest mental asylum. Like I was the crazy woman I'd told him I was.

"Who the hell hears some lame excuse about a

mental breakdown, which is obviously just someone trying to be nice while breaking up with someone else, and *believes* it?" I demanded of my friends. Robin smirked, and settled back into the chair she and her boyfriend Zack were sharing, despite the heat and humidity of the June evening.

"Evan, of course." She exhaled a crisp stream of smoke and shrugged. "Like that's a big surprise. The guy's a dork."

Zack and Robin had been together only a few months, but he was already savvy enough to keep out of any conversation that involved that much gesticulating with lit cigarettes. He only shrugged when I glared in his direction.

"And," Michael added wickedly from the other side of the table, "you did, after all, *deflower* him."

Some months later, I was engaged in a run-of-the-mill existential crisis over my life. Or, to be more precise, my stunning lack thereof. Oh sure, I had friends, but everything else just sucked. I hadn't had so much as a fleeting crush on anyone in ages, and the longer Evan remained my Most Recent Ex, the more convinced I was that he was somehow hexing my future chances. More to the point, there was my "career."

I had been working as a paralegal at Smug, Loaded, Mean & Corporate since graduation, which was just over three years behind me that fall. It was fine, as far as dead-end jobs went. Every year there was a new crop of bright young college graduates, most of whom were spending a year or two toiling for demanding and horrible lawyers as a stepping-stone to their own careers as slave drivers of the same ilk. I had figured out pretty quickly that I wanted no part of law school or, for that matter, lawyers of any kind. I just didn't know what I wanted to do instead.

I was no one's idea of an exemplary employee. Six months into my first job and I was less than impressed with the whole "work for a living" deal. I hated the hours, the drudgery, the having to be nice to people you disliked. You could say I had an attitude problem, one that did not go unnoticed by my supervisors.

I was floating a handful of boring cases and tried to pretend that they filled my days, but this wasn't true. My supervisor trolled the halls for evidence of slackers and caught me out one time too many. She sat me down and told me that it was time to shape up, and as punishment she sent me to Jay Feldstein, the high king of assholes in a firm boasting a roster of hundreds.

No one ever pretended it was anything but a punishment. In return, I didn't pretend to misunderstand the truth: they were giving me to Jay to run me out of there.

Unluckily for them, he liked me.

Jay Feldstein took over my life. I became, for all intents and purposes, his property. I worked only on his cases, subject only to his mercurial moods and unreasonable demands. The most immediate benefit of this was that it made me untouchable as far as my supervisors were concerned. Unfortunately, it also meant I had to field Jay's phone calls night and day, be available around the clock, and jump when he bellowed. And the man did a lot of bellowing.

After two and a half years of his shit, I was well beyond burned out and into a whole different realm. Cue the existential panic.

"Evan is not hexing you," Zack assured me around his drink one October night as I was bemoaning my singlehood while dodging calls from Jay on my cell phone. "Why are we still talking about that guy?"

"Maybe it's not such a shock that you haven't been doing so well in the romantic department," Robin offered, watching my phone vibrate across the tabletop as if performing an electronic belly dance for the overflowing ashtray. "For all intents and purposes, Jay is the man in your life."

A wake-up call if ever there was one.

Except—wake up and do what? All I knew was what I didn't want. I didn't want to stay in the mess and mayhem that was New York. I loved New York, don't get me wrong. I thought everyone should be lucky enough to live there at one point or another, but you could definitely stay too long. Something happened after too many years in New York: you curdled, or maybe it was just the last dregs of your optimism drying up, and then the next thing you knew you were a forty-two-year-old "career woman" too mean to even bother with cats.

But I didn't know where I wanted to go. Or what I wanted to do when I got there. I had dreams, but they were vague things with no real substance. I wanted to be famous, or really rich, or wildly successful, but that was as far as the dream went. My whole life was fill-in-the-blank.

• • •

It was coming up on Thanksgiving when I ran into Evan in a bar I would have told you was far too cool for the likes of him, something Michael was quick to reiterate. This was due to Evan's mild yet pervasive homophobia, and Michael's avowedly fragile loser threshold. Nonetheless, I was feeling like a beacon of friendship—the result, no doubt, of tequila.

Poor Evan, I actually thought, as I unwound my scarf from my neck.

"You look good," I said. This was technically true, given what he had to work with. He still repulsed me. It was unimaginable that I had ever allowed him to touch me. I could tell that Michael was entertaining much the same thought.

"I feel good," Evan said, as if agreeing. "You look tired."

"Work," I said lightly, shrugging.

Over Evan's shoulder, Michael was rolling his eyes. *You look tired?!* he mouthed. I ignored him.

"I thought you wanted to quit?" Evan asked, in a tone that suggested I had lied to him and he was onto me.

"I don't know," I said breezily. "I'm thinking I might go to graduate school." I hadn't thought much about graduate school one way or the other, but Evan had always been intimidated by the college I'd gone to, so why not attempt to be intellectually superior?

"Huh," he said. "Graduate school. Where?"

"Who knows?" I asked grandly. Robin and Zack, who refused on principle to speak to Evan, were off down the bar trying to con free cocktails from Nigel, the British bartender of indeterminate sexual orientation. "I'm thinking about Oxford," I drawled, aiming for blasé. "In England," I added, as if I didn't expect him to recognize the name.

And Evan laughed.

Evan, who had attended an unknown college somewhere in backwater Michigan and found tabloids intellectually challenging, laughed. He tilted back his great big dork head and let out a hoot of laughter. Derisive laughter, it goes without saying.

"What?" I said then, edgily, my eyes narrow. I felt like punching him. Michael pursed his lips as his eyebrows inched even higher.

"Like you could get into Oxford," Evan said dismissively.

Which was how I decided, right then and there, that I would.

Not that it was that simple.

Evan—and I can't stress how much this annoyed me—turned out to be right about Oxford. I would eventually announce to an old college professor that I had been rejected from Oxford, which would make him cackle. "You're in very good company," he told me.

But first things first.

I woke up the morning after running into Evan with my mind made up. This was a new sensation—maybe the first time in my twenty-five years I'd ever felt a sense of purpose.

"I think I should go to grad school," I announced at a very hungover Sunday brunch. "In England."

"Of course you should," Robin agreed. Despite being dragged out of Zack's bed for this summit meeting, she was looking perfectly composed—her specialty. "It's perfect for you."

"And it beats the hell out of working," Michael contributed in a surly growl from behind his dark glasses. He was opposed to rising before 3 p.m. on weekends and was there under protest.

"I could escape from Jay," I mused.

"You could find Mr. Darcy," Michael said, rallying. "That's reason enough."

And that was that. I requested application materials from the top ten British universities and started firing off applications to those that had master's programs I found even vaguely interesting. With my applications headed across the ocean, it was time to turn my attention to the more pressing issue of funding. I could apply for a loan from any number of places, but I thought the best interest rates and repayment schedules were likely to be offered at Bank Dad. With that in mind, I spent hours when I should have been filing Jay's cases writing up a graduate school proposal I thought might appeal to my father, Captain Corporate America. I took it home with me for Christmas—the actual day of Christmas, which was all the free time Jay would begrudge.

"What do you need another degree in English for?" my father wanted to know. He looked stern and disgruntled. Possibly the effect of his jolly red and green sweater, which I was trying to ignore. "Are there actually jobs if you do more of it?"

"Well." I went for a pensive expression. "There's teaching."

His fantasy of a comfortable dotage spent in style at my expense took a serious hit. His brows lowered.

"Teaching," he said, eyeing me. The way someone might say "grave digging." We were sitting in his study, on opposite sides of his desk, almost as if I was applying for a job. "And why exactly do you have to go to England?"

I was actually prepared for that one. "Master's programs in England are only a year long," I told him. "So if I hate it, I'm not trapped for two or three more years."

He liked that. He'd had to foot many a bill over the years, and he knew a little something about my attention span.

"I'll have to think about it," my father said gruffly, which, historically, meant yes. "Let's see if you get in anywhere. Wasn't there some problem with your grades?"

"My grades were fine," I said through my teeth, and then returned to what remained of Christmas Day.

Oxford was the only rejection I got, having been too chicken to apply to Cambridge. I then had to choose between two northern British cities I'd never seen—one I'd never even heard of. My parents had been to the more famous of the two and vouched for its beauty. The university there offered the most exciting program I'd located across England. The campus, moreover, was arranged around a small lake in the glossy brochure, which reminded me of my undergraduate days. So that was that. All I had left to do was wait for school to begin next fall.

I took great delight in giving Jay a month's notice on an airless August day when he was already in a foul mood, and even enjoyed training my terrified replacement.

"You must be kidding me," Jay bitched on my last day. "Why are you doing this? What kind of money are you going to make with an English MA? At least go to law school."

"I'm not so impressed with lawyers," I said. He let out the bark that was his version of laughter. This was probably the closest we ever came to having a moment.

"Well," he said gruffly, the moment over with a flick of his cunning little eyes, "good luck to you. And send that moron in here on your way out."

I spent my last days packing up my small, cramped studio apartment into boxes and sweltering in the summer heat.

The closer I got to my departure date, the more at ease I felt, which went against the grain. I was nothing if not a coward. I'd been a disaster before leaving for college. The unknown usually filled me with panic. But for some reason, maybe because it was all still too huge and too unimaginable, the prospect of going to England was nothing but exciting. As if I'd finally located the path to my destiny and knew it, and could therefore simply relax into it.

"Are you nervous at all?" Robin asked. She was taking one of the rare lunch breaks her workload allowed her.

"I guess so," I said, although I wasn't. "But I think I'm going into it with the right attitude. I get to do nothing but read books, talk about them, and then write about it. What's there to be nervous about?"

The week before I left was crammed full. I visited my grandparents. I moved the last of my possessions into the attic of my parents' house and argued with my mother over the things I needed to take with me across the ocean. I drew the line at canned vegetables.

"It's *England*," my mother kept saying darkly. "You don't know the kinds of things they eat there. Spotted dick is a *dessert*."

I didn't think I wanted to know what spotted dick was, but I did know I was unlikely to eat canned succotash. Rather than argue, I just removed the cans she secreted in my luggage and returned them to the pantry.

I commandeered my mother's car and road-tripped around the greater New York metropolitan area. I spent time with my friends and shopped for things I was sure I wouldn't find in England. Like coffee.

I ran into Evan while Michael and I were having a goodbye dinner. It was one of those gorgeous September nights; leftover summer weather that made the city shine.

"Oh lordy," Michael hissed, "you won't believe who just walked in. And he's with a *girl*."

Sure enough, Evan was toting a petite blonde with ruthlessly styled hair. He saw us, grabbed the girl in an aggressive handhold, and swaggered over.

"Oh my God, sweetie," Michael exclaimed under his

breath, "I think you're supposed to be jealous of his little Kewpie doll."

The girl visibly reacted to my name, which made Michael and me smile.

"Evan's mentioned you," the girl said. With a definite tone. I decided she wasn't in and of herself offensive, despite her choice of man. After all, I'd been there too.

"I just bet he has," Michael murmured.

"Behave," I warned him, and smiled up at Evan. Guilelessly.

"And what are you up to?" he asked. He was smug, his round face triumphant. As he hunkered there over our table, I could see his thoughts traipse across his face. All of them insulting.

"Not much," I said. "I'm just hanging out. I finally quit my job and I'm going to England next week." I could see Michael's widening grin from the corner of my eye.

"A weird time to visit," Evan said, visibly failing to make the connection.

"No," I said gently. "Not to visit." I waited for it. "To graduate school."

It was even better than I'd thought it would be, in those months I'd plotted it. The perfect moment and a fitting end to the story of Evan.

And so what if he thought I was going to Oxford?

Clearly, I thought now from the depths of my narrow cot, I needed to learn when and where to throw down the gauntlet with irrelevant people.

Two

The fact that Evan was my first thought in my new life was so depressing that I sat up too quickly and rapped my bruised elbow into the wall again. The good thing about the paralyzing pain was that it completely blocked out any further thoughts of Evan, along with my creeping self-pity. I might not actually *feel* the way I thought an ace world traveler ought to feel, but I decided that I was more than capable of *acting* perfectly confident. Happy Graduate School Me, in fact, exactly as planned. There would be no lurking around in bed. There was a whole country to explore! Moreover, my mother had given me strict instructions to call home, so I kicked off the comforter and set off for the little nearby village to scare up some supplies and one of those red telephone booths everyone knew dotted the landscape.

To get to the village from Fairfax Court, my new home, I had to walk through a courtyard to the fence and climb over a stile, then amble along a "public foot-path" past a field and a farm with numerous geese, and then eventually to a single street containing a handful of shops and two pubs. The phone booth, depressingly, was glass and not in the least red, and my mother was less than amused to be woken before seven in the morning her time.

"You must try to find some vitamins," she told me, her voice foggy with sleep. Was she dreaming about vitamin compounds? "While you still have the strength."

I sighed. "Go back to sleep, Mom. I have vitamins."

The walk back to my new home was actually kind of pretty. Wet greens and russets laid out beneath the gray sky. The quiet of the countryside all around me. I felt a surge of something I interpreted as confidence. Look at me! Wandering around a foreign country, independent and intrepid, responsible and free!

I spent the rest of the day alternating between unpacking more clothes that were never going to fit in my wardrobe and hovering around the communal kitchen, striking up conversations as housemates wandered in to arrange such things as their pots and pans. It made the day go by pretty quickly, and before I knew it dark had taken over outside.

I was standing at the window with a cigarette, and smiled encouragingly at the dark-haired girl who came over and joined me. She asked for a light. We squinted at each other through the smoke.

"Cristina, right?" I asked. Someone had introduced us briefly over the rationing of refrigerator space. If I remembered correctly, she was Spanish.

"Yes, Cristina," she said. "And you are Alexandra?"

"Just Alex." We smiled at each other.

"So," Cristina said, exhaling a stream of smoke. "This Graduate Welcome Party tonight could be fun, yes?"

"Definitely," Happy Graduate School Me replied.

The only other American in the house, a midwesterner named George, bustled in. He did not exactly fill me with national pride. There was his midwestern twang. And flannel plaid pants. George, I should state for the record, was just a little guy, kind of like a young Ron Howard—all red hair, brown eyes, and corn-fed obliviousness.

"Hey," I said. We'd met after discovering that we shared both a wall and a nationality in the upstairs hallway. "Are you coming to this graduate thing?"

George sniffed. "I can't really invest the time," he said. "I'm only going to be here for a year, so why waste all that energy meeting people? Anyway, I'm already really busy."

Cristina, I saw, was gaping at him in astonishment. *Pompous little twerp,* I thought. I forced myself to smile.

"Obviously," I said, "the lure of free alcohol is the best part of the whole thing."

"I'm going only for a small time, and then to the pub," Cristina interjected quietly. "If you want to do that instead."

"I only go out drinking when I want to pick up women," George told her, expansively. "And I'm not in the mood for it tonight."

In the stunned silence that followed this proclamation, we watched him march back out of the kitchen, clutching a can of Coke to his chest. Cristina and I looked at each other, then at the single British member of our household, who stood across the kitchen, also staring. Melanie's eyebrows were high on her forehead.

"That," Melanie said into the silence, her lips twitching, "is a tremendous disappointment for us all, I think you'd both agree."

We all started laughing. And so began Orientation Week.

Way back when, when I arrived at my undergraduate college, I formed a tentative friendship with Robin, my roommate, but otherwise found the whole college experience overwhelming and upsetting. I dealt with this by hiding in my room. I didn't really come out of it until second semester, when Robin dragged me. She and Michael had drunk their way through first semester, the way you were supposed to, to get it out of your system.

It's only during those early weeks that people really let loose, when no one knows anyone and identities float around, up for grabs. As time goes on, you become known and you are accorded a certain place in the social order and a personality to match, and it's much more difficult to let go. Which I thought might be a good thing, when all was said and done. Letting go had never led me anywhere I wanted to be.

Fast-forward to England and a case in point: his name was Karl, and he was from Germany. Karl was the first German I'd actually met. He resembled all the blue-eyed, blond-haired, preppy boys who had failed to notice my existence throughout my youth, like Billy Peterson, High King of the sixth grade. Over the course of that first incredibly drunk week I slept with him on three separate occasions, which made me feel better because at least it wasn't a one-night stand.

For a change one night, I was staying in until around nine, trying to work out Internet access from my room. I was determined to figure out how to check my email without having to trek all the way to campus to use one of the ever-crowded computer rooms. I was cursing at the stupid telephone system when there was a knock at the door.

"Come in!" I called, intrigued. No one had knocked on my door before. I lived directly over the kitchen—the house's single communal space—and could therefore hear people banging around, so I usually went down and investigated if I craved companionship.

Cristina poked her head around the door.

"I'm sorry to bother you," she said, "but I just ran out of cigarettes—"

"Oh, come in," I said, waving my pack. "I have lots of cigarettes. I imported them all illegally."

She laughed, and came in to perch on the end of my bed.

"Are you going out?" she asked, taking the cigarette I offered.

"There's that disco," I said. "I might go later. It's open until two."

"In Madrid," Cristina said sadly, "we go out at midnight. Everything is so early here."

"Tell me about it," I muttered. "I've never heard of anything closing at eleven."

We settled into the cigarette, using my bed like a couch. We analyzed our housemates, particularly

George. We started off shyly but quickly realized that we had similar opinions.

"He really makes me ashamed to be American," I admitted.

"He makes me ashamed to be human," Cristina retorted. "It's terrible that he's right next door to you."

"I never hear him," I said, frowning at the wall. I sighed. "Although I wouldn't be surprised if he's heard me. Someday I hope to grow past the need to get wildly drunk in the company of men I wouldn't ordinarily speak to." I shrugged.

Cristina froze, and grabbed my arm.

"You too?" she squealed. "I've been going crazy! You wouldn't believe what's been going on. And who can I talk to? George? It's all a mess!"

"I think it's this place!" I told her in a sudden rush. "I think it does something to people. I don't normally behave this way, really."

"The happenings, the craziness . . . " Cristina sighed. "And no one at home can understand." She waved her hand in the general direction of the window. "I think in this rain, everyone goes a little mad."

It was the most comfortable moment I'd had yet. I was delighted.

"More than a little mad," I said. I lit a fresh cigarette and eyed her.

She laughed. "What is it?"

"You tell me yours," I offered, "and I'll tell you mine."

Cristina considered for a split second, then grinned. "Fine," she agreed, "but it stays in this room. No one can know."

"God, no!" I shuddered. "I'd actually deny it ever happened to the guy it happened with."

"Exactly!" Cristina exclaimed, with a cackle. She stole a new cigarette of her own and curled her legs up beneath her. "Okay. Have you met any of those Greek guys yet?"

Cristina and I toasted our new friendship with nightly tequila and cruised through the graduate functions together, sometimes joined by the calming influence of the much more sensible—and usually sober—Melanie. The three of us forged an immediate bond, based on Cristina's and my bad behavior and Melanie's ability to soothe.

Cristina's theory about her own encounters with the brooding, not even attractive Yannis was that he was a necessary introduction to life in the global village, and her actual boyfriend had yet to turn up. We all liked this theory. I felt it went a long way toward explaining Karl, who I saw around a lot but had managed to avoid after round three.

"It's to do with acclimation," Melanie soothed. "Perfectly acceptable behavior."

It was not until the second week that I remembered the reason I was in England in the first place: that whole master's degree thing. Cristina and Melanie were both doing MSc degrees in economics, along with what seemed like half the graduate school population, and they'd gotten started at once and with vigor. The English department didn't seem to be quite so worried about getting into the swing of things.

Our introductory meeting was at noon on a Tuesday. I arrived about five minutes early and saw the only other person I'd met from my same course already there. She was another American, a girl named Suzanne, and all I really knew about her was that she was my age, had an impressive mane of blazing red hair, and giggled. A lot. I had elected to overlook the giggling, what with my vow to be Happy Graduate School Girl.

"We think this is the right room," Suzanne told me in a confiding tone, a touch too intense for the situation. "Do you think this is the whole class?"

I looked around at the handful of people scattered along the hallway and couldn't see a single person I could imagine wanting to talk to. There was a very tall girl with the hunched shoulders and crooked neck that spoke of years of body issues. There were three Asian girls murmuring to one another, the melodic notes of their language and laughter cascading around the echoing hallway. There was a scruffy-looking guy who was actually crouched down on the floor, his nose in a book. I thought that was an obvious and irritating attempt to curry favor with the professors, should they ever turn up, and disliked him immediately on principle. The fact that he was also kind of hot just made it worse.

I smiled my Happy Graduate School Girl smile at Suzanne. "I'm sure more people will show up," I said.

Suzanne returned to her activity, which looked like some drooling over the scruffy-and-yet-hot guy on the floor, and I was suddenly gripped by panic. What was I thinking? Did I even *want* a master's degree? I could hurl bullshit around like a master, but I hadn't had a single academic thought since I left college. We'd all received a list of suggested reading with our entrance packets, and I'd read all eight of the novels, but that was it. I didn't have any opinions to go with the books. What if I just wasn't cut out for this?

My panic attack was interrupted when the door to the room swung open and a throng of students were let out. Dutifully, our group straggled in. It looked to be a group of about fifteen. I didn't think the students who filled the room were much of an improvement on my initial analysis, though I allowed for the fact that I might just be scared. They were all strange and stiff. All dressed oddly. I tried to modify my expectations of what clothing meant about the wearer. I was probably the one dressed oddly. This wasn't my country, what did I know? They were probably a group of fashionistas.

The scruffy-and-yet-hot guy was no longer crouched on the floor—he was standing and I was staring at the big threadbare patch of sweater on his elbow. He looked bedraggled, including his hair, but I suspected gel was involved. What kind of affectation was that? I wondered. If you were that hot—and since he was standing there was no getting around it—why pretend to be scruffy?

"Welcome," he said. I jumped. "I'm Sean Douglas, and I'm the course convener of the MA in Contemporary Literature: Fictions of Choice."

I could feel the flush heating up my entire face and crawling down my neck. I was probably beet red. Worse, Sean Douglas, course convener, had a wicked little gleam in his hazel eyes, which suggested he'd tracked my thought process. *Not hard to do,* I snapped at myself, *when he's all of three feet away from you and you were staring at him.*

I missed whatever welcoming remarks he was making, and when I could look again he'd started a round-the-room introduction session, another one of my least favorite things. I didn't have time to worry about my embarrassment, as a fresh one loomed. I hated all of that stuff. I never remembered anyone's name, or even what they said, unless it was particularly funny. For one thing, I had a terrible memory even when not augmented by alcohol. And for another, who had time to listen while mentally rehearsing speeches?

"Hi," I said when it was my turn. I reminded myself to smile. "My name is Alex. I'm from New York and I don't have a favorite book."

Short and sweet and to the point, I thought, and not annoying like Suzanne's ode to some Salman Rushdie carnival of cleverness, delivered from behind a cascade of red locks.

"We'll have to see what we can do about that," Sean murmured, smiling, in what felt like an incredibly intimate tone. I felt it in my toes.

Oh no.

He went on to talk about the schedule of classes, and to hand out photocopies of an article we were expected to read for our first theory seminar.

I studied him. He was young, maybe thirty? Thirty-five? It was hard to tell. He didn't look like any professor I'd ever seen. Sean looked like another graduate student. He had too-long dark hair and those disconcerting hazel eyes, and was wearing a pair of jeans that looked far too old to actually stay in one piece. And that threadbare sweater. And sure, everyone had a British accent, but that didn't take away from the impact on my susceptible little American system. Sean's accent sounded Scottish. Of course, I then allowed myself to notice that he appeared to be in excellent shape—

Just stop right there, I ordered myself. *Is there a bigger cliché? Get a grip*.

But there was no getting around it. Sean was way too hot for a teacher.

I was happy to escape into the rain, away from his far too knowing gaze. I started the long slog toward Fairfax Court and was joined by Suzanne.

"Wow," she said, in that *I have a secret* tone. "I totally have a crush on our professor."

My first literature class finally rolled around, and I was excited. Literary theory was a muddle, but books I was confident I could do. Bring on the books! I found my way to my seminar room with only minor difficulty—the first floor in England, I discovered, is not the same as the ground floor. I exchanged polite smiles with the other people in the room, all eagerly anticipating our 2:45 class, and settled into an empty seat.

We waited. And we waited.

I doodled in my brand-new notebook. The only people speaking were two girls, far down the table from me. The rest of us stared dully into space, or out the window at the approaching dark, or flipped listlessly through the book we'd been instructed to read. At 3:10, a professor I'd never seen before rushed into the room to inform us class was canceled. Our regular lecturer was unable to make it, having mixed up the times and gone off to Edinburgh for the weekend.

I wasn't very impressed. I would one day have to pay my father a lot of money for that class I hadn't just had. In my head, I started composing fiery emails I would inflict on my New York friends.

People were filing out of the classroom, and the disheveled guy in front of me turned around and aimed a smile at everyone behind him. Which was just me and one other classmate.

"Anyone fancy a pint?" he asked.

As it turned out, we all did.

"I'm Toby," he told me as we walked down. "You're American, aren't you?"

"Do I have a sign over my head?" I asked, smiling. He had dirty-blond hair and eyes like dark chocolate.

"Not at all," Toby said. "But you don't look English."

"Is that a compliment or an insult?"

"You're from New York," he said. "I can hear it."

The guy behind me finally chimed in. "Also, you prat, she announced she was from New York at our first meeting." He grinned at me, displaying laser-blue eyes and dimples. "I'm Jason."

The three of us ended up arranged around a table in one of the campus bars. Jason plunked the first round of drinks on the table and grinned. He threw himself into his seat.

"Right then," he said. "First, a toast." We all lifted

our pints. "To lectures that never were and pints at three in the afternoon," he intoned. Glasses clinked together. Jason took a healthy swig and waggled his brows at Toby and me. "Now—impressions. Is Sean Douglas a ponce? Was that book a waste of a decent, oxygen-producing tree? We'll start with you, New York. Don't feel you have to hold back simply because you're a cultureless Yank."

Three

"And actually," I said forcefully, some days later in one of the village's two pubs, "I hate theory. Obtuse, circuitous, impossible stuff. We are all here because, at some point in our lives, we decided we loved books. It's as simple as that." I slapped my palm on the table for emphasis. Jason, in the midst of lighting his roll-up cigarette, flinched, and fixed me with a warning glare from his pretty-boy blue eyes.

"Steady," he warned, laughter spoiling his attempt at a stern expression.

"It's about *love*," I ranted intensely. "Love of stories, love of novels, love of writing! It comes from *love*, this desire to pursue advanced degrees in something pretty much the whole world will never see as valid or useful! It comes from love, and in return they give you narrative theory! Love turns to semantics! It's the tragedy of higher education!"

"Brennan," Toby sighed from his position in the corner, his head tilted back against the wall, "you're pissed out of your mind and talking shit. Please reign in the philosophizing and tend to your pint."

"That's very deep, Alex," Jason agreed. He let out a stream of smoke and cocked an eyebrow at Toby through the haze. "No more vodka for Brennan."

"Obviously," Toby said.

I was entirely too far gone to care about vodka restrictions and waved them both off. Plus I was currently drinking a pint of delicious lager.

Toby raised his head and focused on me, which took just long enough to indicate his own intoxicated state. "In any case," he said, "you still have to write the paper, and I suspect a bit of literary theory would be appreciated. That being what we're here for."

"Enough moaning about papers," Jason decreed. He pointed his roll-up at me. "Get the drinks in, Brennan. I'm having coherent thoughts."

"That's terrible," I murmured in sympathy. I gulped down the remainder of my pint and set off to remedy the situation.

The next day, however, I was completely out of coherent thoughts as I sat in my little cell of a room and stared balefully at my computer screen. Our first assignment was a relatively short "position" paper. Its purpose was to allow our teachers to assess our standard of work, and it was left ungraded in case that standard was low.

It was driving me crazy. I didn't know how to write academic papers any longer—in point of fact, I wasn't sure I had ever known how. I'd just winged it back in college. This time around, I felt drastic measures were called for and sat there in misery with the MLA Handbook on one side and the university's Graduate Handbook on the other. Notes on style, format, and footnotes, however, weren't terribly helpful when one had yet to write anything.

Toby and I walked to campus on class days and were sometimes joined by Suzanne. All of us lived in connected houses around the same courtyard. Suzanne's kitchen was directly across from mine, which I was already starting to find a bit wearying. She was nice enough, but had a tendency to both drop by and vent at great length. Within a few short weeks of meeting her, I knew far too many of her outrageous personal details and was amazed that there were any stories left for her to tell. But there always were. One night she kept Melanie, Cristina, and me up for hours as she shared, in detail and without solicitation, the experience of losing her virginity to a playboy named Jim at summer camp.

"She seems very nice," Melanie ventured when Suzanne had gone, and our kitchen seemed to echo her revelations. "But perhaps a bit lost. And even a little bit mad."

"She is always here," Cristina groused, emptying the wine bottle into her glass. "Are you her confessor? Must the entire campus know that Jim claimed to love her in exchange for her body?"

"And yet returned to Nina, his long-suffering girlfriend, despite their night of love," I reminded her. Cristina rolled her eyes.

Melanie sighed. "I had no idea American summer camps were so filled with intrigue. I was under the impression it was just sport and a lot of very agitated singing."

The three of us spent hours around that kitchen table, having coffee and cigarettes and watching our fellow students happen back and forth in front of our windows. It was better than television. When Suzanne came, Cristina would recede behind her accent and Melanie would simply smile. Not that it stopped Suzanne, who was the sort of person who believed intimacy involved the spilling of her soul at short notice, and without embarrassment. I thought Suzanne's visits were a handy distraction from work, she certainly seemed to need friends, and we could talk about how hot Sean Douglas was—a subject Jason and Toby seemed understandably uninterested in, given their heterosexuality. And he was really hot. I tended to blank out whatever incomprehensible bit of theoretical nonsense he was talking about and focus only on that hotness. "*Which is probably not a good plan*," Robin assured me in one of her daily emails from the advertising job she never seemed to leave, "*as it significantly decreases any chance you might have of saying something intelligent in class*."

"Yeah, he's great, could you stop wittering on about it?" Toby groaned as the three of us slogged along the muddy footpath toward campus.

"He's a towering intellect," I said. "You're just intimidated by him."

"As if I'd be intimidated!" Toby retorted, and launched into mock bluster. "I'd like to sit him down and have a chat about the things a man ought to study, none of which are Thomas Pynchon."

"Come on, Toby," Suzanne almost purred. "It's manly to study literature. You do, don't you?"

"I find that the manliness depends on the man," Toby said, grinning.

"So you would be equally manly studying, for example, women's studies?" I asked dryly. Toby laughed.

"Men *should* study women's studies," Suzanne said, with sudden passion. "The more men know about women the better." She looked at Toby as she tucked a chunk of her red hair behind one ear. "It can only improve male-female relationships."

I shot Suzanne a sideways look. Was that as flirtatious as it sounded? It was hard to tell: she was possessed of a little giggle that made everything sound flirtatious. I tucked the possibility away in the back of my head and went back to worrying about my paper.

Literature class was grueling, once the professors actually turned up. I felt sluggish and dull, which I blamed entirely on Jason and his insistence on nightly excursions to the pub. Toby and I acquiesced, of course, and I spent most mornings hungover.

Jason caught my eye from farther down the seminar table and rolled his eyes while one of our more earnest classmates was ranting on about some aspect of the latest book that I hadn't even noticed while reading it. Toby kept his own eyes straight ahead and his serious face on. He was afraid to look at Jason or me, for fear we'd make him laugh and embarrass himself. We were deeply intimidated by the professors, who were all great intellectuals and brooked no inattention. Over our pints, we imagined them into huge monsters and looming figures. We created fanciful lives for them to populate, and I spent more seminars than I cared to admit with a hand over my mouth, trying not to laugh, while a particularly nasty suggestion from the previous night ran through my head.

Most seminars broke for coffee in the middle—a stilted affair if ever there was one. The nicotine addicts puffed away, and everyone was on good behavior, following the lead of the professor. Some professors sat in silence, peering at us as if we were a separate species. Others attempted to have jolly conversations. Still others were waylaid by one of the students and compelled to answer questions or expound upon points. I always found the whole ten- or fifteen-minute experience excruciating. Only Sean ever interested me in the breaks, and that was usually because he behaved as if he couldn't care at all if we sat with him. His amused and always aloof gaze took in all of our shuffling and awkward attempts at lecturer-appropriate conversation and did absolutely nothing to put anyone at ease. I thought he was probably laughing at us.

Today, however, I was listening to my peers. Jason had gone from pulling faces to incisive argument in the time it took for our professor's head to turn. He was giving a monologue about naturalism versus political allegory, making some deft comparisons and drawing intelligent parallels to our reading. Toby looked disgruntled. I'm sure I did too. Jason was entirely too silver-tongued under pressure for the committed lush I knew him to be.

"And you?" Jessica Ferrar, the middle-aged battle-ax of a professor, was peering at me. "You haven't contributed much to our discussion today."

"Well," I stammered, turning crimson.

I hated having to introduce myself to groups, but being forced to opine on the spot was a thousand times worse. What was I supposed to say? That Sean Douglas was hot and aloof?

"Well," I said in a much stronger voice, frowning thoughtfully and clearing my throat. I didn't dare look at anyone. "What I found interesting in the reading was the . . ."

In fact, I wanted to say, *I didn't find anything interesting in the reading. Had I found anything interesting in the reading you would have known, you evil old hag, because I would have offered a spontaneous contribution to this discussion.*

"Was the, uh, love story," I said lamely.

Had I really just said that? As if I'd opted to view the collected works of Meg Ryan while everyone else was researching political allegory?

"What I mean," I continued, and had a sinking feeling I identified as my vocabulary jumping ship. "What I mean is that the, uh, central relationship just didn't work for me. I didn't really buy it. Why would they be *so* into each other? Why would she care? So—"

So? So what? Who cares? It's a freaking novel about Northern Ireland! I felt as if I were hovering above the room, watching myself twitch and sweat and stammer. And there was no light to turn away from, just the shining bright beacon of my stupidity.

"*So*," I continued desperately. "So, ultimately, I found the novel ultimately empty. At its core. Which—"

It was time to finish up and pretend I had never spoken. And then, possibly, kill myself.

"Which was what I found the most interesting as I

listened to everyone else's comments." I suppressed a moan and tried to become invisible. But at least I was finished.

There was a small silence.

"Thank you," Jessica Ferrar said in a tone that didn't have to bother lowering itself to sarcasm. "But let's talk for a moment about the religious imagery."

"That looked painful!" Toby snickered as we hurtled down the stairs. I was taking them two at a time, desperate to put distance between myself and the scene of my humiliation. I was thinking a quick swim across the Atlantic might just be far enough.

"I really can't talk about it," I moaned. I careened to a stop once I threw myself through the doors and into the inky darkness. It was just after 4 p.m. and already the dead of night.

"Excellent work!" Jason exclaimed, sailing through the doors behind us. "Nice to see you maintain your calm under pressure, Brennan. Ultimately you found the novel ultimately empty? I was ultimately impressed."

"I hate you," I said calmly.

"Are we going to the lecture?" Toby asked impatiently. At my blank stare, he rolled his eyes. "There's an important lecture tonight, and all the tutors will be there since it's the new addition to the department speaking. Therefore we should also be there as proper graduate students, which might impress them." He raised an eyebrow. "Which I should think you'd be keen on, after today's display." I ignored that.

"But—" I'd had quite enough of the department.

Also, I hadn't ruled out suicide. "But our papers are due tomorrow!"

"The less said about that the better," Jason said, shuddering. He lit a cigarette and flipped me his lighter when mine failed to ignite. "I think this will be a pleasant interlude. The whole night stretches before us, in which I plan to clean my room for the eight millionth time and attempt to pull five thousand words from my arse. Might as well take in a lecture."

"What's it on?" I asked plaintively.

"Do you ever read anything in your mailbox?" Toby demanded.

I experimented with both the British two-fingered salute and the more internationally recognized middle finger.

"Look!" I said, switching back and forth between the two. "I'm bilingual!"

"You," Toby replied, "are a complete idiot." But he was fighting a grin.

Jason and I smoked our cigarettes in the cold before we trudged into the lecture hall, which was surprisingly full. Maybe everyone was aiming to impress, like us. I snagged a seat in the back and watched the professors file in to various seats closer to the podium, laughing among themselves. I saw Suzanne in a seat directly in front of them—an act of unnecessary courage, I felt. What if you were expected to take notes? What if one of the professors read your notes from behind you and thought you were a moron unfit for graduate study?

Which you clearly are, I berated myself. *Having just*

won the prize for the most appallingly stupid thing ever said in a graduate-level seminar. You're lucky they don't ask you to leave.

I slumped into my seat.

I was scoring points, I reminded myself, trying to rally. I was procrastinating *and* scoring points. All was well.

The man I knew to be head of our department, who always seemed to be in between his tenth and eleventh drinks, offered some blurry introductory remarks, and we all clapped dutifully as the stage was taken by a perky-looking woman who, Toby had informed me scornfully, was a very well-known Shakespearean scholar from Cambridge. She rustled her papers and then launched into her lecture. Which concerned—and it took me a few moments to process this—toilet signage. Signs in public places announcing the placement of public toilets.

Yes.

The girl passed out next to me was beginning to emit faint snores. The professors, all in their little clique, were making faces at one another. It occurred to me that they might have been forced to attend just as we graduate students were. The lecture droned on. And on. I stared at Professor Toilet Signage in awe and found myself thinking the words "toilet signage" over and over and over and over . . . *Toilet signage*. And I was concerned about my ability to succeed?

Sean Douglas, I noticed, was sitting apart from the professor clique and looked even more bored than I felt. I could see the glaze over his gorgeous eyes from halfway across the lecture hall. He never even glanced around, just stroked his chin as if he was considering the merits of a goatee and stared off into the space above the lecturer's head.

The only thing that broke through my coma was Sean's voice, as he asked his dutiful question when the lecture finally reached its end and we had all turned to stone.

"Tell me," he said in that silky smooth voice of his. "How does one reconcile the placement of signage with societal preoccupations of waste? What, if any, ramifications do you think the modern psychological disassociation from waste will spur in the conception of signage?"

Okay, *what?!*

I had to force myself to stop gaping across the lecture hall at Sean's little smirk as the perky professor dove into the question with gusto.

Who thought like that? Who would even *want* to think like that? My conviction that I was unfit for scholarship was only growing with every class, and every word that came from other lips, Sean's lips in particular.

"Thanks," I snapped at Toby as we straggled out when the irritating questions were finally over. "That was a complete waste of my time."

"Because you might otherwise have done sweet fuck-all?" Toby retorted.

"I'm off to the library," Jason announced, ignoring us, "and don't either of you disturb me with any pub calls tonight. I have work to do."

Toby was off to check his email, I didn't care to wait, and so, filled with righteous indignation—and a bit of pique that Sean Douglas hadn't noticed my conscientious presence, though I would have denied that if questioned—I took off for home and my waiting paper. The way home involved the dark English night and the slightly dangerous, unlit path through the woods to my house. I took off at a fast pace.

Cristina jumped a little bit in her chair and studied me when I burst into our kitchen, flushed from the long walk home. She had books spread out before her and in the corner, my mother's latest care package. Like its predecessors, it was filled with my mother's version of my favorite American foods. Like Twinkies, which had indeed been my favorite food. In the second grade. I had taken to leaving the packages out on the kitchen table for the amusement of the international community.

"Look at you," Cristina said mildly. "It must be really cold out there."

"I just wasted an hour and fifteen minutes I will never get back, and I have three to five hundred words left to write," I announced in an extremely aggressive tone. "None come to mind."

I threw myself in a chair and shook out a cigarette, shrugging out of my coat and scowling at my care package. The Twinkies were gone. I blamed George. No self-respecting European would ever voluntarily consume such a thing.

"The whole house is aware of your paper," Cristina said nonchalantly. "You've been stamping around and smoking even more than usual."

I smirked at her, and lit my current cigarette with her

lighter and an unnecessary flourish. She wrinkled her nose and waved a regal hand.

"You'll find the right words, Alex," she told me, "all three to five hundred of them. I have every confidence."

Despite all the items I'd managed to sneak past British customs in the nine duffel bags I'd brought with me, from pots and pans to a coffeemaker and an electric toothbrush, to say nothing of stray cans of vegetables, it had never occurred to me to tote a printer with me. I had never had cause in recent years to evaluate my writing style, so I'd failed to prepare for the fact that I required numerous drafts. Write some, print, read, revise, write some more. Words on my computer screen were all very well, but I couldn't trust them there. I needed to see them on paper.

The nearest university printer was located on the main campus, a good ten-minute walk (at a brisk pace) from my room. In order to print anything, I had to save my work to disk and storm across the fields and the dark. Once on campus, I had to contend with the inevitable queue for available computers. Once at a computer, I had to go through the laborious process of logging on to the university network and sending my paper to the printer. Once in the networked printer queue, the paper was ready, but I usually had to wait on yet another line for my turn to log on to the single printer they had in each computer room. Then the closing down of my computer, the trek back home . . . The whole thing could take anywhere from a half hour to an hour, depending on what time of night I went, and it always enraged me.

"This," I would shout at Cristina when she was unwise enough to accompany me, "is absolutely outrageous! How can the university pretend to be cutting edge when it doesn't even have computer facilities anywhere in Fairfax Court?"

Cristina would laugh. "Does the university pretend to be cutting-edge? That is indeed outrageous."

It was almost midnight, and I was in a foul mood. Cristina was nowhere to be found, which, while not unusual, was annoying me. She seemed to know nine out of ten people on campus and fluttered about like a social butterfly. She was all Spanish eyes and glossy dark hair, and everybody was drawn to her. I wandered up the nearest stairs in search of her.

I moved along the empty corridor, which was dark and spooky. There was another staircase that led down into the college bar—more of a canteen, really—where I spent most of my days hanging out with Toby and Jason while we waited for our classes to begin. Sometimes we just met for very bad lunches. It, too, was dark, with only a few emergency lights in far corners. Cristina was there, just straightening up from the soda machine. She smiled at me.

"Ah, Alex," she said grandly. She tossed a diet Coke at me. "Caffeine," she said.

I debated being snippy about her disappearance, but decided against it when she presented me with a packet of cigarettes she owed me. I was easily bought.

We sat at one of the tables near the big windows,

where we could look out at the college's interior courtyard. The college, like the rest of the campus, had been built in the sixties and was a triumph of concrete over aesthetics. The entire university was deeply and profoundly ugly. Despite being advantageously situated around a lake. You could sometimes sense the enthusiasm and original vision of the architects when you walked across the little bridges that spanned the water, and squinted so as to avoid looking at the nearest hulking concrete monstrosity. The university was far better in concept than in practice.

Cristina and I watched the clouds shoot past the nearly full moon and had a contemplative cigarette. All the lights in the section of the college before us were out, save one. We both stared at it. I was pretty sure that was the professors' wing, filled with their offices and a handful of seminar rooms. The single light flickered and went dark. Cristina was telling me a story about her latest crush—the Physicist—when we saw the figure stride through the doors and start down the opposite pavement. Cristina's voice trailed away into nothing.

He was tall and imposing and gorgeous, wrapped in a black coat that looked like a cloak and with the eerie wind blowing through his dark hair. The courtyard lights picked up his angular face and those incredibly clear eyes. I had the sensation of free fall, of being transported into one of those books I'd wept and dreamed over as a child. He was Heathcliff, Darcy, Rochester, all rolled into one lean man with intelligent eyes against the night. My mouth went dry. I lost feeling below the knees.

"Wow," Cristina murmured from beside me. "Who is *that*?"

"That's him," I managed to say.

He never glanced our way, just swept around the corner and was swallowed up in the dark. Cristina and I stared after him, mouths ajar.

"Him?" Cristina echoed weakly. Her fingers, I noticed through my daze, were gripping my forearm.

"Sean Douglas," I said quietly. I met her gaze and smiled. "My teacher."

Four

After some angst, some drama, several more trips to the printer, and a very short, very troubled sleep, I was finished. Or at least I had written all that I could, had ceased caring, and was ready to take my chances. I handed in my paper in the early afternoon and was immediately elated.

"Don't talk to me," Toby snarled from the computer station he'd commandeered sometime the night before. His hair was standing up in dirty-blond spikes all over his head. "I'm having a nightmare involving footnotes and I can't discuss it. Please take your triumph somewhere else."

I took my triumph to lunch with Cristina. She was glowing with excitement, having had an interaction with her Physicist, which had seemed to indicate he was sane. Sanity was no small thing in our village of the damned. We talked strategy. Melanie joined us, taking a break from her dutiful studying, and it became a summit meeting.

"You should do something about your teacher,"

Cristina said, when we'd exhausted strategic maneuvers and were enjoying a postprandial cigarette.

"Like what?" I laughed. Not that I was likely to get that vision of him out of my head. Sean and the elements. Heathcliff for the new millennium. Too cool to rage against the night, too gorgeous to—

Right. *Get ahold of yourself, Alex.*

"You should definitely do something," Melanie agreed, after Cristina finished a lurid description of Sean's appearance the night before. She picked up her bag and grinned at me. "I think I have a crush on him too."

"Who wouldn't?" Cristina sighed. She made a theatrical gesture with both hands. "He is epic!"

I was mulling that over as I walked back across campus, heading for Jason's favorite pub, in which, he'd claimed, he would be taking up residence the moment his paper was in the possession of the departmental secretary and he was thus free again. I didn't actually feel as if I had a crush on Sean; I felt as if he was beyond the reach of mere crushes. Sean loomed a little too large. Cristina was right: he was epic. You couldn't actually have a crush on an epic. You just appreciated, sighed, and went about your less epic life.

Toby had sunk further into misery while I'd been at lunch and was even less approachable when I dropped back into the computer room.

"I have thirty minutes left to produce genius," he spat at me, "and no time at all for conversation."

I didn't bother responding, and decided I would head

over to the pub on my own. I ran right into Suzanne and a handful of other classmates just outside the room.

"Finished?" Suzanne asked me, her green eyes glittering.

"I finished earlier," I said. I glanced over at the open door of the computer room, through which I could see Toby, hunched over his keyboard and typing madly. "But maybe," I continued in a whisper, tilting my head back toward Toby, "we shouldn't talk about this here."

We walked over to the pub, sharing our various war stories. Only Suzanne claimed to have had no nightmares and no difficulties in the paper-writing arena.

"It was only a small paper," she said, frowning. "And it isn't even graded."

"Sure," I said, "but Sean will read them and decide whether or not you're an idiot. Far more terrifying than a simple grade."

"I'm not an idiot," Suzanne retorted. I arched a brow at her.

"I didn't say you were," I replied mildly. "It was the universal 'you.'"

We had reached the pub, which was already doing a brisk Friday afternoon business. Jason was slumped in a corner booth, smoking and reading the paper. He smiled as we surged through the door.

"Jason is the cleverest person I know." Suzanne sighed. I felt my eyebrows hike even higher.

"'Cleverest'?" I repeated, laughing, in the same almost-English accent she'd employed. "Suzanne, come on now. You haven't been here long enough to pick up an accent!"

She smiled—a bit frigidly, I thought. "I pick up accents quickly," she said.

Many supposedly sensible pints later, with Toby in attendance and marginally calmer, the class as a whole decided that it would be an excellent idea to attend, en masse, the party the English department was throwing as a kind of welcome for new students.

"I don't know if this is a good idea," Toby complained, staggering slightly as we poured ourselves into the night. "I haven't slept in days. I just drank loads of pints on an empty stomach. At any moment I could slump over."

"That's fine," I reassured him, patting him on the arm. "We'd pick you right up again."

This is what I remember. We all barreled into the room, a surprisingly lovely one in the single pre-1960s building on campus. Our professors were sipping terrible wine out of plastic cups and mingling with the horde of graduate students. At first, intimidation kept us all in tight student groups. Jason kept up a running, quasi-hysterical commentary on the professors, almost under his breath.

"The head of the department is quite clearly drunk. Uh-oh, Brennan, Jessica Ferrar is here with what appears to be her life partner, best hide. Ooh, someone's just approached Sean Douglas—no, he didn't smite the poor bloke down with a single glance—"

"He's a complete nutter." Toby sighed, rolling his eyes at Jason. I smiled at them both.

"More like a hyperactive little elf," I said. Which was

true. Jason was all blue eyes, dimples, and a mischievous smile that seemed so at odds with the intimidating intellect he unleashed only in class.

Jason and I tripped outside to have a cigarette, with a knot of other similarly intimidated—and much less drunk—students. Jason declared he had to rest, which meant slumping down to the ground right there and tilting his head back against the stone wall. I went back in alone.

Toby and I loomed about near the drinks table, which led to innumerable refills, which led, inevitably, to my belief that I should make spontaneous decisions while quite severely impaired.

I lurched up to Sean Douglas, his mouth in that fascinating little smirk and those eyes gleaming with suppressed laughter, and launched into an impassioned monologue.

"Postmodernism," I ranted at him, "is absurd and irritating. It's the emblem of the intellectual bankruptcy of academia."

"Indeed," Sean murmured, in the same deceptively silky tone he used in class. In class he would stare at you with that condescending smirk lurking around his mouth and in his eyes, as you labored to make some attempt at a point. He would laugh slightly when you wound down and say, in *the tone:* "Well—no. Moving on . . ." It was a tone calculated to make you feel like a deeply stupid child. It was a tone that usually produced respectful silence and a clenched gut.

I completely failed to heed it.

I was very, very drunk. Sean was not. I carried on

without pause for what seems, in my fuzzy recollection, like roughly two thousand years.

"Perhaps," Sean murmured at one point, when I was presumably taking a breath or swilling back more wine I didn't need, "you might wish to read a bit more widely before roundly condemning an entire theoretical school of thought."

I remember that with perfect clarity, yet the humiliation that should have accompanied that obvious slap-down eluded me. I blinked and charged ahead, and only stopped talking when Toby appeared and trod on my foot. I yelped and looked away, and Toby decided to question Sean about opportunities for doctoral study within the department.

It was only then, as I limped away to tend to my foot and to swill back some more anesthetic in the form of boxed wine, that the horror began to take hold.

For the love of God and all that is holy, I thought in a sudden swirl of panic, *what have I done?*

I stumbled outside for another cigarette and found Jason still propped up against the wall, napping. Or possibly passed out. Hard to say. I shook him awake.

"You must be mad," he said in something like awe, when I'd woken him sufficiently, told him the story of my humiliating Sean interaction, and lit his cigarette. He raked his hair back from his forehead.

"Maybe it's not as bad as I think it is," I considered. "He already thinks I'm an idiot, so my confirmation of that can't actually make anything *worse*."

"True," Jason said. He exhaled thoughtfully. "But that's not likely to be much of a comfort."

"There is the slight possibility that he was not as sober as he appeared," I continued. "Slight. He was drinking wine, after all." I frowned. "Well. He was holding a glass of wine. I was the one drinking."

"Did Toby witness this?" Jason grinned. "Maybe he can analyze the extent of the damage."

"Toby?" I considered. "Actually, the last time I saw him, *he* was going on about professional advancement."

Jason laughed. "Going on to who?" I clapped a hand across my mouth in sudden horror.

I stared at him, my eyes wide. "Oh no," I whispered.

I collected Toby, who was still going strong when I reached his side. Sean was listening with that same aloof air about him. *As if,* I thought grimly, *he has an idiot checklist in his head and he's ticking us off one by one.*

"Alex," Sean said in greeting, his wonderful accent not really concealing the underlying sound of patience sorely tried.

"I'm just here to get Toby," I said in a small voice. "Since we're leaving."

Toby turned to look at me, his dark eyes widening. I took that to be the same moment I'd had—when the silence after you stop speaking rings with the horrible sound of what you were actually saying, and to whom.

"I hope you have a marvelous evening," Sean said smoothly. One of his brows was arched arrogantly. I felt the urge to curtsey and ruthlessly quelled it.

"Are you going to crucify me in class on Tuesday?" I dared to ask.

He considered me for a long moment, and his hazel

eyes narrowed. Then he smiled. A full smile, not his usual patronizing smirk. I felt my stomach thud and my heart sink to my knees. Sean raised his plastic glass—still full, I noticed in despair—in a mock toast, and turned back to the crowd.

"We," I said dully to Toby, "are dead."

Saturday was a really bad day.

"It's not actually clear that you were drunk," Suzanne told me when I accosted her through my window as she walked through our shared courtyard. "You were just really, really intense." She continued on toward her door.

"Oh," I said hysterically, hanging halfway out my bedroom window, "that's a great comfort. So I'm not a run-of-the-mill drunken idiot, I'm an extraordinarily *intense* idiot. Fantastic!"

"Fuck her," Cristina said mildly, from her usual position in my chair. "She's jealous of you because you're friends with those boys and she is not. Ignore her. She wants you to feel bad."

"I couldn't care less about Suzanne and her 90210 issues, Cristina," I told her, crawling back inside and standing on my bed. "I have to decide whether I should commit suicide or just calmly wait for the English department to kick me out of the university."

"So you were drunk, so what?" Cristina shrugged in that supremely unconcerned Spanish way, involving her chin and her mouth. "He is the kind of man who is probably used to people drinking too much to cope with him. If he wasn't so scary, people wouldn't need to get so pissed." I loved that word. Pissed meaning drunk, rather than annoyed.

"I wasn't pissed, I was *intense*," I reminded her. Acidly. She lit a new cigarette and sipped at her coffee. I flopped down into a sitting position and picked up my own coffee.

"What are we doing tonight?" she asked.

"I plan to sit right here and contemplate my sins," I said piously. Cristina let out a hoot of laughter.

"That could take weeks." She made an imperious gesture. "I want to go eat a real meal, in town. I demand that you come."

"I couldn't possibly. First of all, I'm hungover."

"Not that hungover, or you wouldn't be throwing yourself out of windows to speak to Suzanne, of all people," Cristina replied crisply. I couldn't really argue. She slid me a sideways look. "We are going to a Mexican place."

"Mexican?" I perked right up, intrigued. Then I scowled. "Do you see how easy I am? I have no willpower whatsoever!"

"Willpower is overrated," Cristina said, and laughed.

"My problem is that I have the emotional maturity of a sullen teen," I told Michael later, when I woke him up in the early Manhattan afternoon and was thus enjoying the image of him cowering from the daylight under his designer sheets. "Emotionally I'm seventeen years old."

"Did you assault your high school teachers with your drunken witticisms?" he asked.

"Ha-ha." I sighed. "I don't know that I would use the word 'assault,' anyway. And you could argue that this guy had it coming, since he's kind of a notorious asshole."

"Alexandra. Are you planning on teaching Mrs. Tingle, just like a bad teen movie?"

"Not at all. As you might recall, I have a fatal weakness for assholes."

"I sympathize," Michael said, "although I'm not convinced that shrieking at a man for untold hours, while inebriated, is necessarily the best strategy to win him." He paused. "Although that was more or less how I started dating Elliot."

"Good point." I stared up at my ceiling. "But we're not actually teenagers anymore—my behavior to the contrary. We're twenty-six years old. Aren't we supposed to evolve?"

"Please," Michael sniffed. "The universal shared characteristic of adulthood is a nostalgic yearning for idyllic youth. Having had a shitty youth which gives me daily posttraumatic stress, I can do without the nostalgia. I *prefer* my emotional adolescence!" He had worked himself up to ringing tones.

"Listen to you," I said admiringly. "Little Miss Voice of a Generation."

Michael was touched. "I do try," he said humbly.

I was pleased to discover I had only the faintest of hangovers the next day. It was so strange not to wake up with a pounding head that it took me several moments to figure out what was different. We had had a dinner that wanted very badly to be Mexican in a restaurant that wanted very badly to be posh. And I had stopped drinking after a couple of pints. Hence the clear head. It was only two in the afternoon—pretty early, considering the hilarity had gone on until after five and Melanie and I had had to drag Cristina up three flights of stairs and put her to bed.

"*You are totally mature and not in any way a sullen teen*," Robin had emailed me late in her Saturday night. "*And don't you dare call me before noon tomorrow*." A glance at the clock indicated that it was still well before noon in New York, so I removed my hand from the telephone and shuffled down the stairs to the cold kitchen and set about making my coffee.

I didn't just "drink coffee" in England. Oh no. I brewed myself an entire pot of Lavazza espresso every morning and at several other points during the day. In response to a nation of tea drinkers, I mainlined my caffeine. Other people claimed to have drug-like reactions when confronted with its strength, but I was blissfully unaffected by the pounding pulse and jumpiness. I was comfortable with the knowledge that this was because I was a hard-core coffee junkie.

I was just settling down with my big cup and a fresh cigarette when the door swung open. I looked up, hoping to see Cristina in all her morning-after agony.

Sadly, it was George instead.

"Hello, George," I said politely. With the advent of classes, I rarely saw him anymore, which suited me fine.

He rocked to a stop and glared at me. Today, I noticed, he was sporting what could only be called a math-geek-meets-rapper outfit. Genres collided and performed a drive-by incident on one little redheaded troll of a guy. It was very confusing. I kept my face carefully blank.

"How dare you," he said. And actually he was already pretty loud.

"How dare I?"

"You woke me up with your party last night," he accused. I wasn't a big fan of the belligerent tone, but sucked it up in the greater interests of house peace. There'd been noise, after all.

"I'm sorry," I said. "You should have told us to shut up." I may have stressed the word "us."

"I couldn't be bothered to get out of bed," he said. Loudly.

I immediately realized that I couldn't be bothered, therefore, to care.

"George," I said, leaning back in my chair. "It was a Saturday night."

"You wouldn't like it if I had *my* friends over until six in the morning! How about if we decided to make noise right outside your door? How would you like that?"

I would probably be astonished, I reflected, that George knew anyone with whom he could throw a revenge party outside my door.

"Actually," I said, considering, "I probably wouldn't care. I would either join you or just deal. Or"— I threw in a meaningful pause—"I'd ask you to keep it down."

"My girlfriend and I were trying to sleep!" George roared. His *girlfriend*? Huh? "We had to get up early this morning! You have no consideration for anyone in this house but yourself! I'm going to party directly outside your door and see how much you don't care!"

I didn't exactly laugh—I may have smirked. I was thrown by the "girlfriend" but I rallied.

"George," I said, very calmly. This was a tone Robin had once called my "insulting calm." "The only thing outside my door is a toilet. Do you think people would enjoy partying in a toilet?"

Okay, that was snotty.

George turned purple and pink, not the most flattering colors for a redhead, despite the claims of a certain Molly Ringwald film. As I watched him, wondering idly if he'd really lose it or possibly explode, Cristina hauled herself in through the door.

George made an inarticulate frustrated noise—at high volume—and thundered out of the kitchen. Seconds later I heard the front door slam shut, and then saw George race past the window at great speed.

"What was his problem?" Cristina asked without much interest. She was in her pajamas, looking as if she had recently been run over by a fleet of trucks. She slid into a chair and propped her head up with her hands.

"Why do I get yelled at and you don't?" I demanded. "And more to the point, the point being totally unfair things—did you know George has a *girlfriend?*"

"Impossible."

"He said he did. He said he and his *girlfriend* couldn't get to sleep last night. Which is by the way my fault because it was apparently my party."

"He can't have a girlfriend," Cristina said. "It must be forbidden by some law."

"That must be the same law that ensures that all I have are horrible flashbacks of Aryan Karl while Horrible George enjoys the horizontal lambada with fetching supermodels."

Cristina shuddered and raised a palm. "No more. My stomach is weak." She glared at me. "I can't believe you allowed me to drink so much whiskey. You are the elder. You should take better care of me."

I snorted and took a soothing hit of my coffee. "You're a crazy Spaniard," I said, "not to mention a disaster waiting to happen."

Cristina moaned. "I think it already happened. I think I am the disaster."

Sundays were just as gloomy in England as they had been at home in New York. All I wanted to do was curl up on my couch, order pizza, and watch bad Lifetime movies for three days. Pizzas in England, sadly, involved bizarre ingredients like sweetcorn and scary ingredients like mad cow. And the only television around was in the central building and generally tuned to what the entire world called football, but I felt compelled to argue was soccer. I tried to do some of my reading but found myself brooding instead.

My behavior in front of Sean aside—and I couldn't bear to think about that yet—it wasn't so clear to me that I belonged in academics. My classmates were constantly worrying about trying to impress the professors with their comments in seminars, which was diametrically opposed to my own view that *they* ought to be concerned with impressing *me*. If we were the next generation of scholars, surely the present generation would be advised to pay a bit more attention to cultivating us from our MAs into PhD programs.

I liked the idea of Doctor Me. I just wasn't so sure I wanted to chain myself to three years of PhD research into some subject I had yet to imagine. I had no burning desire to write about anything, nothing that jumped to mind, anyway. And three years was a long time, during which you were by all accounts expected, encouraged, and fully destined to go off your rocker.

That sounded kind of fun for maybe a summer, but as an entire life? I wasn't even convinced that I loved the whole literature thing. I was afraid I was living my life by default. The thought of the corporate world filled me with horror, so it was best to stay with the academics. Except I couldn't really say I was approaching academia as a *choice*. More like the best of uninteresting options.

Which brought my thoughts back to how much of a fool I'd made of myself in front of a professor. Not just any professor: the most superior professor I'd ever encountered. The professor I most wanted to impress and had had the least chance of ever impressing even before *the incident*.

I sighed and reached for my cigarettes. Cristina had retreated back to bed, and I was unable to shut off the instant replay images of me cornering Sean. Reliving my lost youth was one thing; embarrassing myself in what was likely to become my professional sphere was something else entirely. The things I'd left New York for—all those dreams of claiming my life and making sense of it at long last—seemed as out of reach as they'd ever been. The drive that had inspired me to cross the ocean didn't seem to be around any longer, and Happy Graduate School Girl wasn't keeping me out of trouble.

I took a long drag and stared out my window, where the world blurred into reds and greens and was muted by the constant wet. The wind came rushing in from the fields so hard that it raised an eerie howling along the courtyard. Sometimes the windows even rattled. There was no escape from the chill, and the dark came earlier every day. Winter was coming, I'd shamed myself, and I still couldn't understand the theory assignment.

It was possible, I thought darkly, that I was losing my sense of humor.

Five

Tuesday dawned, despite my and Toby's best efforts to prevent it, which mostly involved dire mutterings down at the pub. We were trudging up the stairs together as if a firing squad awaited us in the classroom.

"I'm not sitting near either of you," Jason had informed us cheerfully over a pre-class cigarette. "I don't wish to be infected with your shame."

Toby and I stopped outside the door and looked at each other. We shuffled back down the hall a few steps.

"Go on then," he said.

"I'm not going in there first. You go."

"I insist. It's actually a courtesy."

"Over my dead body."

A brief shoving match ensued.

"Excuse me."

That rapier-sharp voice. Toby and I froze like two naughty children. Sean was standing behind us in the hall, eyebrow cocked, hazel eyes alight, but not too actively contemptuous, as there was no sign of the vicious smirk. Which in such circumstances was as close to a good sign as I was going to get.

Just once, I'd have liked to be able to disappear at will.

"Sorry," I whispered. I could feel myself flush several shades of red. Toby tripped over his own feet and thudded into the wall. He was descending into slapstick while I stood frozen in horror, staring at Sean like the proverbial doe in headlights.

"After you," Sean commanded, his tone deadly.

We slunk into the seminar room, humiliated, to see Jason laughing so hard he had to wipe his eyes and hide his face in the crook of his arm.

Sean never changed expression.

Though I was sure I would bear internal scars for the rest of my days, that was the worst of it. I quickly had other things to worry about. I learned that the reason I had fewer classes than my housemates in economics was because I was expected to read extremely long novels and significant pieces of critical theory. There wasn't enough time to get to it all, not that this translated well. George, for example, felt that the lack of mathematics and daily classes meant that my work wasn't really serious.

"You can't be stressed," he scoffed one night in the kitchen. "All you ever do is lie on your bed and read novels."

"That's a really good point, George," I said. "No wonder I never get my work done."

Idiot.

Cristina and I spent hours in my room next door to George's, trying to hear through the walls and spy through the little peephole in my door. So far I'd only seen the side of the mystery girlfriend's head.

"Her name is Fiona," George had informed Cristina very severely. "She's a *nice* girl."

"Meaning we are what?" Cristina demanded later, laughing.

"Meaning we are *bad*. Duh," I said.

We were fighting for position on the peephole.

"If this girl is at all attractive . . ."

"She can't be." I was positive. "And if she is, she's obviously visually impaired."

"And deaf."

"And they can't really touch, because then she would realize he was a little troll and run, or, assuming she was bound and gagged, roll away. Screaming."

"So we are left with very few options," Cristina concluded. "She must be a monster."

"I can't stand the fact that George has love and I don't even have a crush on anyone," I whined, very late one night. Cristina, Melanie, and I were polishing off a bottle of wine after a night of study. We were clustered in Cristina's room, listening to music.

"You have a crush," Melanie said. "An inconvenient one, true."

"Sean is not a crush," I said. "He's like . . . this elemental being. He just *is*. Also he's sarcastic and mean."

"Which you like." Melanie shrugged when I glared at her. "I'm not making a judgment, I'm just saying you do."

"He doesn't count as a crush, given the ethical dilemmas and the fact he thinks I'm among the lowest forms of sentient life around. Shellfish rank higher with him, I'm pretty sure."

"What about those boys you hang around with?" Cristina's voice was sly. I frowned.

"Jason is like a British, human version of Yoda, and Toby is just . . . Toby."

"Ah . . ." They grinned at each other.

"What 'ah'?"

"You and Toby," Melanie said. "We think he likes you."

I snorted. "I don't think so," I said. I threw back some more wine. "It's not like that with him."

We talked until the early hours about Cristina's touch-and-go thing with the Physicist, and by the time I crawled into bed I was exhausted and tipsy. Too much work, I thought. Too many books keeping me awake with my head spinning. And then when I finally slept I had strange dreams about Toby and Sean, all of them sexual and unsettling.

I woke up feeling dislocated, and stayed that way until long into the day.

We decided to have a party.

"And why not?" Cristina demanded. "All the parties we go to are boring."

"So you think we should invite all the same people here and it will somehow be less boring?" I wasn't entirely skeptical, just incredibly tired of the huge Günter Grass novel I was trying to finish.

"Less boring and less distance to walk," Cristina said. "You must tell everyone you know."

This consisted of a few announcements to classmates and the random people on other courses I'd met in those chaotic first days. Between them, however, Cristina and Melanie seemed to know every other postgraduate student around.

The day of the party I woke up with every intention of doing some work, an intention I vetoed halfway through my first cup of coffee. I called Toby and we met up for lunch. We walked along the fields behind our dormitories, into the little village. The village sported a sandwich shop, which could usually be counted on to provide that rarity of British cuisine: tasty *and* safe.

We sat on a bench and ate our sandwiches, watching other students and locals mill about. While not what I'd call sunny, it wasn't actually raining, which was all the encouragement most people needed to get outdoors.

"Jason's not coming to your party," Toby said. "He has to go see his girlfriend."

"Thank you, Toby," I said sarcastically. "Jason and I actually do speak, you know." Jason's girlfriend had never been seen by any of us, and we periodically suggested that she was imaginary. He claimed to go up to Edinburgh to visit her regularly, and seemed unmoved by our skepticism.

"I'm coming," Toby continued, with a big grin. *You should therefore need no one else*, the grin said. I rolled my eyes.

"I'll notify your fans," I said. "Assuming you have any."

"What about that Suzanne?" Toby asked. He grinned again. "I reckon she fancies me."

"Really?" I frowned into my unaccountably empty bag of potato chips. Or "crisps," as they were Englishly known.

"Jason and I reckon she's after the accent, and what's a bloke to do but surrender?" He sighed, manfully, polishing off the remains of my crisps he held in his hand. "I might offer myself as a sacrifice."

"Do you fancy her?" I was reeling a little bit from a sudden vision of Suzanne and Toby together. Her bright red hair and his dirty-blond spikes. I supposed they could each be considered attractive. I wiped the accompanying images from my head and yanked Toby's bag of crisps from his hand to finish them. He didn't bother putting up a fight.

"I'm equal opportunity," Toby said. "I fancy until proven otherwise."

"There's that discernment women appreciate so much," I said ruefully. He shrugged, gathering up our trash and lobbing it toward a nearby bin.

"I do what I can," he assured me.

He abandoned me to hit the library, and I headed back to my house. I didn't really know how I felt about a Toby-Suzanne connection. The fact was, I didn't know Toby well enough. For all I knew, Suzanne and he were perfectly matched. I'd spent almost every night of the past two months in his company, but personal details were kept to a minimum. British people reserved that kind of thing. We talked about general issues and people we knew. Or differences in American and British culture. Or a whole lot of rubbish, more often. There had been no deep, emotionally wrought testimonials about anyone's psychology, or scarring first love, or any of that nonsense.

Alternatively, I thought that if the whole literature thing didn't work out I could probably write my MA dissertation on Suzanne's childhood traumas, her insecurities, her intellectual issues, and her worst fears. Why did Americans shift so quickly into the murky intimacy of personal revelations? But maybe it wasn't fair to tar all my countrymen with the same brush. *I* certainly didn't act that way. I liked to give the impression that I was sharing bits of my soul, when the truth was, that was a privilege reserved for a very select few. I didn't understand people like Suzanne. I tried to give her the benefit of the doubt—maybe she kept her real self hidden—but I couldn't imagine that was possible, given the volume of the information she gave out. She was either so much deeper than any other human being I'd ever encountered—and I suspected sometimes that this was her take on things—or this was the package, the whole enchilada. I was far more comfortable with Jason and Toby and all that British reserve than I ever was with Suzanne.

I wandered into our courtyard and there was Suzanne herself. I could see her through her kitchen window, sitting alone and looking blank. She looked up and I waved. I started lecturing myself on being such a hypocrite. If I didn't like her . . . But that was the problem. I didn't dislike her. I just thought she was a bit misguided.

She invited me in and we had a coffee.

"I'm so glad you came by," she said. "I was calling you." On-campus phone calls rang and rang and were never forwarded to voicemail. Only off-campus calls were. I had been rendered speechless over this and refused to allow myself to think about it anymore, for fear of apoplexy.

"I'm really psyched about your party tonight," she said. "I have a big crush, but you can't tell anyone if I tell you." She giggled.

Okay, that right there. What was this, seventh grade?

"Let me guess," I said dryly. "Toby."

"Oh my God, you could tell?" She covered her face. Theatrically, I thought. "I'm so embarrassed!"

I could have told her that Cristina had called it earlier in the week. I could have cleaned up Toby's comments from earlier and told her he'd mentioned her to me. I did neither.

"Toby's really cool." I smiled at her over my coffee mug. "But you never hang out with him."

"Well," she said, "you three are a unit, aren't you? And I think he has a crush on you." She sighed. My eyebrows shot up.

"Toby? No way. You couldn't be more wrong."

"I think both he and Jason do," Suzanne said. "It's obvious to me, anyway." She watched me with those disconcerting green eyes.

I laughed. "Jason's girlfriend lives in Edinburgh, and even if she didn't, Jason doesn't strike me as the kind of person who would have a crush on anyone. He's too . . . bookish."

"Come on, Alex," Suzanne said, abruptly serious. "You can't deny that you lead both of them around. They're like your acolytes."

"They're my friends," I said. "I don't lead them anywhere."

Suzanne shrugged. "You get all the male attention on the course."

"What?" I was gaping at her.

"You're dynamic and you have a strong personality," she said. "It's not surprising that people would feel drawn to you. Why do you seem so surprised?"

"I don't think it's true," I said, thrown. And I wasn't sure how much I liked the idea that Suzanne clearly spent time thinking about me in such a weird way.

"Well," she said. "It is."

I blinked.

"I *really* like Toby," she said fiercely, her eyes locked on mine.

"Then you should go for it," I said, relieved the conversation had veered away from me. "Except I would be careful of getting romantically involved with someone you'll have to see every day if things go wrong." I shrugged and tried to smile. "The gospel according to me."

Later, I flopped across my bed and wondered.

For the first time, it occurred to me that behind all the deep emotions and heartrending tales of angst, I actually knew very little about Suzanne. I knew enough: like me, she'd chosen to abandon home and everything she knew to study in a foreign country. When your own country boasted some of the finest institutions in existence, and you could find your subject matter in any of them, it meant you were running away from something. Or running toward something. I knew I was.

"Guess what," I said to Michael, propping up my feet against the wall and holding the phone against my shoulder. "According to Suzanne, I have acolytes."

"What kind of acolytes? Because the wrong acolyte can destroy an entire reputation, you know." He laughed when I sighed. "Why was she telling you this? Does she want to be one of your acolytes? Is there a waiting list? Do people really talk about things like that over there?"

"She's that American one," I said. "I told you. She went to Smith," I reminded Michael. A point Suzanne brought up in entirely too many conversations.

"Good God," Michael murmured. "Tales of patriarchal oppression and radical feminist tracts at the breakfast table. That's half her problem right there."

"Then she lived in Oregon or something, teaching maybe." I considered. "Or, more likely, she was involved in the struggle to take down big lumber companies or some other endless fight against The Man."

"You shouldn't joke about things like that," Michael warned. "Do you know, there are people who are actually living in trees, in protest?"

"Can you imagine that?" I asked. "Do you believe in anything strongly enough to go live in a tree for a year?"

"Well, no," he admitted. "But then, I wouldn't go live in the suburbs for a year in protest of something, either. Do you really think we're supposed to? I think those people whose lives are all wrapped up in some big idea or some big cause are pretty dreary. Fundamentalism is a disease, as far as I'm concerned. If you can't defend something rationally and unemotionally, without getting all dramatic and chaining yourself to a tree, you're a big freak." He paused. "In my humble opinion."

"Okay," I said, "but what do we feel strongly about? Anything?"

"I feel strongly that it's nobody's right to thrust their issues into my face," Michael retorted, "or to legislate so that I don't have the option to exercise my opposing choice. Choice always wins over narrowing the field. I believe that."

I closed my eyes. "We're not going to have a debate about abortion, Michael, since I am actually a woman and I agree with you, which never seems to keep you from ranting at me."

"I just think that having the ability to choose not to do something is meaningful. Having no choice at all is fascism. You can quote me in one of your graduate papers if you want."

I waited a beat. "You're awfully vehement today," I observed. He sighed.

"I just wish everyone would keep their beliefs and their issues and their drama to themselves. If everyone did, we'd be a much happier species."

Robin wasn't answering any of her telephone numbers, so I posed the same question to Melanie and Cristina at dinner. We were in major party preparation mode, and so we were bolting down dinner in our strangely clean and presentable kitchen. No overflowing trash can. No stacks of dirty dishes in the sinks and cluttering up the washboards. Gleaming counters. It was both creepy and festive.

"The British are much calmer about these things," Melanie said after a moment's consideration. "For the most part."

Cristina eyed me narrowly. "Did Suzanne actually chain herself to a tree?"

"I don't even know her opinion on trees." I shrugged. "She's just the sort of person who, given the opportunity, would leap at the chance to believe in something. Particularly if it brought her attention."

"I believe that she's an idiot," Cristina said. "If that helps."

"Suzanne also has a crush on Toby," I said. "She was quick to tell me."

"I knew that from the beginning," Cristina scoffed.

"Hang on," Melanie said. "She has a crush on that teacher of yours. She said a few days ago that she had an 'intellectual crush' on that Jason. Wasn't there someone else?"

"That really hot Italian guy," I supplied.

"The one who you were talking to that night in the pub." Melanie waited for my nod. "Is there anyone she doesn't have a crush on?"

"Cristina's Physicist?" I smiled at her.

Cristina made a face. "The girl claims to have a crush on every male you know," she pointed out. "I think she is staking a claim. You should tell her that she must choose one. Just one."

"Apparently," I said, "I'm very dynamic and popular. All the men want me."

Melanie nodded. "Obviously, that goes without saying."

"That Suzanne," Cristina muttered. "I don't like her at all."

Hours later, the party was in full swing. Melanie and I were taking a breather by sitting up on the counters.

"I can't believe so many people fit in here," I said.

Melanie grinned. "Free drinks."

The two of us were particularly interested in the animated conversation Cristina was engaged in with her Physicist over near the wall.

"I think he likes her," I said now, watching the way he leaned down to catch her words. "They laugh a lot."

"I don't know," Melanie said. She frowned. "There's something about the way he looks at her. It's a bit too indulgent, as if he can't take her seriously."

We watched some more, until a new song came on the stereo and people screamed and began dancing with even more energy. There wasn't exactly space to dance, which was why Melanie and I had pulled ourselves up and out of the way. The Europeans liked their pop music, which offended my American rock sensibilities. They danced in discos and listened to girl and boy bands. It was like waking up and finding myself transported to my own Wham!- and Duran Duran-filled youth, except without bands I actually had that teen girl connection to. The scariest part was that it grew on you. When I'd arrived in September I'd been appalled. These days I just surrendered. Even sang along.

I saw Toby and some of our other classmates push in through the crowd, and began making my way toward them. People had cameras, and I found myself posing with classmates, housemates, and taking my own pictures of people. I was taking a group picture for some of our neighbors when a familiar tall, golden presence appeared.

Aryan Karl. Ugh.

"This is my house," he announced in his deep, unnecessarily severe voice. Referring, I presumed, to the group and not the house he stood in. I stared at him in dismay over the top of the camera. I'd actually forgotten about him.

"Smile!" I ordered, and took the picture.

Karl's housemates evaporated, with an interchange of knowing smiles I really didn't care for.

"Hello!" he said abruptly. To me.

"Karl." I showed my teeth in an approximation of a smile and noticed Toby from the corner of my eye, peering in my direction.

"This is a large party." Karl's endlessly blue eyes and high forehead were too much for me. I couldn't bear staring up at him. I had the slightly hysterical urge to do something unforgivably fucked up, like offer a Heil Hitler salute.

Best to shove that right out of my head.

"Uh-huh," I said. "And how are you?"

Toby appeared at my side and slid Karl one of his xenophobic stares. I didn't even have to prompt him.

"All right?" Toby drawled. The first time I heard that particular greeting, I was deeply confused, until I worked out that they were just cutting out the "are you" in front of the "all right."

"Toby, this is Karl. Karl, Toby."

They stared at each other. Toby looked insolent and rude, which made me grin.

"You are a friend of Alex?" Karl boomed.

Toby stared at me. I grabbed his arm and excused us from Karl's line of sight. A little bit rudely.

"What was that?" Toby asked, laughing.

"My sins in human form," I replied. I reached for a new drink. "God."

The night wore on.

Karl was never more than a foot from my body, though he had given up attempts at conversation.

"He is looming over you," Cristina said in a brief non-Physicist moment. "I think he wishes to resume your relationship."

"I think I would rather sleep with George," I retorted.

There was dancing, and toasting. Cristina and her Physicist adjourned elsewhere, and Melanie and I celebrated her victory. And then George strolled in, hand in hand with a girl.

"She's not a monster," Melanie said, surprised. "She's quite pretty."

"Pretty is overstating things," I said, checking the girl out. "You're just giving her bonus points because she's standing next to George."

"Standing over George, really."

Fiona was a good head taller than George. She had uneventful hair, an unobjectionable body, and unremarkable clothes. What made her stand out from the crowd, aside from the troll at her hip, was her nose. It was what my mother would have called prominent, to be polite. It was huge.

"She's like a vulture hunkering above him," I breathed. Melanie and I stared at each other in delight, and the Vulture was christened into being. This made it her karmic right to come right up to the two of us and glower.

"These are my housemates," George said. He nodded at me. "This is the American." *The American*. As if he wasn't.

"I've heard about you," Fiona said. She had rather obviously heard unpleasant things.

"I've heard about you," I replied, easily.

"I also heard you that night you threw the party without asking our permission," she continued.

"'Our'?" Melanie queried politely. "Sorry, but you don't live here."

I noticed that when Melanie said it, no one turned purple or started shouting. I was going to have to learn tone control.

"That's hardly the point," Fiona said primly.

That was more than I could bear, and I broke for freedom, looking back to see George talking very close up in Melanie's face. Fiona was simply looking vulture-ish and peeved. Melanie glared at me, then returned her mild attention to George.

"Who's the ginger bloke?" Toby asked. He pronounced it with a hard g, to rhyme with "ringer."

"My horrible American housemate," I said. As if I wasn't.

The alcohol supply was getting low, something I noticed only when an extraordinarily wasted Welshman started raging about it. This meant it was time to break into my private collection. Toby and I climbed the stairs to my room.

"What do you want?" I asked. "Beer, red or white wine, or vodka? I think I have some orange juice somewhere."

Toby just flopped down on my bed and sighed deeply, as if exhausted.

"What's wrong with you?" I asked mildly, cracking open a beer.

"Lager, please," Toby said, and I threw him one. I settled into my chair and lit a cigarette.

"Where's that Cristina?" he asked, sitting up.

"Her crush turned up, they talked only to each other for ages, and have now disappeared." I grinned. "We can only hope for the best."

Toby considered. "It's not going to happen. The bloke hasn't actually made his position clear. He's not going to. He wants Cristina panting after him. He's a wanker."

"So far he's been compelling and exciting," I argued.

Toby looked at me over his can of lager. "A wanker," he repeated. "I'm a bloke. I've also behaved like a shit with every girl I've ever been with, so I'm an expert." He smiled at me. "Trust me."

"Right," I scoffed.

"Go on then," he said lazily, leaning back again. "Give us a fag."

"You don't smoke," I reminded him.

"I do when I'm pissed," he contradicted me. I never felt that it was my place to lecture people on the evils of tobacco, given my raging addiction. I just shrugged and tossed him one. He lit it and puffed away, almost pensively.

"Enjoying it?" I asked.

"It's hard to say," Toby said. "I don't know how you can smoke as much as you do."

"Years of practice."

We finished the cigarettes, and then each took a bottle of wine.

Toby laughed. "They might be rioting by now. With no drink."

"Hopefully they're all too drunk to actually riot about anything." I locked my door and traipsed down the stairs.

Toby and I were laughing when we walked back into the party, directly into Suzanne.

"Oh," she said, looking back and forth between us.

"I'm going," Toby said. He had to shout a bit.

The kitchen was even more packed than it had been earlier. Melanie and I were crowded into the corner, where I had gone to flee Suzanne and her wounded expressions. She had turned them on Toby in the absence of me, and I'd been more than happy to leave the two of them to it for the bulk of the night.

"Going?" I made a face at him. "It's early."

"It's two in the morning."

"As I said—early."

"I," he said grandly, "am a committed student, Alex. I have a great deal of reading to do tomorrow morning."

"What about you and Suzanne?" I probed. "You looked pretty cozy over there."

Toby shrugged and made an unreadable sort of face. "I don't know. She left. She's having a bit of a strop."

"Did you make your position clear?" I asked lightly, remembering what he'd said about Cristina's Physicist. An arrested sort of expression flickered across his face, then disappeared. Maybe it was the music, which was currently a terrible pop duet involving faded British stars.

"I have no position," he said. "On Suzanne," he clarified after a brief pause.

"All right then," I said. "Call me tomorrow if you want to get some lunch. I'll probably be getting up around then."

"I can't believe how lazy you are," Toby said, smiling at me. "It's why you Americans will never amount to much, all that lolling about and lying in till the afternoon."

"Weren't you leaving?" But I was smiling.

Which is when he leaned over and kissed me.

That's right.

I might have concluded that in the presence of so many cheek-kissing Europeans, Toby had had a few too many and gotten carried away in the spirit. But this was no brief peck. Nothing parental or platonic about it. It was an "okay, baby, I'm going to bed, I'll see you there" kind of a kiss. The fact that there was no tongue didn't make it any less carnal.

I was so stunned and so unprepared that I didn't react. At all.

"Okay," I said in a perfectly normal voice. "Bye."

Toby turned and left. I briefly wondered if it had even happened. Maybe it was just a strange flash from those weird dreams I'd had about him that night. Maybe I needed to drink less and pay more attention to my unhealthy sleep pattern—

"He kissed you," Melanie observed from beside me.

"Yes," I said. Maybe I was dazed. "I noticed that."

Six

All of a sudden, it was Week Eight. I wasn't really sure where the term had gone. I could remember the first days so clearly. Then everything seemed to have picked up speed. Each term began with Week Zero, during which time everyone milled around without classes and I got myself into trouble with Aryan Karl, who looked like the concentrated version of Billy Peterson, who broke my heart in the sixth grade. Then came the nine weeks of classes, though normally the final week was packed full of exams and papers and other such fun. It was as if I looked up from my desk one day and it was December. I couldn't believe it was time for Christmas already.

First, however, there was my final seminar of the term. Having been a profound coward all term, I had failed to volunteer for the opening presentations Sean liked students to make in our theory classes. He liked them, we'd decided, because he was a sadistic bastard and also because he could have a quick chuckle at our stupidity to begin each class. Everyone had had their inevitable turn at the chopping block. When Sean had pretended not to know who was left, who hadn't presented, I'd imagined briefly that I was saved. No such luck.

"Alex," he'd said. He looked almost affectionate as he gazed at me. "I believe you have yet to have a go."

I had been staring at a big book entitled *Feminisms: An Anthology of Literary Theory and Criticism* for hours—days maybe—but it wasn't going away. I was going to have to make a presentation in front of the one person I could be certain (a) already thought I was an idiot and (b) I would freeze in front of because (c) I had such a huge crush on him I could hardly breathe through it. More than this, my mother kept leaving increasingly emotional messages on my voicemail about my plans for Christmas vacation and how her home was not a hotel, Robin had disappeared off the face of the earth, which I was interpreting as her suddenly hating me, and I was strangely nervous about going home to New York in the first place, because what if everyone thought I'd changed? Or worse—what if they didn't? And oh yes, Toby had kissed me, which I refused to think about, much less discuss with anyone. He had probably been drunk, and I knew better than to accord drunken incidents any meaning. Melanie wisely refrained from mentioning the subject beyond a single morning-after raised eyebrow, and Toby himself behaved as if nothing had happened. Which it hadn't. Why couldn't anything ever be simple?

It seemed as if it were always dark. The days were short and grim and very cold. There was too much work and too many social implosions. Cristina, for a start, had suffered a complete sense-of-humor failure.

The night of our party, she'd spent the entire evening with the Physicist, having a fascinating conversation that spanned all kinds of topics, for hours on end.

"This man is so intelligent," she told us. "The way his mind works. I could listen to him talk for days."

They sat up talking of philosophy and physics, poetry and passion, economics, politics, ethics, graduate school, history, literature. They fell asleep curled up around each other on the Physicist's narrow little bed. It was very chaste, very beautiful. She didn't see him again for a week. As each day passed, she became more and more withdrawn.

"Go pound on his door," Melanie advised.

"I really can't," Cristina said. "I was the one who followed him around that night with stars in my eyes. It is up to him to find me if he wishes. He knows where I live too."

That was the week of Thanksgiving, a tremendously odd thing to celebrate in the midst of the mother country. I made a celebratory chicken pasta and forced Melanie and Cristina to share the meal with me. It didn't take much forcing—we were all pretty much whores for any meal prepared by someone else.

"It's about being with those you care about," I said, raising a glass.

"Salud!" Cristina said.

"Cheers," Melanie chimed in.

Our glasses clinked together and we all grinned.

This touching moment was, predictably, interrupted

by George and the Vulture. The Vulture sneered down the length of her nose. Quite a sneer, in other words.

"Quite a celebration, Thanksgiving," she snapped. "Did you Americans kill the Indians before, during, or after the meal?"

"*I* never celebrate it," George sniffed. "It's barbaric."

I refrained from giving voice to my suspicion that George's American life was probably singularly lacking in celebrations of any kind, if his ability to irritate others on this side of the Atlantic was anything to go by. I glared at his girlfriend instead.

"Who is 'you Americans,' exactly?" I demanded. "Do you mean the English expatriates who fled the religious intolerance over here? Or all the British second sons and commoners who were after a better life? Where do you think Americans came from?"

The Alex Brennan Thanksgiving Address: we *all* killed the Indians, so shut up, eat your turkey, and save the PC sermonizing.

"I think that's glossing over the facts," Fiona retorted snippily. She was, she had informed Melanie grandly, a student of political philosophy. "I study political philosophy," she intoned as if on cue. "And I think you'll find that—"

"Fiona," I cut her off wearily. "I think *you'll* find that we all agree that the United States was a British colony until roughly 1776."

Cristina interrupted at this point to utter a malevolent-sounding stream of incomprehensible Spanish. Given the fact that we were sitting in a room lit only by candles, and Cristina herself was slouched into a chair and glaring evilly, the effect was like something out of a horror film. It was chilling.

"Good riddance," Melanie sniffed, as Fiona and George made a dramatic exit.

"My life is shitty enough," Cristina snapped. "I don't need those two compromising my appetite." She knocked back her wine with a graceful flick of her wrist.

"Yeah," I agreed, darting a worried look at the former social butterfly. "Why does she think she can talk to us like that in our own house? What's that all about? I don't think she'd like it if I busted up into *her* house and started getting in her business."

"She is unlikely to live in any house," Cristina said, topping up her wine from the bottle in the middle of the table. "That one is more likely from beneath a rock."

Melanie and I dragged her out to the pub that weekend.

"You might as well have tequila," I said. "It pretty much cures all ills."

"Or renders you utterly insensate," Melanie agreed. "The next best thing."

Cristina had spent the entire week in the same Angel of Death mode as at Thanksgiving. It wasn't that I was opposed to it—quite the contrary. Most of the people I loved dearly were equally morose and embittered. It was just that Cristina had previously been so upbeat that the abrupt change was alarming.

We claimed a corner of the crowded pub, and Melanie demanded Cristina and I fetch the drinks. It was hard to even get near the bar, but I had been weaned on far more frightening mob scenes. I weaseled my way in, and turned back around slightly to look at Cristina.

"I don't know why you're so glum," I said. "You don't know anything yet. For all you know, you and the Physicist could be declaring your love for each other by the end of the night." I should really learn not to make statements like that.

"True," Cristina said, although she didn't look convinced.

I passed her the drink she ordered, then paid. I loved the whole lack of tipping in bars. After all, why did they deserve a tip for handing you a bottle of beer? How hard was that? This was not something I planned to take up with the bartenders back in New York, however. Better to just pay them and attempt to curry their favor. The wrath of a New York City bartender was never something to be taken lightly, as I had cause to know personally. There were places I could never enter again, thanks to some youthful antics best left forgotten.

I was thinking about some of those antics, all of them unsavory, when I nearly tripped over Cristina. Who had come to a frozen standstill in the middle of the pub. Confused, I followed her gaze, and found the Physicist standing with another woman, laughing.

"Cristina, we can just leave," I said into her ear.

She said nothing. So I watched with her as he left the other woman near the entrance and sauntered toward the bar. I watched the exact moment he spotted Cristina and the odd look that flickered across his face. He changed direction and walked toward us.

"I'll see you at the table—" I began in an undertone.

"Don't you dare leave!" she hissed.

The Physicist ambled over and stopped directly in front of her. I stared off into the middle distance and pretended I couldn't see him. He flicked his dark, surprisingly intense gaze over me, and then returned it to Cristina.

Okay, I thought, I could see how that was kind of hot.

"Hello, Cristina," he said. For some reason I was surprised that he was British, and that his voice was so clearly posh. Cristina was stiff.

"Hello, David," she replied in a cold tone. David, I thought. Such a nice and normal name. I hadn't actually known he had a name, previously.

"I wanted to see you," he said. "I meant to come round."

"Well," Cristina said crisply. "Clearly, you didn't really. Since you didn't."

"I had a really nice night, Cristina," David said quietly.

"I did also," she snapped.

There was a pause. I felt as if there were all kinds of things happening that I didn't understand, undercurrents and messages and an awareness that passed me right by. The two of them stared at each other for a long, wordless moment. Cristina was the one who broke it, worrying her drink with her free hand. I saw her lips tighten, as if to ward off words she didn't want to utter.

"I'll see you," David said gently, and moved off into the crowd.

"Let's go," Cristina snarled, and swept back to the table Melanie had been holding down all this time.

"What's happened?" Melanie asked, sounding a bit alarmed at the sight of Cristina's face.

"What just happened?" Cristina demanded. "Did he feel obligated to speak to me? And if he did, what was he saying? '*I meant to come round*'?" She lit a cigarette with jerking motions and nodded at me. "You heard him. What did you think? What the hell was he doing?"

"I don't know," I said cautiously. "I don't think he was actually being nasty, Cristina. I think he was trying to be nice."

I related the exchange to Melanie as Cristina fumed and smoked her cigarette.

"Or in any case," Melanie agreed, "not *trying* to be horrible."

"Is he still standing over there?" Cristina asked me. "With that girl?"

I looked. He was laughing, angling his body down toward the woman in much the same way he'd done in our kitchen, with Cristina. "He's still there," I confirmed. "And if that's his girlfriend or even his shag for tonight, I have to say, I'm unimpressed."

"Deeply unimpressed," Melanie agreed immediately. "In general, but particularly when stood next to you."

"She's skanky, and I don't know why people who dye their hair that eggplant color—"

"Aubergine, Alex," Melanie corrected me automatically.

"—never seem to realize that as it grows out it looks silly. She's flat-chested and has big hips, and if he really wants the pear-shaped girl over you he's a complete fucking asshole idiot who—"

"That's the problem," Cristina said quietly. "He's really not."

Just before Christmas the English department chose to return our papers, with comments. Sean Douglas, course convener, was on call to read the comments provided by two separate members of staff and add his own, smirking spin.

Our first papers were, happily, ungraded. Sean spoke to us about them during the coffee break of our theory class, following my surprisingly unremarkable—by which I mean I managed not to shame myself, which is not the same thing as being impressive—presentation. The coffee break thing was supposed to suggest an air of casualness and nonchalance, but in reality just made me hyperaware that all my classmates could probably overhear Sean denigrating my attempts. On the other hand, like that was anything new, and I was just pleased I hadn't fainted during my little spiel about feminism. I was finding class difficult enough these days, what with inconvenient memories of Toby and his lips intruding at the strangest moments. Which I refused to think about. The very thought of that kiss made my stomach tense. Not that I was considering it in any detail.

"You're very passionate, Alex," Sean told me in that rich voice, and Toby and his lips disappeared from my head entirely. I no longer really heard British accents, but I could feel Sean's in my toes. He actually smiled, a bona fide smile, with no supercilious undertones. "Passion is good, and the profession always needs it."

He went on to point out some weaknesses here and

there, which involved leaning his head in closer to mine. He smelled like pine and something soapy. I broke out in goose bumps.

"Overall," he was saying, "I'm quite pleased with it."

I must have been giddy from the unexpected lack of sarcasm, coupled with his dizzying proximity.

"I wasn't really sure I was cut out for this," I told him in a rush, as if he'd asked.

"Anyone who thinks they are tends not to be," he said quietly. "This is a solid piece of work."

"Thanks," I said, delighted.

"Even," Sean continued, deadpan, "within the constraints of the bankruptcy of academia."

I felt myself jerk, and then blush deep and bright. The sound of my drunken words coming back at me was not the most pleasant of echoes.

"Um," I said, intelligently.

"Keep it in your papers, Alex," Sean suggested. He leaned back and offered me that lazy smile.

I had the strangest feeling then, as if I could actually read what went on in his baffling eyes. I was suddenly *absolutely certain* that he knew how he affected me. And that he enjoyed it.

"Please ask Evelyn to come over next," he said.

By the time I got to my feet I was convinced it was just my hyperactive imagination. Who could possibly read an enigma like Sean? And even if I could—as if he would be intelligible, much less even peripherally interested in getting me rattled and breathless. *You wish, Alex*, I jeered at myself.

That was a problem, though. I really did wish.

Seven

There's just nothing pleasant about the night flight from JFK to Manchester. It's always impossible to actually get any sleep, unless you happen to be traveling in first or business class. Which I didn't happen to be able to afford. You leave at about 8 p.m., have an uninspiring if not revolting in-flight dinner, and then it's still only about ten o'clock and you're wide awake. When the plane lands at eight or nine in the morning British time, it is only three or four in the morning in New York. And in your body. The five minutes you closed your eyes and fruitlessly ordered yourself to sleep were not at all rejuvenating. Which means, if you were me, you ended up staggering around the airport with as much luggage beneath your eyes as on your trolley. And if you were me, that's a whole hell of a lot of luggage.

Some people are addicted to illegal drugs or unsuitable lovers, gambling or shopping sprees. I was addicted to books. Which is why each one of my two duffel bags weighed in at about forty pounds. I had been veering toward the psychotic while packing up after Christmas at home, and could therefore blame only myself when I wanted to weep from exhaustion and yet still had to lug all that weight around the city of Manchester.

And I do mean the *whole* city of Manchester.

The great thing about Manchester Airport on a normal day is that the train station is attached, and you can just pop off the plane and wheel yourself down to the train tracks with minimal fuss. This was not a normal day. I had to wrestle my enormous bags onto one bus, then onto another completely different bus, then across a largely underwater Manchester city street, then onto a train that turned out to be taking a scenic route across the country. Thus becoming a three-and-a-half-hour journey as opposed to a two-hour journey. By the time I discovered that I was on the wrong train, I was too tired and cranky to bother myself to move. Also I had used up what puny arm strength I possessed.

The extra-long train ride gave me time to think. If you could really call it thinking. More like jet-lagged obsessing: heavy on emotion and light on sense. I had, very deliberately, chosen not to think about my life in England at all while I was home, beyond the glowing press releases I issued to family members and the slightly more in-depth descriptions of Sean's hotness I shared with friends. When it came to compartmentalizing my life, I was already a master.

I felt like I needed a vacation to recover from my vacation. Holiday cheer took a lot out of me. Too much racing around the city pretending to be back in college with Michael and pretending to be grown-up with Robin. Thirdhand tales of the happy new life of my hex—I mean ex. Unpleasant fights with my father that

I had the sneaking suspicion were word-for-word reenactments of battles fought when I was thirteen, and would probably still be fighting when we were both toothless and in diapers.

Nor were my battles over, I discovered when I arrived in my frigid university town. It took ages to get to a taxi when I got into the train station, and even longer to lug my bags into my house, and even longer than that to drag them up the stairs and into my room. Once they were inside my bedroom, stacked haphazardly in the center and therefore taking up the entirety of the floor space in the little cell, I passed out across my bed. The moral of this story: leave the books at home.

I slept the sleep of the dead, and when I woke I saw that it was dark already. I stumbled down into the kitchen and was faced with the complete lack of anything edible on my shelf in the house's shared refrigerator. I looked at Cristina's and Melanie's respective shelves, from which I often pilfered in times of need, and saw that they had nothing either. This meant that I had to go out of the house.

I stamped back to my room and yanked on the nearest coat. Muttering crossly, I shoved my feet back into the boots I'd worn on the plane—and which had not exactly helped during the later Manchester trek, what with their three-and-a-half-inch heels—and rummaged around for appropriately British currency. I paused as I shoved a handful of pound coins into my pocket and got a glimpse of myself in the mirror above my sink. The Bride of Frankenstein had nothing on me after a transatlantic journey. My hair was piled around on the top of my head and my eyes were still carting hefty bags. I was dressed like a homeless person in a flannel shirt three sizes too big for me, sweats, and the incongruous boots, all bundled under a black trench coat. This made me cackle at my own reflection. If you have to look like a wildebeest, you might as well look like the queen of the wildebeests, I always said.

I pushed my way out into the dark. It was barely four-thirty and could as easily have been midnight. The small convenience store—and I call it that not because it was actually convenient at all, with mysterious hours and odd personnel, but because it was close—sat in the center of Fairfax Court and sold the kinds of things students were most likely to want. This, apparently, meant pasta of every description, milk and yogurt, beer and wine, cigarettes, and minor toiletries. No produce, just canned goods. I could whip up an excellent pasta with cream of mushroom soup as a sauce, but that was pretty much the extent of my range. Mostly I used the place for cigarettes and beer.

I stormed into the little store and didn't even bother looking around, just went and gathered the few items I required to get me through the night. Milk. Beer. I was trying to summon the enthusiasm necessary to choose between a questionable British boil-in-the-bag curry and an even dodgier, supposedly Thai dinner. Which would be the least likely to nauseate me? A hard call to make.

"Alex?"

I knew that voice, but it was impossible that I would

hear it in the tiny little Fairfax Court shop, so I was scowling when I turned my head.

And because my life is an endless farce, it really was Sean.

He was holding a bottle of wine and looked delicious. Dark trousers, a dark sweater, his dark hair slightly damp from the weather. Gorgeous. Much more so than I'd remembered, and my memory was both detailed and vivid. I felt his hazel gaze flash over me, and suddenly found myself much less amused with the whole "queen of the wildebeests" thing. His mouth curved.

"Did you have a pleasant holiday?" he asked.

I was clutching my beer and my milk and my revolting dinner choices. I stared at him.

"I did," I said. "I actually just got off the plane. I mean, earlier today, but I'm pretty jet-lagged. So."

The usual witty repartee.

Sean smiled.

"Welcome back," he said. He nodded at my armful of horrible curries. "You can't eat that. It will remove your stomach lining. I speak from sad experience."

Why was he being nice to me? Why was he talking to me at all? And why wasn't he off living in his cerebral little world in his professorial refuge, wherever the hell that was?

"What are you doing here?" I blurted out. His eyes lit with suppressed laughter. The look I was more familiar with.

"I moved into one of the faculty houses," he said. He gestured with one hand. "That way."

"Oh."

"You look like you could do with a decent meal," Sean said. "And as it happens, I'm a decent cook. Why don't you come round? It's a vast improvement over boil-in-the-bag curries, I promise."

"Um—"

"It's quite all right, Alex," he said, grinning wickedly. "I don't bite."

So that was how, without even meaning to and without necessarily being fully conscious, I agreed to have dinner with Sean Douglas. In a few short hours. In his house.

Oh. My. God.

I stumbled back toward my house, telling myself that a shower and a change of clothes could absolutely transform me into a vision of hotness Sean would be powerless to resist. From wildebeest to hottie in one quick shower? No problem! I was so out of it I was completely unaware of my surroundings until the figure leaped out at me.

I screamed.

Okay. It was more of a wimpish yelp, and some truly embarrassing hand flapping. And actually the figure wasn't leaping out at me at all; I just hadn't seen her until the last possible second. Because she was looming in the dark, waiting for me.

"I had no idea you were so girlie," Suzanne said.

Bitch.

"Jet lag," I snarled. "How are you? How was your Christmas?" My heart was still pounding. Which could as easily have been a reaction to Sean as to Suzanne leaping from the shadows to accost me. I tried to breathe deeply.

"My holiday was fine," Suzanne said. She was watching me closely. Too closely. "I saw your bedroom light on," she told me. "That's how I knew you were back."

"Oh," I said. "Well." Then, weakly: "Want a coffee?"

Of course she did.

"I wanted to talk to you," she said, very solemnly.

I sat her down at the kitchen table and bustled about preparing coffees for us both. Instant for her, since the British were so big on drinking Nescafé and Suzanne was so big on being British, and a very serious pot of espresso for me. It occurred to me that the reason that last sentence of hers sounded familiar was because it was: right after our party, when she'd freaked at the sight of Toby and me coming down the stairs together—fully clothed and bearing wine—she had said much the same thing.

"*I want to talk to you,*" she'd said. "*I think we need to.*" I had thought we needed nothing of the sort, having heard enough talking from Suzanne to last me years, and so I was happy to use excessive work as an excuse to avoid it. Which had happened to be true—we'd all had those awful papers I still couldn't permit myself to think about without shuddering. And Cristina had had that whole thing with the Physicist. And, of course, there had been the kissing incident, but I didn't think she knew about that. And anyway, I wasn't thinking about it. I had been really happy to forget all about the various dramas of life in England while caught up in the whirl of my Christmas at home.

I smiled as I sat down, presenting her with a mug and immediately sipping my own. Suzanne toyed with hers.

"What's up?" I asked brightly. Or as brightly as can be expected when you were jet-lagged, had just had a mind-altering interaction with the smartest man you'd ever met whom you happened to have a serious crush on, and most important, when you really didn't care about whatever she was going to say.

"Something's happened," she told me. "And it's changed everything. I wanted to be the first to tell you. I wouldn't have been able to live with myself if you'd heard it from someone else."

"Oh," I said. "Were you in New York or something? Because if you slept with my ex-boyfriend Evan, it's really not such a big deal. As I'm sure you now know." I waved a cavalier hand. As I did so, I thought about how strangely perfect Evan and Suzanne would be as a couple. Evan could impress Suzanne with his stolen witticisms, which she, being one of those people who refused to have a television, would find new and hilarious. Suzanne could rant at Evan for hours and he, being so genial and unassuming and (dare I say it) dull, would enjoy it. A match made in heaven.

"Alex," Suzanne said. "I'm really serious on this."

"Sorry." I took another gulp of hot coffee and smiled encouragingly, while visions of Evan and Suzanne's eco-friendly wedding danced in my head. I managed not to grin, and ordered Evan out of my head.

"It's between Toby and me," Suzanne said. She sighed. "I know how close you are with him, Alex, and I want you to promise me that no matter what, we'll keep the lines of communication open between us. I don't want you to feel as if you're losing friends, either Toby or me."

I had a little inkling with that, but was far too annoyed with her dragging it out to pretend to understand. I thought: *Toby, how could you?* I utilized a handy blank stare.

"I also want you to know that I would never poach on your territory, but you did say you and Toby were just friends," Suzanne said. She was looking at me with a great earnestness that I somehow couldn't believe.

"Suzanne, I'm tired and I'm out of it," I said evenly. "I had a very strange trip home, which I am still processing. I have two duffel bags the size of elephants to unpack, and I have laundry I should have done before I left. I have a headache and I desperately need a shower." I smiled thinly. "But what I do not have is ESP. So please, please stop talking in circles."

Her green eyes gleamed with something that could have been malice, or even triumph. "Toby and I are together now," she said. "This will obviously change things, and I wanted you to be prepared for it. I didn't want you to walk into something, not knowing how everything was."

"You sound as if there's been a coup," I said lightly. "I'm glad you and Toby are together, if that's what you wanted." I thought about that kiss at our party. When had he decided Suzanne was what he wanted? What happened to not having a position on Suzanne? Not, of course, that I cared.

"It is." She watched me. "But I think you wanted something else."

I groaned. "Suzanne, I really couldn't care less if Toby dates you or Margaret Thatcher or no one at all. I couldn't care less who you date either, as a matter of fact. Go crazy." And again: *Toby, how could you?*

"You were the leader," she said. She propped her chin on her hand and stared at me. "Everything is different now."

"Whatever." I rolled my eyes. "I mean, okay, fine. I really don't care. Is this what you wanted to talk to me about before the holiday?"

"Toby and I only got together recently," Suzanne said, frowning. She sat up. "Oh, you mean after your party?"

"I guess."

She laughed. It was a girlish, innocent peal of laughter. "Can you believe how paranoid I was?"

Suzanne then performed one of those intricate hair flips that you can only do in public after extensive practice in private. One of those flirtatious, self-aware girl moves that looks sexy and is all about power. That single motion completely undercut her attempt at innocence. I watched her through narrow eyes as her bright red hair settled back down into place.

"Paranoid?" I asked. Which was as good a word as any to describe her, I thought.

"I just wanted you to promise me that you and Toby weren't going to get together," she said. Smugly. "Silly, right? Anyway, I just hope you're not too disappointed." Her eyes swung back to meet mine.

"You can stop letting me down easy," I said, with a ghost of a smile. "I'm really fine with the whole thing.

You clearly don't believe that, and I don't know what else to say."

"I believe you," she said.

She could just as easily have said: *I believe that you want me to believe you.* It hung there in the air between us, unsaid.

"So," Suzanne said, leaning back and smiling at me. "What was so strange about your trip home? What happened?"

I thought about telling her. Family and friends and all the joy and horror that entailed. The unsettling realization that lives I used to star in ran with perfect smoothness without me. Robin's disappearance, which had turned out to be Robin and Zack moving in together, like grown-ups, and so okay with that decision, like grown-ups, that it had just happened without the usual twenty thousand phone calls. The predictable issues with my parents and the typical misadventures with Michael. Or the current excitement of dinner with Sean, which I knew would really, really bother her. I really wanted to tell her, I realized, and only to make it perfectly clear that I had better things to think about than any piddling romance she was having with Toby.

Reason prevailed.

So I just smoked a cigarette and talked about the wonders of life in Manhattan.

I stood in the shower with my eyes closed and let my brain try to work through the overload. The shower stall I shared with the entire house was what I imagined a gas chamber would be like. It was just a large rectangle with tile. Fluorescent lighting and no fan. You shut yourself in and hoped for water.

I let the water run over my face and thought about Evan and Suzanne, which made me snicker, and then about Toby and Suzanne, which didn't. I allowed myself thirteen seconds to think about Toby *that way* and thought: *Whatever*, may he and his crazy new girlfriend live happily ever after. I thought about that kiss of Toby's and then I thought about Toby kissing Suzanne, and then, in defiance, I thought about kissing Sean. Hot, delicious Sean, who was having me over for dinner and who would never in a million years consider the likes of Suzanne. Sean, who would know how to kiss someone in such a way that there would be no pretending it had never happened. That was so much fun that I ran with it until my skin pickled up.

Back in my room, I was faced with a serious clothing issue. What exactly did you wear to have dinner with your gorgeous and mysterious professor, when it *definitely* wasn't a date and he'd already seen you doing your impression of *Night of the Living Dead* and anyway he thought you were an idiot and *anyway* you really couldn't *dress up* to impress him because what would impress *him* anyway and you certainly didn't want to give off the impression that it had ever *crossed your mind* that this was a date or even *date-like* and *in any case* he was only feeding you because you'd looked like some lost stray and he probably wandered around the countryside feeding stray dogs and alley cats with exactly the same total lack of romantic intention—

"Oh my God," I said aloud, and called Michael.

"Jeans and a casually hot top," he said immediately. I heard his pen tapping against his desk. "Or black pants and one of those V-neck sweaters you like so much. Boots, of course, and your hair down. No jewelry, minimal eyes, sheer lip gloss."

"No black trousers," I said. "That's too dressy for a casual campus dinner, don't you think? This is someone who sees me in what I wear to class."

"Oh, good point." Michael thought for a minute. "But you said you just got back, so obviously you just pulled on whatever was on top of your bag."

"No." I rubbed a hand over my face. "Then I'll just be desperate to slide that into conversation and will be obsessed with it and will end up shrieking it at some totally inappropriate moment. He'll say hello and I'll maniacally scream that I just yanked on whatever was on top . . . Not worth it." The scene was all too vivid for me. I shuddered.

"Jeans, then," Michael said. "And that black thing you wore that night at Robin and Zack's housewarming thing. You looked great in that." He transferred the phone from one ear to the other. "Are you okay? You sound a little stressed."

"Michael!" I almost dropped the phone. "Why do you suppose I'd be stressed?"

There was a sudden knock at my door.

"That's random," I muttered. "I didn't think anyone else was around." I peered through the peephole and sighed. "I have to go. It's Toby, and this is probably going to be an annoying conversation."

"Call me the minute you get home," Michael

ordered. "I want to know every single detail about the un-date."

I hung up and hurriedly yanked on some jeans and the nearest bra. "Hold on," I yelled, as I looked around for something I hadn't worn on the plane and pulled it over my head.

Toby raced right past me the minute the door swung open.

"Thank God you're back," he said. He flung himself into the desk chair and stared at me. "I've got myself in a terrible mess."

"Hello, Toby," I said dryly. "I'm great, thanks. And how are you?"

Toby had spent entirely too much time on campus over the holidays, thinking he'd get a head start on our next paper and also avoid too much time in his own childhood home, a small village in Devon. These plans, he told me now, were foiled by the library's lack of reasonable opening hours during the holiday and his own lack of motivation.

"Once everyone left, this place was well depressing," he said.

"So you should have gone home," I told him. I had brushed my wet hair and was sitting cross-legged on the bed.

"Thank you, Brennan," he snapped. "Do you mind?"

He'd gone home for Christmas and spent New Year's Eve with a pack of disreputable blokes with whom he'd spent his equally disreputable undergraduate years.

"A load of drunken louts," Toby said, his dark eyes

bright with laughter. This from a man who drank ten pints and considered himself only mildly tipsy.

He'd returned to university and had attempted to impose a strict work schedule upon himself.

"I got up every morning and had a brisk jog along the lane, ate a healthy breakfast, and then cracked the books." He glared at me as I snickered at this image.

And then one day he'd run into Suzanne.

"Who I think might have been spying on me, actually," he confessed. He looked a bit pink around the cheeks at that.

"Spying on you?" I frowned at him. "What do you mean?"

"Well." He cleared his throat.

Every time he'd left the house, she had appeared. Which he realized she could do if she was sitting in her kitchen and keeping a watchful eye on the courtyard beyond. After the first few times when they'd run into each other—"or when she stalked me, call it what you like," he said—they'd had a nice cup of coffee and walked together to the library, and then Suzanne had asked if he fancied a drink.

"Which I have to say, I did." Toby sighed. "I do fancy Suzanne, you know. She's really lovely."

I kept myself from an eye roll with the iron control I'd always suspected I had in there somewhere. *She must have done a lot of hair flipping,* I thought.

This was, Toby said, the night before last. "*Recently,*" Suzanne had said. I'd had no idea just how recent. They'd met up and walked to the pub, and as Suzanne talked, Toby got shitted.

"I didn't make a conscious decision to get wankered," he said. "It just sort of happened."

The more intense Suzanne got—"and I have to say, she was getting well into it," he said—the quicker Toby drained his pint. He'd started having a shot at the bar with each newly ordered pint—"for extra strength and charm, of course."

"Of course." I sighed.

By the time they called last orders he was seeing triple—

Toby sighed heavily. "And would have happily snogged a dog's arse if it were presented to me."

Which is how he reckoned he found himself snogging Suzanne.

"I don't really know how it happened," he said.

"But you're *a couple* now," I replied, with relish. I was congratulating myself for never alluding to our own drunken snog by word or deed. Obviously, this was something the guy just ran around doing. Jackass. Toby looked sick.

"It's all a bit hazy to me," he said. "And much as I fancy her, I don't want anything serious. Not with anyone. It's really not her. I think she thinks we're . . ." His voice trailed off.

"Oh," I said, eyebrows high, "she definitely does." I gave him a look. "You must have done more than snog the girl."

"I swear I didn't." His eyes were wide. He blinked. "Well, it was quite a bit of snogging, actually, and possibly a grope—"

"You're such a *guy*, Toby."

"—but that's it, I swear it. No clothing was removed. No skin was involved. Certainly no fluid—"

"Okay, stop. Enough." Ew. I lit a cigarette and blew out a stream of smoke, pensively. "You're fucked," I said. "She thinks you're dating. More than dating. She came over here so she could be the first to tell me that you two were together and I would have to prepare for the new group dynamic."

"The *new group dynamic*? What?"

"Whatever. Why are you telling me all this, anyway?"

He looked a little sheepish. "I thought you could sort it out."

"What can I do?" I laughed. Why should I do anything for a serial snogger?

"You're both American, aren't you?"

"There's no national consciousness concerning dating disasters, Toby," I said. "I can't wave the flag and have her stop thinking there's something going on between you. Only you can."

He slumped in the chair and made a face.

"Do you do this kind of thing a lot?" I asked, grinning. "Didn't you tell me that you behaved like a shithead to every girl you ever knew?"

Toby grinned. "I don't think I said 'shithead,'" he replied. "But I have a certain reputation, it's true."

"And you're sure you don't want to just . . . give it a go?"

He made a face. "Not really, no."

"Why not?" I was curious. I was uncomfortable with Suzanne, but I'd always thought men lapped up her kind of thing like cream. Her whole *I'm helpless and yet sexy* thing.

"I don't like her that way," Toby said. He laughed. "I mean, I wouldn't mind having a go in one sense, but not as a girlfriend."

"You wouldn't mind having a go." I shook my head. "You're a horrible little shit, Toby."

"I'm not trying to be horrible." He shrugged. "I just don't want a girlfriend right now. You know what I mean?"

I shrugged. "Then just tell her you were incredibly drunk, events got out of control, and you apologize if you gave her the impression that you wanted anything more."

"As if I can just say that," he scoffed.

"Fair enough," I said. "As an alternative, you can employ the tried-and-true dickhead method and just avoid her until she corners you, at which point you can act like she's insane, hoping to confuse her into thinking she hallucinated the entire event." I smiled. "But I warn you, that way lies madness and the possibility of angry poems."

Toby just shook his head. "I would never do something like that," he said piously. But there was a little smile on his face. I wondered if what he would do might not be even worse.

I saw that it was nearing seven o'clock. It was time for Cinderella to go to the ball, but I definitely didn't want Toby to know where I was going. I didn't want him to know I was going out in the first place. *He* might choose to run around having a soap opera life involving the entire university, but I preferred to be a little bit more cagey.

"I'm really tired," I said. Which was true, if irrelevant. "I've had you and Suzanne and too many stories today, on far too little sleep."

Toby looked nonplussed. "Don't you want to go to the pub?" he asked, almost plaintively.

"After the story you just told me?" I laughed. "I may never go to the pub with you again."

He slumped his way out of the house, and as I heard the heavy outside door thump shut I wondered if I should be offended that kissing me had led Toby directly to drunken shenanigans with Suzanne. I wasn't sure I wanted to be on any list of conquests that included Miss Hair Flip. Who would be next?

I moved over to my window and watched Toby cross the courtyard. He glanced up and grinned at me, and then performed some kind of 007 maneuver past Suzanne's window before sneaking into his own house. I stood there for a moment, and had to shake myself out of it.

Walking over to Sean's house some time later, I reasoned that it was unnecessary to work myself up into a state about the situation. It would be like dating George Clooney. So unimaginable and absurd that why not just relax into the fact that he would never in a million years ever find you even slightly attractive? Or even if he had a slight moment of finding you kind of appealing, like a dog, that would be that and he would be back to dating size zero supermodels by the end of the night. This, rather than being depressing, was freeing. There was no pressure. There wasn't even anything to gain. And so there was really no need to be stressed. Might as well just have fun, shoot for that moment of being mildly appealing, and maybe at the end of it all he'd consent to a photograph you could show your buddies back home.

Not that I'd spent a lot of time thinking about dating George Clooney.

Sean had cooked chicken with vegetables and rice, nothing too exciting, and all of it surprisingly edible. He poured wine and we sat at the small table in his kitchen. Faculty housing was much nicer than student housing, I noticed. Sean's kitchen was actually homey rather than institutional. He seemed to have no problem at all making nice conversation, almost as if our theory classes had been conducted by his evil cerebral twin.

George Clooney, I hissed at myself. And sort of relaxed into the whole thing. Maybe it helped that I was so jet-lagged. I had a limited emotional range, which certainly cut down on possible ways I could embarrass myself.

After dinner we sat and had some more wine, and talked.

"So tell me," he said, his hazel eyes warm. "What makes a New Yorker pick up stakes and come to a tiny city in the north of England?"

What I usually say when people ask me that is something like, "*Well, I thought that if I was going to go to graduate school I might as well go in England.*" It seemed to be a crowd-pleaser back home, particularly among friends of my parents.

So I opened my mouth to say it again and instead

said, "Somebody told me I couldn't." I sort of grinned.

"It doesn't surprise me that that would motivate you," he said.

"What about you?" I dared to ask. "Why are you an academic?"

He played with his wineglass and smiled. "Somewhat by default, I suppose. I didn't know what I wanted to do when I finished my undergraduate degree, so I just stayed on. And that led to the doctorate, which led here. Nothing very exciting, I'm afraid."

"How old are you?" I couldn't believe I'd asked. His eyebrows arched up.

"Thirty-four," he said mildly. "Mephistopheles."

"Hey," I said. "I'm twenty-six. That makes me the old lady compared to my classmates."

Sean laughed. "Not quite an old lady." He topped up my wineglass and crooked an eyebrow at me. "Are you sure you want more? I'm not certain I can fend off another attack on postmodernism."

"I think you know how embarrassed I am by that," I said, and I could feel myself turning pink.

"You shouldn't worry," he said, grinning. "I won't tell you some of my own embarrassing stories, but take comfort in the fact they exist."

"Sometimes," I dared, "I think you take pleasure in scaring us all."

"Of course." He agreed, and then sat back in his chair, his body lean and lazy. I reminded myself to swallow. "It's a tutor's prerogative." He smiled again. "And what about the rest of your life here, outside the course. Are you settling in well?"

"Sure," I said.

And maybe it was the wine, maybe it was the exhaustion. Maybe it was neither of those mundane things and I was just a little drunk on all that personal attention and how relaxed Sean was. Maybe it was because I felt safe there, cocooned in the kitchen with his wise eyes and a kind smile.

Maybe I was just insane.

I said, "Sometimes I think I'll never really belong anywhere, or trust anyone. I think I need to learn how to stop caring about that."

"You can't decide not to care," Sean said. "You can only control your response."

"Is that really possible?" I asked.

"It really is," he said. "It even starts to get a little bit easier."

"Really?" My voice sounded like a stranger's. "When?"

There was a small silence. It seemed to fill the room.

I felt prickling at the back of my eyes and realized with some horror that I was about to cry. I excused myself to the bathroom and splashed water on my face. I stared at my reflection and could see the darkness in my eyes. And if I could see it, Sean and his laser eyes could no doubt read me like a Dr. Seuss book.

"Time to go, jet lag," I whispered at myself. "You can't do this."

I smiled slightly when I returned to the kitchen. I began shifting my weight from one foot to the other, a nervous habit I thought I'd outgrown in the fifth grade. The moment I realized I was doing it, I locked my knees and stood straighter.

"I should get going," I said. Years of my mother's tutelage sprang into use. By rote, I said, "Thank you so much for dinner, Sean. It was really nice of you to have me over. I would never have made something so delicious for myself."

Sean stood and gave me that half-smile of his. He reached over and touched my shoulder very briefly, then dropped his hand. I imagined I could feel the place he'd touched through my sweater, as if he'd branded it.

"You're welcome, of course," he murmured, almost impatiently. He caught my eyes and held them. "Alex, I don't know if it helps, but I have every faith in you and your abilities."

His eyes were so warm then, almost like some liquid near gold and twice as precious. I felt a lump in the back of my throat. His kindness was almost too much to bear. I thought maybe the sarcasm was better, in the long run. For my heart. It was protection from what he could do with a little tenderness.

I stared at him for what felt like ages, as if I could crawl into his gaze or his arms and stay safe there for a very long time. It was a bizarre feeling, one I'd never experienced before, and it unsettled me. I even found it a little tough to breathe. He smiled again, and I returned it. I could have sworn that for at least that brief second I could read his eyes and I could see there his awareness of what I was afraid was written all over me.

Don't be an ass, I snapped at myself. *This is your George Clooney moment*.

"Thank you," I said quietly, and made myself walk away.

Eight

The first night all three of us were back, Cristina, Melanie, and I threw a little impromptu party in my room. We ordered takeout and drank entirely too much and sang along to terrible songs for numerous hours. *Bon Jovi's Greatest Hits*, which Melanie inexplicably owned, was only one among many eighties-based groups who figured prominently.

"I wouldn't eat food I don't like," Melanie moaned the next day. "Why do I drink things I *know* I'll regret? I wouldn't eat something that I had demonstrated a consistent allergic reaction to. Why did I drink gin?"

"If these are your regrets," Cristina muttered from where she was, facedown at the table, "you have no regrets."

"I have no regrets at all," I chirped. "I'm just pleased the two of you are back, so I don't have to navigate my life here alone anymore."

I was maybe a little too cheerful. All that drinking with Toby and Jason had left me much more prepared and much less hungover. This meant I had the tolerance of a seven-foot-tall burly truck driver, but I wasn't concentrating on that part. I chose to concentrate on my mother's latest package instead. Cheez Whiz and Triscuits, which had entirely disintegrated on the trip across the pond. I aimed a squirt of processed cheese at my forefinger and licked it off.

Melanie eyed me, and shuddered at the Cheez Whiz. "Perhaps you'll reconsider your regrets when you recall that you were belting out 'Born in the USA' at two in the morning. Quite on your own."

I eyed her right back. "Fine," I said. "And who was that who made an even bigger scene to 'Livin' On a Prayer'?"

Melanie pinkened.

Cristina raised her head and glared at us both. "I don't really think either of you is in a position to throw stones," she said. "Do you?"

"And by the way, I still think you should sort out that teacher," Melanie continued in an uncharacteristically aggrieved tone. Clearly the hangover at work. "He's not actually a celebrity, you know."

"Weren't the three hours we spent on this last night enough?" I rubbed at my eyes.

"You must show him who is boss," Cristina said, or anyway I think that's what she said as she cradled her head in her arms.

"Just get pissed and snog him," Melanie suggested, sounding more like her normal self. "It's a great British tradition."

Having nothing at all with which to reply to that, I returned to my room to place a dutiful call to my mother.

• • •

"Brennan." Toby said my name with great resignation when he swung by to accompany me to the library. "What was going on last night?"

"I don't know what you mean," I said coolly.

"I think you do," he said. "In case you wondered, you woke me from a sound sleep. You were screaming American rock anthems at full volume. And I do mean screaming and not singing."

"Don't be ridiculous," I said with tremendous dignity. "I was in bed last night by ten." I glared at him as we set off along the footpath. "And don't you have better things to do than worry about what I might or might not be doing? Like worrying about your girlfriend?"

Toby winced. "She's not my girlfriend."

"Yeah," I said. "But she doesn't know that."

Although, in truth, I kind of thought she ought to.

I was actually a little amazed that Suzanne's expectations of a single drunken snog were so high. If it had been me, I would have *assumed* that Toby was never going to speak to me again. In fact, when it was me, I had automatically assumed that we would never discuss the incident, and, sure enough, Toby and I were as okay as we'd ever been pre-kiss. I would never have run in the opposite direction altogether, claiming a relationship. The very idea made me cringe.

Not that I could really claim that my behavior was a guide, given the profound lack of any reasonable romantic interests in my life. In fact, maybe Suzanne had the right idea. Those girls who made assumptions and refused to slink off into their shame tended to end up with the man after all. Michael, Robin, and I had watched this phenomenon play out repeatedly. Okay, sure, we didn't much care for the tone of the ensuing relationships, but they *had* the ensuing relationships. We just had painful tales to tell one another over cocktails.

When we got to the library, Toby disappeared immediately into the stacks. I arranged my notebooks and my books and my study materials very carefully around my workspace and stared at them. I decided I required a cigarette for motivational purposes, and sauntered right back down the stairs and outside into the cold. The smokers huddled together in the entranceway in smoky solidarity. At least it was covered over. You might freeze, and you would definitely damage your lungs, but you could avoid the ever-present rain. I was trying to pep myself up into a frenzy of academic zeal—with only moderate success—when Jason appeared from around the side of the building. I flicked my finished cigarette off to the side and grinned at him.

"Excellent!" he cried. "Let's have a cigarette! May the dark night of the soul never rob us of these moments, Brennan. Though the pub calls, know that it can only be sweeter by our working for it. What could be better than a smooth pint after a long day's toil?"

"You haven't started either?" I asked dryly.

"Not a word," Jason said cheerfully. "And I have a shocking lack of interest."

"I would take comfort in that," I said. "Except I know you, Jason. You'll moan about everything and whip us all into the heights of panic, and then you'll sit down and dash off a paper in the course of a single night. *And* get distinction on it."

He grinned mischievously. "Or I might simply have a heart attack," he said. "I can't take the pressure. All these expectations. I might just choke." He sounded as if he might find that amusing.

The papers we were all working on were supposed to be five thousand words long. As we had all theoretically started them before the holidays, we were all theoretically well along the way now. Let me stress *theoretically*. Five thousand words worked out to only about fifteen pages. Fifteen pages didn't scare me. When I'd been at college, I had once memorably pounded out a twenty-page paper overnight, fueled by nicotine, caffeine, and a total lack of interest in the subject that was outweighed only by my fear of the teacher. I'd gotten a really good grade. But this was different. It wasn't the length that worried me, it was the quality. Suddenly every word counted. Suddenly I was a graduate student, and bullshit papers just weren't permitted anymore.

It was terrifying.

Jason and I made plans to meet in the pub that night for restorative pints and a collective moan, and I decided to have one more cigarette while he raced inside to bother Toby. I stared out across the expanse of campus before me. It looked like some kind of small city, all those flat-topped concrete rectangles and antennae. It was a profoundly ugly place. Just when I thought I'd acclimated to it and gotten over it, I was struck anew.

I saw Suzanne barrel up the path toward me, her head

tucked down toward the ground and her legs eating up the distance in impressively long strides. I had the opportunity to duck inside and avoid her, but I didn't take it. Something perverse in me stirred to life and waited for action. I wasn't sure what it meant, but I lounged against the doorframe and waited for her to glance up.

"Hello," she said when she reached me. "Have you been here long?"

"A while," I said. No need to advertise that I hadn't actually done any work yet.

"I heard your party last night," she said. I got the accusing green-eyed stare.

"I guess everyone did," I said. I laughed. "I guess we got a little carried away."

"I'm surprised no one called security," Suzanne said.

Lines like that were the ones I reported, with great umbrage, to my friends. And whether those friends were in England or in New York, they all groaned and demanded that I stop giving the girl the time of day. I never knew why I didn't heed their advice. Except, I supposed, it was simple arrogance—I thought Suzanne needed my friendship to function as some kind of voice of reason in her personal cacophony of drama. I figured that the fact that she annoyed me wasn't reason enough to avoid her.

"You should have called security yourself," I said lightly.

"You can tell me if Toby was there," she snapped. "I won't hold it against you."

Although she quite evidently already did.

I sighed. "He wasn't." I was watching her closely. "It was a house thing."

Something shimmered behind the impassive face she was trying to wear. "Whatever," she said bitterly. It occurred to me that she might think I was lying.

"He really wasn't there," I said. "He wasn't invited and, Suzanne, why would I lie about it?"

"I don't know." She sighed. Her eyes were dark. She tugged her coat tighter around her and shook her bright hair away from her face. "I don't know why anyone would do anything. I have to get to work."

She smiled at me, though. It was meant to be a reassuring kind of smile, I thought. As if to smooth over the fact that she thought I was a liar. And something else, something worse.

We walked in together. I got the impression that she wanted to run away, but she didn't. We climbed the first set of stairs in tandem.

"I'm sitting with Toby," I said without inflection.

"I'm meeting people," she retorted.

She looked at me. I kept my face blank, and she sighed again. "Are you going out tonight?" she asked.

"Probably," I said. I smiled. "I usually do."

"Call me," she said. "Depending on how much work I do, maybe I'll come."

I watched her hurry away into the stacks and frowned. Maybe it was right then, right at that moment, that I first considered the possibility that Suzanne very seriously disliked me.

• • •

"Which kind of sucks, I guess," I told Cristina later that evening as we were getting ready to go out. "But on the other hand, why should I care?"

"Because who knows what she might do," Cristina said darkly.

"Please. What can she do? So she doesn't like me and she thinks there's something between Toby and me when there isn't. So what?"

"You should be worried that she has always thought there was something with you and Toby, and still declared herself for him, and still jumped him. Now she blames you." She shrugged. "I think maybe her real crush is on you."

"I don't think she's gay, Cristina," I protested.

"I don't think she is either."

Cristina and I stared at each other. I frowned, thoughtfully.

"Huh," I said.

We both lit our cigarettes and blew it all away like smoke into the night.

I wrote like a madwoman. I felt like a madwoman. The paper crunch was on.

Toby and I ranted down the phone to each other, and sometimes met for emergency coffee and in-person ranting sessions throughout the long nights. There was very little sleeping. I tended to wake at dawn with a jolt, gasping for breath, and would leap up and return to work no matter what time I'd crawled into bed the night before.

My housemates gave me a wide berth. I stormed back

and forth to the printers and cursed everyone and everything. I read, I wrote, and then I tore everything up and wrote again.

First there was a blank screen. Then some quotations, and then a few sentences. Then suddenly there were pages, and the kernel of an argument. And then somehow there was a paper. It was always a mystery.

Cristina and I were lounging in the kitchen, sharing a bottle of wine. We'd both had work and had avoided the pub, and so decided a later drink without the hassle of socializing was the way to go.

"You seem sad," I said. I didn't dare say the words "Physicist" or "David." She shrugged.

"I'm not," she said. "Or anyway, there's nothing to do about it."

"I hear that," I muttered ruefully. We wallowed for a moment, and then we both snickered at our own wallowing.

And then we both jumped when someone pounded on the kitchen window from outside. We stared, and then stared at each other. A figure had attached itself to the window with the side of his face, and was sliding off. A figure that looked suspiciously like . . .

"It can't be . . ." I breathed.

We watched him topple over. Cristina and I stared at each other for a moment and then leaped up and raced for the door.

Outside, now lolling about on the ground, lay George.

"He's drunk!" Cristina was agog.

"Maybe he's just really sick," I said. "Does he even drink?"

Closer inspection showed that George thought Hawaiian shirts were best paired with patterned trousers and high-top sneakers. And that he smelled like a brewery. George moaned incoherently. Cristina and I looked at each other.

"Good Samaritans," I ventured. "Very good karma."

We each took an arm and pulled him to his feet. He staggered, but we were able to direct him inside. We sat him down at the kitchen table and began plying him with pint glasses of water.

"What's going on, George?" Cristina prodded. "Why are you in this state?"

"I gave her my heart and she gave me a pen," he replied, though not quite so distinctly. Exposure to Evan had sharpened my ear for quotations, and I scowled at George from across the table.

"Don't you dare quote *Say Anything*!" I gasped. I jabbed an accusing finger at him. "You are not Lloyd Dobler! That's sacrilege!"

In response, George did a header onto the table.

"He is too drunk," Cristina said dismissively, losing interest.

She settled back into her chair and sipped at her wine. As if we were alone. We resumed talking, moving away from depressing subjects and concentrating on sharing wild and unsubstantiated rumors about some economics students we knew.

"Let's talk about Sean Douglas," Cristina said with a leer, when we exhausted the gossip thing.

"Sean . . ." I sighed, smiling.

"I do not agree with this George Clooney idiocy," Cristina said sternly. "You are a woman and he is a man. You must claim him." She waved her cigarette at me. "You must declare yourself to him!" She smirked as her ringing tone echoed around the room.

"And that would lead directly to him declaring me mentally unstable," I told her gently. This was not the first time we had had this conversation since the Jet Lag Dinner.

We both sighed dreamily. It was still a great fantasy.

After about an hour's snooze, George reared up again and stared around in alarm. Cristina and I had polished off one bottle of wine and were working on our second. We'd segued from Sean to celebrity crushes.

"It's all fine," I told George in what I hoped was a soothing tone. "Cristina and I rescued you."

For some reason, that didn't appear to really comfort him. Cristina and I watched in horror as his eyes welled up and he began to wail. It wasn't a pretty sight. It was kind of scary. As much as I thought George was a tool, I didn't wish him ill, and pain was pain. I didn't know what to do with his. A hug was more than I could bear, and whispering "there, there" while patting him on the forearm seemed somewhat shabby.

I was briefly alarmed when Cristina ran out of the room, but she returned at once with a roll of toilet paper in place of tissues and thrust it at his head. She and I were stricken into silence. Also trapped. You could hardly bolt for cover when someone started bawling. Although as he continued I was giving it serious consideration.

"She left me," George cried. "She said our politics would never mesh. She said I represented everything she hated about American cultural imperialism."

"Oh, for God's sake," I snapped, immediately roused from my quasi-respectful silence. "You should have told her to get a grip. No one's begging her to watch American movies or shop in American stores or eat in American fast-food restaurants. She's like a political vegetarian who storms around at PETA rallies in leather boots. I saw that Gap sweater she was wearing! Her hands are totally dirty."

"Alex!" Cristina made a quelling sort of face at me.

"I can't believe Fiona dumped you for political reasons," she said in a soft, compelling voice I had never heard come out of her mouth before. I stared, and she winked at me. "That seems so cold and impersonal."

"Sounds like our Fiona," I muttered. Well, he was too drunk to really hear.

"Political philosophy is Fiona's *life*," George moaned. Even with the moaning, he sounded far less slurred than before. Apparently his nap—or brief coma, call it what you like—had perked him up. He was now wasted, a big step up from paralytic.

He blotted at his face and seemed to be finished with the actual sobbing. Which came as quite a relief. I was used to my own crying, but anyone else's made me uncomfortable. You never knew what to do, or what they wanted you to do. Some people wanted hugging and some people wished you would just leave them to it. It was all too confusing.

"But to dump someone over such a thing seems so

harsh." Cristina's voice couldn't have been more encouraging. She was hanging on George's every word—a sensation that must have been new for him.

"We got together because our sexual attraction was so intense," George confessed, to Cristina's and my absolute shock. And to our equally horrified delight. It was like a tabloid come to life! Troll and Vulture in Sex Escapades!

George laughed hollowly, and heedlessly continued. "We barely got out of bed for three months."

The visuals that accompanied that statement nearly made me swoon. Cristina and I engaged in a brief kicking session under the table, each of us near hysteria and yet maintaining completely straight faces where George could see them.

"That's always the way," I commiserated. "But eventually, the real world must intrude, no matter how fantastic the sex." My voice rose a little on that last word, and I had to gulp back the laughter as further visuals flooded my brain. Cristina managed to change her bark of laughter into a serious cough.

"And if Fiona felt that your political views were so far apart . . ." she said, frowning very thoughtfully as she let her voice drift away.

George covered his face with his hands. I took that as an opportunity to reenact my hulking bird of prey impression. Cristina turned red with her effort to keep from laughing.

"Shh!" she hissed at me. "George," she said to cover it, "you can't blame yourself. Did it just happen tonight?"

"We were supposed to spend the weekend in Dublin," he said miserably. "She said she couldn't go because of work. But then tonight when I called her she was going to the pub with her mates. So I confronted her and told her I wasn't the kind of guy who put up with being jerked around."

"Please tell me you didn't actually say that," I interjected. This time Cristina didn't pretend—she just kicked me. Hard. "Okay, ouch, I'll shut up."

"And that's when she told me that she couldn't see me anymore, no matter our attraction to each other. She said she needs a man who can fulfill her mentally *and* sexually." George sniffled, as Cristina and I digested the image of him as sexual animal. That was the kind of digestion that led directly to antacids. "But I think she's already found someone else," he confessed.

I perked up. Emotional wallowing was beyond me, but drama I could handle. "Why do you think that?" I asked.

"I can tell," he said. If he said anything about sensing it in her touch I was prepared to vomit, but he just shrugged. "I can just tell."

"Then she's a heinous bitch," I said dismissively. "Not to mention a liar. You should find out. I guarantee that if you find out she's been carrying on with someone else, it will allow you to hate her, and that always speeds up the grieving process."

"I agree," Cristina said. Her eyes glittered. "Hate is always better than pain." I eyed her askance and then turned back to the subject at hand.

"How would I find out?" George seemed baffled.

"She'll never tell me. And her friends don't really like me."

"That shocks me," I said. "But it's easy to find out."

"Oh yes," Cristina agreed, grinning. "A covert operation."

"A simple reconnaissance mission," I said with a smile and an expansive gesture. "To see if the Vul—if Fiona is entertaining any overnight guests."

George simply stared.

Nine

The great thing about the university was that all its houses had huge windows, past which you could saunter and into which you could always look. The faculty houses, for example, offered two separate views inside, one into the kitchen and one into the living room. I had learned that a simple five-minute diversion from my usual walk home from campus allowed me to skulk right past Sean's windows with him nary the wiser.

He was never there, but stalking wasn't about immediate gratification. Immediate gratification was for wimps. I could wait.

This experience was why I felt qualified to be skulking through the night, Cristina and George on my tail.

"I should have changed into something black," Cristina whined. "I will stick out in these clothes."

"Not really," I hissed. "Of course, the fact that the three of us are crouched in the shrubbery might raise a few eyebrows."

I glanced down to where George was bringing up the rear, his clashing patterns resplendent in the shadows.

"To say nothing of your *Hawaii Five-O* look, George," I muttered. Cristina slugged me in the arm.

"Fiona lives in that house," George said. He pointed, and his lip quivered. "That's her window."

We were in a section of campus into which I rarely ventured: St. Stephen's Court. It was the older version of student housing, which was troubling as it meant my little concrete bunker was considered new and improved.

"Stay here," I whispered, and took off in a lope across the grass. I came up against the wall and glanced around, my heart thudding. I wondered in passing why I thought I had transformed into La Femme Nikita.

Oh, right—wine.

I was pretty drunk, I admitted to myself, but why let that get in the way of a simple reconnaissance mission? I was highly trained. I'd attended a small liberal arts college.

There was a tree outside the house on the slight slope right near Fiona's slightly ajar window, and I wasted no time trying to shimmy up the few feet necessary to get a view inside. I've never been able to perform a single pull-up in my entire life, much less shimmy up anything, as many repressed junior high school gym classes would attest if I allowed myself to remember them. It was amazing what alcohol could do. It was as if I'd suddenly been blessed with the arms of an action hero.

I was leaning over, hoping to get a good listen if not a peek, when I heard an ominous rustling from across the way.

"FIONA!" boomed a Spanish-accented voice I knew all too well.

First I froze, then I spazzed. And then I let go.

I landed on my feet, then lost my balance in the slick grass and the mud and wiped out, tumbling down the little knoll and coming to a stop next to the house.

Cristina was now standing in the shrubbery, cupping her hands around her mouth to form a bullhorn.

"We know what you are!" she shouted. "We know what you did! You will pay!"

I was paralyzed with shock, and maybe had also severed my spinal cord. I saw lights flicker on above me and nearly swallowed my tongue. Covered in mud and probably being paralyzed was nothing. Being caught lolling about in the dirt beneath Fiona's window while my housemate bellowed insults was such a horrifying prospect that I, who would probably not run even if pursued by the entire selection of bad guys from the whole *Scream* trilogy, took off like a bat out of hell.

I hauled ass past Cristina, who had moved on to Spanish insults, which were much more lyrical and sounded twice as vicious, and I hauled ass past the quivering section of shrubbery I took to be George, cowering.

I ran as I had never run before, and didn't stop until I was safely in my room. Where I realized that everything hurt, I was covered in mud, my actions had just been those of the clinically insane, and I ought to be ashamed of myself. Which made me laugh.

I was still laughing when Cristina and George appeared, both out of breath.

"This was maybe not such a good plan," Cristina said, standing in the doorway. She frowned at me. "Why are you covered in dirt?"

"Because I fell out of a tree when some Spanish lunatic started shouting verbal abuse from the bushes," I retorted.

"Yes," Cristina said, nodding solemnly. "I don't know why that happened. I think I am drunk."

We caught eyes and set ourselves off laughing again. When I calmed down a little, I looked at George, who was actually grinning.

"Sorry," I said. "I should have warned you not to listen to any of the nonsense we come up with. It's all destined to end in disaster."

"It's okay," George said. He sounded dazed. "I mean, I just didn't know that girls did stuff like this."

"I don't know why you have to bring your entire house with you wherever you go," Toby groused.

"Just shut up," I suggested mildly. "I had no idea you were such a baby."

Toby muttered something I was just as happy not to have heard, and slunk back to the table with a handful of drinks. We were becoming quite a little group—Jason, Toby, and me, with the new additions of Cristina, Melanie on the rare occasions she wasn't staying in to study, and—unbelievably—George.

I paid the bartender and splayed out my hands so I could transport three pints and my wallet, which was a useful skill indeed and possibly the only one I'd so far garnered from my master's course. After a hair-raising navigation through the crowded pub, I plunked the drinks on the table and tossed myself down. I smiled at the group.

Cristina and Jason were engaged in a spirited debate about an Almodóvar film. My taste in film ran more to the Bruce Willis side of the spectrum, so I didn't bother to pay attention to any in-depth discussion about the meaning of camera angles. I was only in it for the cheap thrills, half-naked heroes, and explosions. Toby had taken himself off to feed money into the jukebox. And George was assuming his usual position: glassy-eyed and near coma.

As far as Cristina and I could tell, George had gotten drunk the night of our doomed reconnaissance mission and stayed that way. That night was at least two weeks gone by now, and George showed no signs of sobering up. I was coming to feel almost affectionate toward him. In his intoxicated state, he wasn't unlike a pet. A dopey Labrador, maybe. Addled and confused, but essentially good-natured. Or in George's case, so drunk that it amounted to the same thing. He was slumped over his drink and far beyond conversation, so I wandered over to the jukebox and tried to look at Toby's selections. He blocked me with his elbow, and then his shoulder when I tried to fake him out.

"You won't know any of the songs I'm choosing," he told me, laughing. "None of them made the American Top 40."

"You're such a snob," I retorted. "Which is amazing, given the fact that I know you get weepy over boy-band ballads."

"That's a bit of vicious slander, Brennan," Toby said, trying to sound hard, but he was grinning at me. "And don't think I'm not prepared to defend my good name."

I sighed. "Just please spare us another round of Radiohead. I beg you. If I have to listen to Thom Yorke whine about being a creep one more time I might have to slit my wrists on my pint glass and then throw myself out the window."

Toby gave me a level stare. "That would be a very foolish thing to do," he said. "As the window is at street level, you'd be essentially unharmed and forced to pay for repairs."

I scowled at him. "When did you become practical?"

He gave me his cheeky little grin. "I think you'll find I'm the very soul of practicality."

I made a face at him, which only made his grin widen. So I punched him. He laughed, and dodged a second hit by catching my wrist and holding it in the air between us.

"I have another arm," I pointed out.

"Go ahead," he invited me in a fake, and terrible, American accent. "Make my day."

I never got to respond to that, because that was when Suzanne appeared at the pub's entrance, in our direct line of vision.

"Shit," Toby muttered. "She's been after me for ages."

"You should try talking to her," I told him. I pulled my wrist out of his grip. "Then you wouldn't have to avoid her."

"I did try," he protested. "I went round her house but

she ran off. Said she would let me know when she could '*bear the disappointment*.' "

"Well, she's headed this way," I said. He groaned, but summoned up that default polite expression the English were so good at.

We both chorused a polite "hello." Suzanne stopped in front of us and shot me a flat look.

"If you'll excuse us, Alex," she said stiffly. "Toby and I need to talk."

"Of course," I said immediately, and sidled over to our table. Toby hadn't moved from the jukebox, and Jason and Cristina had stopped their debate to ogle the coming scene. I slipped into my seat.

"About what?" Toby asked, a touch belligerently.

"About what happened!" Suzanne was making no attempt to keep her voice down. In any case, we were all about three feet away.

"That's the thing, Suzanne," Toby said impatiently. "Nothing really did happen. It was ages ago, anyway."

"I don't know how you can say that." Her voice was low and rough. I was pretty sure she was about to cry, but she was angled away from us. Cristina rolled her eyes and stole one of my cigarettes.

"Because it's true," Toby snapped. "I wanted to talk to you weeks ago, but you refused. I don't appreciate you coming here and having a go at me in the middle of a pub."

"In front of your friends, you mean," Suzanne snarled. She twisted her head around and saw us all watching. "Better make sure you suck up to them, right, Toby? Particularly to you-know-who!"

"I think you've said enough," Toby said in a quiet, angry voice that made him sound much older than he was. "I won't have this conversation here."

He brushed her aside and made for the back of the pub and, presumably, the bathroom. We all sat in uncomfortable silence, except for George, who had started to hum tunelessly to himself. Suzanne balled her hands into fists and stormed over to the table.

"Are you happy now?" she demanded. "Did you all enjoy watching that?"

"Suzanne," Jason said, laughter creeping into his voice as if he wanted to encourage her to laugh too, "we're right here. Of course we watched."

I said nothing. Discretion seemed the wisest course, and I kept my face blank. But her glare found me anyway, and her face twisted with anger.

"Everyone knows how he feels about you," she hissed directly to me. "You just use it to your advantage."

"Hey—" I began.

"Enough," Cristina interrupted, in a tone brooking no argument. "Suzanne, no more of this. You are upset. You should go."

Suzanne breathed in a few ragged breaths and then hissed a succinct, "Fine." She whirled around and barreled out of the pub. No one said a word until we saw her shape fly by on the street outside.

"Bloody hell," Jason burst out.

Toby reappeared, looking disgruntled. "Thank God that's finished," he muttered, sending a dark look out the window.

"You know what?" I interrupted in sudden irritation.

"I'm tired of everything being my fault. What did I do?"

"You exist," Cristina said, waving a dismissive hand. "She is fixated. Who cares? She's a lunatic."

"Why did that happen?" Jason wanted to know, poking Toby in the arm. "I had no idea you and Suzanne—"

"There was never any me and Suzanne," Toby protested. He shrugged. "It all got blown out of proportion."

"American birds," Jason pronounced. He grinned at me. "Mad as you like, every one of them."

I stuck my tongue out at him. "Drink your pint," I ordered.

The doorbell started ringing at seven the next morning. The third time it went off, I stared blearily at the ceiling and realized no one else was going to answer it. Groaning in frustration, I crawled out of bed. I staggered down the stairs in my pajama bottoms and a scruffy T-shirt, my hair no doubt standing on end. I planned to rip into the blurry figure I could see through the glass, and yanked open the door to get started.

"Suzanne." I stared at her. "It's fucking seven o'clock in the fucking morning."

"I need to talk to you," she said. "I couldn't sleep at all last night—"

"So my sleep should be likewise disrupted?" I was incredulous.

"Don't be all sarcastic with me!" she shrieked, throwing her hands up. "I can't take it! I'm not like you!" She burst into tears, standing there in the doorway.

This is how I knew that I would never be a good person: I wanted to kick her right back out and slam the door. I had to strictly forbid my eyes from rolling into the back of my head. I wanted to rewind and get back in bed and pretend no one was home. I think I would have given anything, at that moment, not to have to deal with Suzanne and her tears.

"Okay," I said. My stomach already hurt in anticipation of the coming discussion. I rubbed at my eyes. "Okay, Suzanne, stop crying."

"I can't," she sobbed. "I don't think I ever will."

"Well, you have to," I said briskly. "Or we can't talk."

I stepped aside and sort of tugged her into the house. I thought that maybe I was getting frostbite on my bare feet, I was half asleep, and Suzanne was still snuffling. The tears were real, I saw, but that hardly made me more sympathetic. What was wrong with me? I wondered. Shouldn't I have more compassion for my fellow man? *That's what therapists are for*, I could hear Michael retort. *If they're not going to pay you, why pretend it's your job to give a shit?* I almost smiled, but figured Suzanne would take it amiss.

"Go up to my room," I ordered her. "I need to make myself some coffee if I'm going to be at all coherent." I realized she had yet to apologize for yanking me from my bed. I set my jaw. "Coffee or tea for you?"

"Tea," Suzanne whispered. "Herbal if you have it." She might as well have been Dumas's Camille, about to collapse on her chaise. Just so long as there were no arias, I thought I could just about cope.

"Just go up," I said. "I'll be right there."

She started up the stairs and I went into the kitchen and held my head in my hands. What a disaster. Then I remembered it was Friday, a day upon which I had no classes, and I all but gnashed my teeth. I was tired, damn it. I lived a mostly nocturnal life here. What was more, Suzanne knew that. She could easily peer out her kitchen window and see my bedroom light on until three or four in the morning. What the hell was she thinking, turning up at seven?

I slammed my coffeemaker around and slapped on the kettle, and tried to take calming breaths. I wasn't sure what I would do if faced with another round of Toby's feelings for me according to Suzanne. I didn't know what his feelings were, and I didn't want to know.

I fixed Suzanne's tea with an herbal tea bag stolen from Melanie and trudged up the stairs. I shoved open my door with my hip. Suzanne was sitting in my chair, her knees drawn up under her chin and her face toward the window. Quite affecting, really, except for the twin pigtails she was wearing, which, with all that red hair, rather unfortunately brought to mind Pippi Longstocking. I muffled a sigh and thrust her tea at her.

"Chamomile," I said gruffly.

I settled back into my bed and under my covers and took a long pull of my coffee. I could feel the espresso begin to work through my brain, and resisted the urge to moan aloud in pleasure.

"So," I prompted her. "Seven in the morning. What's going on?"

"I don't know how you can make everything into a joke," she said quietly. "I'm afraid I don't find it funny at all."

Sigh. Spare me.

"What I think is funny," I said, "is that you have no qualms wrenching me from a sound sleep and then expecting me to be able to decipher your drama with a single glance. What I think is funny is your unbelievable self-centeredness in assuming I care at all about whatever trauma has you so overwrought. What I think is funny is, in a word, you."

Of course, I just wish I said that.

Instead, I just sighed a little bit. "What's going on?" I asked again. I put down my coffee and lit up a cigarette. Suzanne required as many vices as possible as a filter. I would have started chugging down some wine if I hadn't suspected that it might make me violently ill. Not that I was ruling it out entirely, depending on how the conversation went.

"I don't know how to say this," Suzanne said. I arranged my face into something I hoped was more encouraging than bored. She turned her head and looked directly at me. "I think you and I are in competition."

"You and me?" I echoed. "Competition?"

"I think it's a direct competition between us," she said, in that low voice. "We seem to have the same kind of appeal. We both went to really good colleges. I assume you also graduated with honors."

"Not me," I said. "I almost didn't graduate, actually." I gave her a big smile on that one. "And I never tested very well, either."

"Well." Her eyes shifted away from me, no doubt to conceal her pleasure at her academic superiority. "We're clearly the two most intelligent women on our course. I think that we have to come to terms with the fact that everything between us is a power struggle, based on the fact we're so similar."

"Suzanne." I struggled to keep my voice even, and not to let myself get snide. "I really don't think we're at all alike. Also," I said, "I don't think we can discount the intelligence of our classmates. Who knows what kind of papers they write? If my intelligence was determined by my performance in class, I'd be asked to leave."

"Come on, Alex," she said, frowning at me. "You know there's been this weird energy between us since the day we met. How else would you describe it if not a battle for supremacy? I'm willing to admit to it; why can't you?"

I didn't think that was the right question. I thought the right question was probably—why wasn't I asleep? I took a drag of my cigarette.

"I really don't feel any competition with you at all," I said. "And as far as any energy . . ." I took a breath. "Suzanne, I know you're upset about Toby. Why are you making this about me?"

"You say you don't want him," she said immediately. "Maybe that's true. But I think you definitely don't want anyone else to have him."

"I don't care who has him. And I don't have anything to do with the decisions he makes." But was that really true? Because I actually hadn't been all that excited about Toby being with Suzanne. Maybe I just thought that what Toby and I had as almost-entirely-platonic friends was much deeper than Suzanne's stupid snog-and-then-bail scenario. After all, Toby and I had also snogged, nothing had come of it, and we were still close. Maybe I was more proprietary than I thought.

"So you had nothing to do with what he decided about us?" Suzanne's eyes narrowed. "Because I would have thought he mentioned it."

"Of course he mentioned it." I took a big gulp of my coffee. "So did you. And there ends my involvement."

"You didn't tell him what to do?" Her voice was rich with disbelief. I stared at her.

"If you mean, did he ask me my advice, yes. And I gave it. I would have given it to you too, had you asked." I shrugged. "You never asked."

"You can't play both sides against the middle, Alex," Suzanne snapped.

"Hey!" I raised a palm. "I don't have a side."

"This is exactly what I'm talking about," she said. "You won't even admit how embroiled you are in this thing!"

"I don't understand what you want me to say." I watched her face. "You came over here the moment I got back from Christmas break to tell me all about how you and Toby were together. I haven't been running around telling him to get rid of you or trying to come between the two of you. If anything, it seems as if you maybe misread the situation."

"And you just love it, don't you?" she said, with tears in her throat. "It just plays right into your hands."

"Suzanne," I said, with a definite edge to my voice. "I don't know how many more ways I can tell you I don't care. I didn't care if you were together and I don't care if you're not. I'm sorry if you find that harsh, but it's true. I. Don't. Care. Okay?" I softened. "I am sorry you're so upset. But I don't see how that has anything to do with me."

Suzanne snuffled and wiped at her nose. She stared at me. I busied myself with my coffee and with lighting a new cigarette, having left the first to smolder out.

"Maybe that's it," she said finally, when I had started wondering if she'd turned to stone and I would be stuck with a Suzanne statue in my room for all time. The upside of that being that I could go back to sleep immediately.

"Maybe what's it?" I asked. I was losing tone control and sounded weary even to my own ears. I wished that she would leave. More than that, I wished that I had the guts to tell her what I really thought of being emotionally accosted at the crack of dawn.

"The mystery of you," she said, and laughed hollowly. "You're completely emotionally unavailable. No wonder Toby finds it compelling. He's British, isn't he."

"Emotionally unavailable?" I didn't like that at all.

"Sure." Suzanne shrugged. "You've never let me in. Or anyone else, I'm sure. You lock yourself away. People tend to find that intriguing." Though her tone was more scathing than intrigued.

I thought: *Too much Psych 101, not enough common*

sense. Suzanne was almost breathtaking to behold. The part of me that didn't want to throw something at her almost wanted to hug her and tell her everything was going to be all right.

"Really," I said. What absolute gall. *Maybe I'm emotionally unavailable to* you, *Suzanne, because I don't actually* like *you*.

"I feel for you," she told me. She gave me a tremulous smile. "I think I might just be starting to understand you, Alex."

"Sweetheart, please," Michael said dismissively. "What sort of availability are you supposed to have? This girl sounds like she just spews out emotion like some kind of lawn sprinkler. Are you supposed to model your emotional health on *that*? I can't believe we're having a serious discussion about what some insane child thinks of you in between her fits of jealousy."

"Hey," I said. "Suzanne's a nutcase but she's not dumb. She may see things about me that I don't want to see myself."

"Let's add the necessary grain of salt, shall we?" Michael retorted. "This is not someone who *likes* you. I do like you, so I'm hardly qualified to judge your flaws as they appear to others. You've always been emotionally available to *me*."

"I don't know." I was unconvinced.

"Look," Michael said. "If she thinks you're emotionally unavailable—well, good. Right? You actually don't *want* her close. She's just obviously too self-involved to realize that *probably* you're not emotionally frigid, you just don't like her."

"I guess," I muttered.

"What do you mean, you guess?" Michael sighed. "Alex, you know I love you, but why do you spend so much time on these losers? That Evan creature, for example, don't think I've forgotten *him.* And this Suzanne chick. The fact that people are around you and aren't actively heinous isn't a good enough reason to hang out with them. You have to learn how to be picky."

I thought about that long after I hung up. I sat and I smoked and let the hours crawl by. What was it that bothered me so much about what Suzanne said? Because Michael was right—I didn't want her close.

The day wore on and I fell into a sulk. The shadows lengthened and still I sat there, chain-smoking. It wasn't that I was upset, or even that I thought what Suzanne said was valid. It was that I couldn't entirely refute it. It bothered me.

"*Suzanne sucks,*" was Robin's concise email response to the voicemail I'd left earlier. "*I don't want to hear that name again.*"

Everything was fading to black outside the window, and my stomach was insisting that I get up and get back to my life. I wasn't one of those people who could suffer quietly or in isolation. I wasn't the kind who dropped fifteen pounds every crisis. My body never let me go too long too lost in my head. Usually it demanded chocolate instead.

I climbed out of bed again and stared around the small room as if I'd never seen it before. I stared at myself in the mirror as if I'd never seen me before. I searched for signs of alteration, but there were none. I wondered if people had spent a lot of time staring at themselves in mirrors before movies came along and taught us that that was how people registered confusion and change.

Stupid Suzanne. And stupid Toby, too, when it came to that. I didn't want to hear those names together anymore. And I definitely didn't want to have another round of My Flaws According to Suzanne. I needed to concentrate on other things.

I shuffled down the stairs and smelled garlic frying as I pushed through the door. Melanie and Cristina were milling around the stove together, chopping vegetables and talking. They both looked up when I came in.

"We're having a stir-fry," Melanie said. "If you fancy it."

"You must eat," Cristina said sternly. "You need vitamins."

"I was planning on cigarettes and coffee," I muttered. I was surprised to hear my own voice.

"Stir-fry and then cigarettes and coffee," Melanie said easily, sweeping more vegetables into her wok.

"You had a very bad day, I think," Cristina said, coming over and tossing an arm around my shoulders. She grinned. "This calls for whiskey and whingeing, my specialties."

Ten

The path we took to campus at night added an extra five minutes or so to the journey, but avoided the muddy black hole of the footpath. When you were all dressed up for a night out, the mud and the dark did not appeal. Cristina and Melanie were collapsing with laughter all over each other, stumbling as if they were already significantly intoxicated, and it was barely eight o'clock. I was feeling virtuously sober, having decided to go without the preliminary glasses of wine Melanie and Cristina had indulged in back at the house. *I* knew that I could have fun without the demon liquor, but I felt it was always a good idea, periodically, to prove it.

"It's true," Cristina said, turning to grin at me. "If you jump a little bit you can see directly into David's bedroom. He is normally alone."

"After that whole Fiona the Vulture thing, I would have thought you'd outgrown reconnaissance missions," I said. "Or at the very least feared arrest."

"Shh!" Cristina made a big show of looking all around. "We must never speak of that night again. I am sure that Fiona the Vulture has spies where we least suspect it!"

"David the Physicist knows you," Melanie pointed out, still laughing. "And he's eventually bound to recognize your little head popping up and down outside his window."

"You would be surprised how seldom people really look out their windows," Cristina said philosophically. "Especially men."

"You think it's a gender issue?" I asked. But it had given me an idea. A delightfully bad idea.

"Men are fools," Cristina pronounced. "Every woman in every country knows this is true. American men, Spanish men, and especially British men. Idiots, all of them."

"I agree completely," Melanie said. "Think of all the wonders of civilization, all brought about by men. Imagine how much more impressive it all could have been if it had been done by women instead?"

"Whatever," I said impatiently. "Then we would have had to fight all the wars and go race around the tundra after woolly mammoths, which is frankly not my idea of a good time. I think women had the right idea. 'Yes, honey, you're a big bad mammoth hunter. You go on with your bad self and I'll just stay here and dig up a few roots and lounge by the fire.' " I warmed to the topic. "And what was so horrible about staying at home and eating bonbons? All you had to do was clean the house and bake a few cookies for the kids and you got a paid vacation for life. I never asked anyone to burn *my* bra."

"The not being allowed to vote, though," Melanie

said. She grinned. "And Alex, not to be picky, but I've seen the state of your room. Cleaning the house might well have presented a bigger challenge than you imagine."

"True." I sighed. "And I don't really like kids." I looked at them both. "But follow me, please. Since you're so into stalking, Cristina, I thought we'd add a little to the night's entertainment."

She caught on immediately. "Your teacher!" she breathed. Melanie's eyes widened.

"You stalk *him*? I thought you were joking!" She sounded thrilled. "Let's go!"

We made our way with unnecessary drama and much flattening of bodies to walls like bad B-movie spies. Cristina kept pausing to perform martial arts moves against imaginary assailants. Melanie was shaking so hard from repressed laughter that I thought she might just topple over.

"Could you stop that?" I asked Cristina, snickering.

"You must never let your guard down," she informed me solemnly.

"I can see why no one has tried to recruit us into any spy organizations," I muttered. "Which I thought was practically de rigueur at British graduate schools."

"Yes," Melanie said quite seriously. "But I think you have to be proficient in languages or bomb making or something. I don't think literature is really—"

"There's his house," I hissed, cutting her off. "I think he might actually be home for once."

Excited, we crept closer and peered inside.

Sean was standing in all his lean and delicious glory,

propped against the counter in his kitchen—the very counter where he had prepared me a meal. Propped against him was a woman. A woman who was not me. They were talking to each other with the kind of smiling awareness that led directly to the nearest bed. I could see the heat in his wonderful eyes.

I was crushed.

The woman was the kind of woman that the British find breathtakingly sexy and I could never figure out why. She had short dark hair that was a little bit spiky on top and a curvy little body. She was cute, I supposed, but was no goddess. She wasn't worthy of him. And yet Sean looked like he wanted to eat her up.

"Let's go," I said, but I didn't move.

And so we sat there, in the bushes outside Sean's house, and stared in through the window as he and Miss Sexy Only in Britain flirted and smiled and eventually began some serious kissing that made my mouth drop open. Whether in shock or profound envy, I couldn't tell.

"Oh my," Melanie whispered, impressed.

And actually, I could tell. I was painfully, surpassingly jealous. I could feel it like arthritis in my bones.

A door opened nearby and we all jumped. I toppled over backward.

"Bloody hell," Cristina hissed. "This is no time to swoon, Alex. It was just a kiss."

She and Melanie each took an arm and yanked me to my feet. In Sean's kitchen, the kissing went on uninterrupted, and I saw his hand—

"Alex!"

I ran for it.

• • •

We approached the college pub, where we'd agreed to meet the others. We hadn't said much since running away from Sean's, mostly because we were all out of shape and had to concentrate on breathing.

"Are you very upset?" Melanie asked me.

"Why would I be upset?" I retorted. As my retort hung in the air, I realized, sheepishly, that it had been a tad on the aggressive side. "He's my professor," I said with tremendous dignity. "His romantic choices are no business of mine. If I were less of a lunatic and hadn't felt the need to lurk in the bushes and peer into his windows, I wouldn't even know about them. So."

"Men," Cristina said darkly. "Idiots."

We walked inside and picked our way through the crowded college pub. It was like walking into a wall of noise. There was some kind of disco-like event going on, in celebration of nothing in particular, and the place was packed and heaving.

"You'll see," Melanie shouted in my ear. "A little eighties music and you'll be as good as new!"

The British, I had discovered, loved to dance. Even the men. Granted, they drank immense quantities of alcohol before taking to the floor, but they danced. I couldn't think of a single straight American man of my acquaintance who voluntarily attended dancing events. Much less leaped out onto the dance floor and boogied, which was the only way I could describe what the people around me were doing. The British had many fancy dress parties, which often seemed to be nothing more than an excuse for straight boys to doll themselves up in drag and for the girls to get tarty. Or, as the case was for many this far north, tartier. In the middle of such displays, it was easy to see why drinking too much and making scenes was considered a very minor social sin.

We found Toby and Jason in a corner, tossing back drinks and delighted to be joined by three females.

"I believe my masculinity was being called into question," Jason said. "Which is difficult to combat when dancing with another bloke to 'It's Raining Men.'"

"Gay is good," I told him.

"Not when you're not gay," he replied.

"Tequila shots!" Cristina cried. "I will get us some, and the dancing will begin!"

She returned with a tray of double shots for all. I decided a double shot only slightly compromised my no-alcohol plan, and then decided what the hell, screw the no-alcohol plan. I'd just seen my teacher and major crush stick his tongue down another woman's throat and his hand up her shirt. With tremendous finesse, but even so. We clanked plastic glasses and downed the shots on the count of three.

"To the dance floor!" Cristina cried, and dove right in.

We'd been leaping around for some time when Toby commandeered a table and he and I dropped into the nearest seats.

"Your housemates are mad," he observed. His eyes were warm.

I grinned. The normally sensible Melanie was like a wild thing on the dance floor, and the less said about

Cristina the better. Together they'd made me laugh too hard to do much dancing of my own. Although I had made a small spectacle of myself to "American Pie." If there was anything more surreal than listening to a packed bar filled with British citizens shouting, "Bye, bye, Miss American Pie," I had yet to encounter it.

"They're both fearless," I said to Toby. "But so is Jason."

"Jason is far beyond mad. He's a complete nutter. Before you lot arrived he was narrating the entire evening. We would get a drink and he'd say, 'Drinks in, thirst quenched' in a very odd, low voice. As if he were speaking into a microphone in his armpit." Toby shook his head. "I can't work out if he's putting it on or if he's just a bit off his head."

"Both," I said immediately. We relaxed into a companionable silence as the DJ began to play Spandau Ballet. The dance floor cleared but for the usual couples and a few very drunk groups who clung to one another and swayed, singing loudly.

Since Toby's altercation with Suzanne, everything had gone back to normal. Toby had never spoken of it again. He and I certainly never discussed any of the accusations she'd leveled at him or at me. I'd told him that she'd cornered me in my house the day following the scene in the pub and he'd just been disgusted. "*She needs to sort herself out,*" was all he'd said. Our relationship was as comfortable as it had ever been. And as platonic as it had ever been. That kiss, obviously, had been a drunken bit of silliness best forgotten and completely without meaning. Suzanne, I thought, could go to hell.

Not that I'd really seen her since that early morning emotional drive-by. She had different classes this term and had stopped dropping by the house. Which suited me fine. I didn't know who she was hanging around with, and if I was honest with myself, I knew I was only curious because I knew she required an audience and wondered who that audience could be. Was I the villain in her tale? I presumed so. Suzanne wasn't the kind of girl who could make the guy his own person. If Toby had hurt her, I could be sure that it was considered my fault.

"Why are you sitting?" Cristina descended on us. "Melanie is getting more drinks." She perched on the arm of my chair. "There are many men on the prowl, Alex. I think it would do you good to prowl yourself."

I perked up. "I could do a little prowling. Who did you have in mind?"

Melanie came over with very suspicious-looking drinks of indeterminate ingredients. They were in pint glasses, and they were pink.

"It's called a Snakebite," Toby told me from where he remained slouched in his chair. "For reasons you will shortly discover if you drink it."

"Ugh," I said, staring at mine. "Just tell me there's no aniseed in here. I can't stand it."

"No aniseed," Melanie said. "But I'm not telling you what's in it. Just drink it. You'll be the better for it." We all raised our glasses except Toby, who was looking mulish.

"I'm not drinking that," he said.

"A wise choice." Melanie laughed. We were all less wise, and drank.

I watched Toby frown at his drink. He took a big gulp when he thought no one was looking.

A very bouncy eighties anthem came on, and the three of us took to our feet, trolling for potential romantic candidates. Toby remained behind, claiming that he was tired and that he would rather wait and see if Jason reappeared from wherever he'd wandered.

"We have to be careful, however," Cristina said. "Because Yannis is here and he is not very pleased with my behavior."

"Yannis?" I stared at her. "But you haven't even really spoken to him since your whole thing with him ended way back at the beginning of the year!"

"I know this and you know this," Cristina said, shrugging. "But Yannis has his own version, of course. It is better to just avoid him."

Melanie anointed herself the Chooser, which meant she pointed out eligible men and Cristina and I would go and try to act fetchingly in their proximity. This had mostly no results. Mostly the "chosen" men looked at us as if we were freaks or ignored us completely.

"I think you suck at this," I told Melanie.

"Me?" She gave me a look. "You're the one who keeps doing *Saturday Night Fever* moves in front of your potential boyfriends. Perhaps that has something to do with why they look at you with fear rather than passion."

"Passion, fear, it's all the same," Cristina exclaimed. She made a grandiose, sweeping gesture with one arm. "You must bring them to their knees."

"Go on then," Melanie challenged her at once.

"That one right there," I said, pointing to the nearest

male—who looked to be still in his teens and who was sporting a feather boa and a bowler hat. "Bring *him* to his knees. Melanie and I will stay right here and watch and learn."

Cristina never could resist a challenge.

"I am a Latin lover," she informed us very seriously. "You watch."

And off she slunk, the light of battle in her eyes, to grab the feather boa.

"She just busted up to this complete stranger and grabbed him!" I laughed. "Poor kid. He didn't know what to do, but, being a man and facing Cristina, he just surrendered." I laughed again, at the image. "She practically snapped a whip and had him jump. It was amazing."

"Whatever," Toby snapped. I eyed him.

"And your problem is?"

"I don't have a problem," he retorted. In a tone that quite clearly contradicted that statement.

We were walking back home together. The music and the mayhem had all proved a little too much for me, so I'd left Melanie and Cristina to further adventures among males and had accompanied Toby when he'd announced he was going to bed. It was already after one. I always felt all turned around when bars had late licenses and stayed open past eleven. It was so disconcerting.

"Right," I said to Toby, in a wry tone. "You were sulking at the disco and now you're storming around, snapping my head off, but you don't have a problem."

"I was hardly *sulking*," Toby snapped.

"You were sitting in the corner with a pissed-off look on your face for the better part of the last two hours," I said. "What would you call it?"

"Maybe," Toby said snidely, "I didn't think it was the biggest laugh of all time to watch you and your mates throw yourselves at every man in the place."

"Excuse me?" I was stunned.

"You think you're so funny, you know, but you're not. You have no idea how you appear sometimes." Toby snorted. "I was embarrassed for you."

I stopped walking and stared at him. Realizing I wasn't keeping up with him, he turned around and glared at me.

"You know what?" I glared at him. "If you were so embarrassed you should have left. And fuck you anyway."

"Oh, that's very nice," he sneered. "Of course, nothing could be wrong with your behavior, because you're always right."

"Who asked you to comment on my behavior? If I'd known you were sitting in the corner monitoring everyone's actions I would have told you to leave myself. As if the way you behave stands up to any scrutiny."

"There's nothing wrong with my behavior," he snapped. "I'm not the one throwing myself at strangers."

"No, you like to throw yourself at people you know!" I snapped right back. "What makes that any better?"

Toby scowled at me. "Exactly what are you talking about?" he demanded. It occurred to me that I really,

really didn't want him to think that I was talking about anything or anyone but Suzanne. I scowled back.

"I'm talking about the mess you made with Suzanne," I snarled at him. "The mess you don't have to deal with yourself, naturally."

I stamped on, headed for home. As I passed the intersecting path that led around to Sean's house, I gritted my teeth. Toby stormed along behind me. When we reached my house, I made to go in but he grabbed me by the arm.

"We have to talk," he said. Why did people keep saying that?

"I don't want to talk!" I practically shouted, incredulous. "What are we going to talk about? How you just attacked me for no reason? How you're an immature little shit who can't deal with—"

"Don't you call *me* immature!" he interrupted. "You're the one who doesn't act your age!"

Asshole. "Let me rectify that," I hissed. "Please remove your hand from my arm, and please leave. I have nothing else to say."

"Fine," Toby snapped, and he stormed off toward his own house.

I shoved my way inside and nearly tripped over the prone body of George, who appeared to be unconscious as he lay sprawled across our entry hall. I prodded him a few times with my foot, but elicited no response. I made sure he was facedown, so he wouldn't choke on his own vomit if there was any vomiting, and then stepped over him and marched up to my room.

I was so angry I didn't know what to do. I threw off

my clothes and threw on my pajamas but was far too furious to actually get into bed. I was standing in the middle of my room, quietly raging, when the doorbell rang.

"Asshole," I hissed, and stamped back down the stairs.

Yanking open the door, I glared at him. "What?" I asked rudely.

Toby just brushed me aside and came into the house. He stopped to stare at George. "You're not just leaving him there?" he demanded in an accusatory tone.

"What would you suggest I do, Toby?" I asked acidly. "Pick him up and carry him? He might not be the largest guy in the world, but I assure you he's too heavy for me to carry up a flight of stairs. But you go right ahead, since you're such a big, tough guy. And why are you even here? How could you possibly have anything else to say?"

He stepped over George and headed up the stairs. "You don't want to wake up your whole house," he said.

"Because I'm sure they're all sleeping soundly now, after you rang the doorbell at one-thirty in the morning?" But I followed him.

Inside my room, he slumped on my bed and I sat in my desk chair and crossed my arms over my chest.

"What do you want?" I demanded. "Do you have any more insults? Or maybe you can tell me all the other occasions upon which my behavior embarrassed you?"

Toby just looked at me, for a long moment. Then he reached over to my windowsill and picked up one of the bottles of wine I kept on hand for late-night sobriety emergencies.

"Let's have a drink," he said.

"Surely there's been enough drinking tonight."

"Maybe for you." Toby went over to my sink, where I kept some glasses, and poured two full to the brim. He handed me one.

"I'm very angry with you," I told him, taking it.

"I'm not too pleased with you," he replied.

It was like a toast. We each took a big gulp.

"I never meant for you to deal with Suzanne," he said. "I don't know why she's obsessed with you." For a moment, it looked as if maybe he was going to say something else. Our eyes held. But he looked down.

"It's one of the great mysteries of our time," I said lightly, to break the spell.

By the time he opened the second bottle, we were both laughing.

And when I woke up the next morning, he was in my bed.

Eleven

Fully clothed, I hasten to add.

"Oh my God!" I practically shouted.

Without moving, Toby muttered, "There's no need to shout."

"That's easy for you to say." I climbed over him and dove as far away from him as it was humanly possible to get in the confines of my little cell. Which was about three feet.

Toby stretched as if he hadn't a care in the world and grinned cheekily. "Come on, Brennan," he said. "Surely you've woken with more horrible things in your bed."

"Out." I pointed at the door.

"I'm just saying, all things considered, at least you needn't worry about your virtue—"

"Out!" I yelled at him.

He sighed and swung himself into sitting position. He rubbed his face with his hands. "That's the last time I try to fulfill your needs," he said.

"I don't even want to know what you're talking about," I said. "Nothing happened, no needs were fulfilled."

"Certainly not mine," he agreed, looking disgusted.

"Nothing happened," I repeated. A small pause. "Did it?"

A delighted grin spread across his face. "Why, Alex," he said. "You can't remember, can you? Don't worry; I don't think anyone saw too much when you ran naked through the courtyard."

"I hate you."

"*Of course* nothing happened," he said, sighing, but he still looked delighted. "I'm sure we both just passed out."

"So you don't actually know," I said. I scowled at him. "Jerk. You're just as much of a lush as I am."

"And just as hungover," he agreed. "Step aside, Alex. I need water."

"I can't believe you had such a fit last night," I said as we walked downstairs. It was barely nine in the morning, but I could tell from the size of my headache that sleep wasn't an option. I needed caffeine and grease. George, I was pleased to note, was no longer in the entryway, which cut down on the possibility that he was dead.

"I did not 'have a fit,'" Toby retorted, yanking open the door.

"What would you call it, then?" I shivered in the frigid entryway. It was gray and misty outside.

"Expressing some concern about a friend," he said primly.

"Oh come on. You totally flipped out."

"How very American."

"How very snotty."

We were grinning at each other when a complete stranger strode down the stairs and into view. Toby and I looked at him, then each other. The guy was tall and attractive and clearly very hungover. He paused when he saw us.

"All right," Toby greeted him, expressionlessly.

"Morning," the guy said. He stepped between us to get out the door, and glanced around for a moment before setting off in the direction of campus.

Toby laughed. "What was that all about?"

Which is when Cristina came rushing down the stairs. She stared at us in horror. She had to visibly collect herself.

"Good morning," she said with dignity, and swept into the kitchen.

I shrugged. "I guess that's what that was all about."

"That Cristina," Toby said, shaking his head. "Mad."

"That's our Cristina," I said affectionately.

"Well," Toby said. He grinned at me. "I really enjoyed sleeping with you, Brennan. It was the highlight of my life."

"You can't even remember it," I reminded him. "For all you know it really was."

"Your morning-after routine could stand a little work," he retorted. "Shouting is generally frowned upon in polite circles."

"You can deal," I said, smiling up at him. "You're pretty tough."

"Well," he said.

"Yeah," I said. "Well."

"Yes," said a third, much less amused voice. "Well."

Surprised, Toby and I turned.

Suzanne stood there, freshly showered and on her way to an early morning at the library. Her eyes were narrow and nasty, and Toby and I just stared at her in shock.

"I hope you're very happy with each other," she spat at us, and stalked off.

"Can you imagine?" I moaned. "And there Toby and I are, looking all rumpled and half asleep as if we'd just rolled out of bed. Which we had, but in a million years that girl is never going to believe that nothing happened."

"We are all having some difficulty with that one," Cristina said archly.

She and I were sitting on her bed, tending to our hangovers.

"I suppose I'm going to have to tell her what really happened," I said, considering.

"Why bother?" Cristina lit a fresh cigarette. "She won't believe you anyway. She will take it as an opportunity to say more horrible things to you." She exhaled. "And the truth is that she is right: Toby prefers you. It's not your fault. Nor is there anything that she or you can do about it."

"Whatever." I sighed. "It's your turn. Who was that guy?"

"Oh," Cristina said in a low voice. "Him."

"Yeah, him," I said. I looked at her. "What's wrong? He was very good-looking."

"Yes." Cristina met my eyes. "He is also David the Physicist's housemate and friend."

I covered my mouth and stared at her. "Oh no," I whispered.

"Oh yes," she said. Her eyes were miserable. "It seemed like a good idea last night, of course." She shrugged. "Possibly I also spent the night platonically, but I don't think so."

"He had a big hickey on his neck," I said. Cristina glared. "I'm just saying that it's probably not a platonic—" I stopped myself. "Who cares, anyway?" I demanded, getting myself riled up. "David has no claim on you. If he wanted one, he had a million opportunities to do something about it."

"That is not the point," Cristina said. "And you know it."

"It's not necessarily a big deal," I countered.

"It's not a big deal at all," she agreed. "It just means that any chance there was of anything ever happening with David is now gone."

"Hey," I said. "You never know. He might never mention it."

"Please," she said.

"He's a guy," I said. "Maybe he doesn't know your name."

Cristina considered. "That's actually possible!" She sounded significantly brighter. "It's very possible. I only know his name because I am a crazy person and make it my business to know everyone who comes into contact with David."

"So you could easily be in the clear." I shrugged. "And if not, just deny it."

A smile flickered across her mouth. "How do you deny it to the person who knows better?" she asked.

"That's the best," I assured her. "They don't know what to do." She looked skeptical. "I speak from experience," I told her. "I've never actually done it, just had it done to me. This guy just flat-out lied and told me—and, more importantly, his girlfriend—that he'd never touched me and didn't know what I was talking about. The girlfriend believed him, and I was actually wondering if I was too drunk and had imagined the entire thing. I still sometimes wonder that."

Cristina was staring at me.

"Sorry," I said. "But that's a true story." I lit a cigarette and smiled. "Nobody knows the trouble I've seen."

"Ouch," Robin said. "I can't believe you brought up that repulsive Chris Reardon."

"As an illustrative point," I said.

"Illustrative of what?" Robin demanded. "Only you would have reacted that way, Alex. I assure you that if he'd denied sleeping with me, I wouldn't have just stood there. Assuming of course that I'd lowered myself to sleep with him in the first place." I was so pleased to finally get her on the phone that I chose not to remind her of some of the low places she'd visited over the years.

"Musicians are very sexy," I said. A touch defensively. "They have a universal appeal."

"He was unwashed, uneducated, and uninteresting," Robin snapped with remembered disdain. "And he was only a musician in the broadest sense of the term. What he did to a bass guitar was really a criminal act."

"Thank you, *Rolling Stone* magazine." I rolled my eyes. "The point is not Chris Reardon, Robin. I was merely pointing out to Cristina that denying things can sometimes be a good idea, no matter how ridiculous it is to try."

"Your poor friend," Robin said. "That's just never a good situation. People always react badly when you sleep with their friends."

"I didn't know what to say," I said. "Of all the men on campus, she had to pick that one."

"She probably picked him deliberately," Robin said. "You know how that is. For some reason, when you're drunk, it seems like the perfect gesture of revenge and adoration. Unfortunately, I've been there."

I hesitated. "You can talk about stuff like this?" I asked, scandalized. "With Zack right there?"

"I actually don't like to talk on the phone when he's sitting next to me," Robin said. "So he's in the other room. But he already knows everything, so there's never anything to hide."

"Even the time you—"

"Whatever you're about to say," she said sternly, "don't. I'm sure I've repressed it, and I'm happier that way. But yes, he knows everything. Some things I probably presented with a slight spin, but so what? According to him, he's never had a cross word to say to another living human being in his entire life."

"He's a lawyer," I said.

"Exactly. Spin." Robin laughed.

"So . . ." I didn't know what to say. "How is it? The whole living with somebody thing."

"It's really good," she said.

"Do you feel like an adult, making adult choices and living an adult life?"

"Not really. I feel like me, living with Zack. He claims he had no idea I was the kind of woman who needed that much closet space. And I had no idea he had an electric guitar he can barely play. He thinks he's a chord or two away from greatness. Small adjustments, but everything's pretty cool."

"You sound happy," I said.

"I am," she said simply.

"Robin's blissfully happy," I told Michael.

"Yeah? So?" Michael was much less so. "Why shouldn't she be happy?"

"I'm just reporting that she is," I said. "What's wrong with you?"

"Nothing is actually wrong with me," Michael muttered. "Nothing that an entirely different life and personality wouldn't cure."

"Michael—"

"Whatever," he said. "I'm sorry, I have to go sit in a dark room and feel sorry for myself. I'll call you back when that gets boring."

"Do you remember Chris Reardon?" I asked.

There was a small silence.

"Thank you," Michael said stiffly. "Now I have to vomit, then go sit in a dark room and feel sorry for myself while fighting off images of *your* horrendous taste in men."

He hung up.

• • •

"Hi, Mom!" I said brightly. "That latest care package was the best yet. Who knew they made marshmallow Peeps in so many different varieties?"

"Oh, hello, Alex," she said serenely. "Lovely to hear from you. You seem to keep leaving messages when we're having Sunday dinner with your grandmother. I don't think I've talked to you live in two weeks."

"Huh." Busted. "What a coincidence."

"Is it raining?"

"It usually is," I said weakly.

"Your father was just saying he needed to speak with you," she continued merrily. "I'll put him on. He's in his study."

Oh goodie, I thought as I heard her cover the receiver and call up the stairs to my father.

"What do you think I am?" my father demanded when he picked up the extension. "A millionaire?"

I'd discovered through years of trial and error that it was usually better not to answer questions like that.

"Hi, Dad," I said with a hearty dose of false cheer. Couldn't hurt. "How are you?"

"I don't know what you're doing over there," he said in a heavy tone, completely blowing the false cheer theory. "I don't know what they're teaching you. But it's certainly not the value of a dollar."

"Well, no," I said. "Since they use the pound here."

It just slipped out. I couldn't help it. Some people had the compulsion to steal. Or lie. I had the compulsion to be a wiseass to my father. This had never ended well for me, in all my nearly twenty-seven years, and yet I couldn't seem to stop.

A very tense silence indicated that this was gearing up to be another bad ending.

"Why don't you write *me* a paper?" my father suggested in a deadly tone. "How about five hundred words on fiscal responsibility? Or better yet, on how to avoid being stranded in a foreign country without a penny?"

"Dad," I said. I covered the mouthpiece with my hand and massaged it with my palm. "I don't know why I say the things I say," I said, speaking normally, although through my hand. On his end, it should have come out something like, "*I—muffled—why—muffled—things—muffled—say.*"

"What? Alexandra?"

"Bad line!" I shouted, and hung up the phone.

And now there was also no one else to call. Unless I wanted to hunt down some high school friends I hadn't bothered to keep in touch with, and that was a whole different level of desperation.

I sucked it up and went to find Suzanne.

I wasn't sure why, but I just didn't want her thinking she'd caught me and Toby fulfilling her worst fears. Okay, yes, I knew why. Suzanne could call all her tree-hugging friends back in Oregon and bitch, she could tell everyone she knew at university that I was Satan, and there wasn't anything I could do about it. But if she was going to hate me and vilify me, I wanted it to be just because she disliked me. And I wanted her to admit that she disliked me simply because she did, with no justification and nothing to sob about into the pillow. If she was going to lie about it to whatever minions she had at the ready, that was up to her, but I wanted to make sure the two of us were perfectly clear what the real deal was. It had nothing to do with Toby. He was just a convenient excuse.

I yanked on my coat and ran out of the house, with a fire in my eye and my head already composing the perfect words.

And therefore felt pretty foolish when one of Suzanne's housemates stood rigidly in the doorway and informed me that Suzanne wasn't home and wasn't expected anytime soon.

All the perfect words faded away as I trudged back home.

And then finally it was time to get our long papers back. On the one hand, it had taken ages, and who did the professors think they were? We deserved to know how we were doing, surely. On the other hand, who really wanted to have written proof that they sucked and were an academic joke? The smaller papers we'd written before the Christmas holiday had been held up for some reason, no doubt professorial negligence, so we were expected to drop by Sean's office and have a small chat about both.

As if I could chat with Sean about anything, much less my grades.

As if I could even look at him, after watching that scene in his kitchen.

I veered between chills of fear and flashes of embarrassment. What if he could somehow sense that I'd been spying on him? Could he change my grade? Would he prefer to have me locked away?

"Get a grip," I snapped at myself.

On Judgment Day, I was so stressed out that I woke up every half hour on the half hour starting at about five in the morning. Finally I just got up and went down to the kitchen to bite my nails, smoke cigarettes, and drink too much coffee so at least I could blame my jitters on something other than nerves.

I completely surprised Melanie, who had a nine-thirty class and had never seen me in the morning before.

"I wasn't entirely certain you'd ever seen the daylight," she teased.

"I could be a vampire," I said, thinking about it. "But I'd probably know it by now. Bloodlust and all that."

"Do you get your marks today?" she asked, and smiled when I nodded. "You'll do well," she said staunchly. "Everything will be fine."

Cristina burst into the room, looking wild and shoving books and papers into a knapsack. "Let's go," she said to Melanie. She looked at me in surprise. "What are you doing? Are you just getting in?"

"Cristina, please," I said. "You know perfectly well I didn't go anywhere last night."

"Stress," Melanie told her matter-of-factly. "She's getting her marks today."

"Ooh," Cristina said, brightening. "You get to sit in a small room with Sean." She leaned toward me and went all sultry. "You must tell him that no display of lust with a trollop can dissuade your love, and that he must—"

"Please go to class now," I ordered.

I heard them laughing as they left. I stared out the window and saw all kinds of people leaving their houses and greeting one another. And all before ten in the morning. I realized that there was a whole different university than the one I knew. There were people whose experiences had nothing to do with pubs and late nights, and everything to do with early mornings and daily lectures. It was somehow comforting. A complete inverse of the life I led.

The kitchen door slammed open and I stared as George staggered into view. I'd forgotten that he, too, had the early classes. I took in the state of him in silence. He was wearing jeans and what appeared to be his bedroom slippers, and looked to have merely tugged on a sweater over some kind of pajama top. I realized that meant he probably slept in pajamas—an image I found unaccountably icky. His eyes looked glued shut and his red hair stood almost completely on end.

"Unh," he said. He smelled, even from across the room, like stale beer.

"George," I said in greeting. I wrinkled my nose at him. "You might want to reconsider that shower."

I watched him upend a carton of orange juice into his mouth. He gulped it down, tossed the carton in the direction of the trash, and then wiped his mouth with the sleeve of his sweater. The carton missed the trash bin by several feet, smacked against the wall, and then dropped to the floor.

"No time," he gasped out, belched, and left.

No wonder I wasn't a morning person.

I had so much time that I was able to take a long shower and prepare myself in a leisurely fashion for the walk over to campus. Unlike the mornings I had classes. I dressed myself in head-to-toe black and then decided the wearing of mourning clothes without a reason to mourn was probably tempting fate. I pulled on some jeans instead. I played soothing music and was talking myself into a philosophical frame of mind. I was Zen. All was well. I had done my best on my papers. The grade was immaterial compared to the sense of accomplishment I should already be feeling. I was heading out the door, feeling serene and in control, when Toby came careening around the corner, startling me.

"Oh my God," he all but panted. "I've been up all night. I went jogging and nearly collapsed in a ditch." He grabbed my arm and stared into my face. "I even tried to do press-ups. I'm a disaster."

My serenity bit the dust. My stress returned, tenfold, with a nearly audible thud into my tensing shoulders.

"If I fail," I told him in sudden hysteria, "I cannot possibly resubmit! I cannot possibly deal with that essay again! Either of them! I hate them both! I'm going to have to work at a gas station to pay back my incredible debt, Sean will eviscerate me and dance a jig on my remains—"

"Jesus, Brennan." Toby frowned. "You're panicking."

"I was fine until you showed up, blathering about jogging and press-ups!" I snapped. I stared at him. "Why did you decide to get all athletic?"

"Because I'm a man," Toby informed me solemnly. "It's what men do."

"I can think of a few things men should do," I muttered darkly.

"Let's not do that scary thing you do, Brennan," he said cheerfully. He eyed me. "Missing me in your bed, are you?"

"The way I miss the plague," I retorted, rolling my eyes. "You idiot. Can we go get our marks now?"

We all sat in the college bar and watched the clock. Meetings with Sean were scheduled in fifteen-minute intervals. Jason kept up a running narrative of panic and horror that did nothing to calm my nerves.

"Please shut up," I finally told him.

Jason looked startled. He took a deep drag of his cigarette. "Do you know," he said as if surprised, "I really don't think I can. I've been like this since early yesterday afternoon."

"We're all doomed," Toby said from where he was lying down across a bench, covering his eyes with his elbow.

"This is great," I said. "Could the two of you be more gloomy?"

"I'm sure I will be as soon as I receive my mark," Jason said darkly. "Possibly even suicidal. I wish we could buy firearms in this country, so I could take to a watchtower. Isn't that what they do in New York?"

"Yes," I said, shooting him a withering glare. "Every single American gets a day up in the watchtower blowing up hapless pedestrians. It's in our Constitution."

"Doesn't surprise me," Toby muttered. "Bloodthirsty colonials."

"Okay, enough," I said and stood up. "I'm going up. Wish me luck."

But I didn't hang around to see if they would, I just ran up the stairs toward Sean's office.

I stood in the hallway alone. The last person to come out had looked pleased, but I couldn't interpret that as particularly good or bad. I suspected other people's happiness had very little bearing on whether or not I was going to fail. I wondered briefly if the MA course was like some I'd seen on television, where the professor only gave out two As, four Bs, and failed everyone else. For no good reason, as I recalled. Just because professors had the power to grade evilly and cause pain.

This train of thought is not soothing, I told myself sternly.

And soon enough the door was opening and a classmate emerged. Sean stood there in his doorway and smiled at me. Just looking at him, at those amazing eyes and his lean body, I forgot all about Miss Sexy Only in Britain. Probably he could see the adoration in my eyes. I actually felt my heart tremble in my chest, and then melt. It had been this way since the Jet Lag Dinner. I had even less to say than before—which meant I spoke in fewer idiotic monosyllables. I just gazed. Sean's behavior remained noticeably unchanged, of course. It had been my George Clooney moment, after all. Not his.

"Hi," I said, like a goofy adolescent with an outsize crush. Which was an apt description, come to think of it.

"Alex," Sean said. "Come in." He was still smiling, his eyes warm and bright. Like the Big Bad Wolf. In a rising wave of hysteria, I was convinced I could see fangs.

The troubling thing was that this in no way detracted from his appeal.

I stepped inside.

"Highlights include him leaning back in his chair and smirking at me," I said. "And saying, 'I look forward to your dissertation.'" I blew out an exasperated breath. "I almost told him that I was glad *he* did, because *I* certainly did not."

"He thinks he's a comedian," Jason agreed sagely. "And who are we to argue? I merely count myself lucky when I actually understand him."

"Which you do about a thousand times more often than I do," I said crankily. "Aren't you taking his class on *Gravity's Rainbow?*"

Jason winced. "I am trying to eat my lunch, Brennan," he scolded. "Please don't bring up Thomas Pynchon."

"Right," Toby said, appearing before us. "That was bracing."

"Well?" I eyed him. "Are you happy?"

"Reasonably," he said, looking pleased. "It will do."

He disappeared, and then returned a few moments later with a sandwich and some crisps.

"Uh-oh," Jason murmured. "Incoming."

Toby and I looked up and saw Suzanne bearing down toward us.

"Terrific," I said sourly. "She still thinks—"

"She can sod off," Toby snapped.

But Suzanne was wreathed in disturbingly authentic-looking smiles. She grinned around the table, and in particular at Toby and me. Well, mostly at me. It was such a shock that I found myself smiling back automatically.

"I'm so glad you're all here!" she exclaimed. "I'll be right back."

We watched her march off toward the food counter.

"I'm sorry," Toby said. "Was that Suzanne, the drama queen?"

"I think it was her cheery body double," I said, still dazed. "I have no other explanation."

"Perhaps she got a good mark," Jason chimed in, shrugging.

Ah, I thought. *Mystery solved*.

Suzanne came back and sat herself right down. "Did you see Sean yet?" she asked me.

"I did," I said. She giggled.

"It's so hard to pay attention to what he's saying, don't you think?" she trilled. "I keep thinking about how hot he is instead."

"That's the problem I have," Jason told Toby very solemnly.

"I think we all do," Toby replied in the same tone.

"He's awfully hot," I agreed. I had a flash image of that kiss, except in the image there was no Miss Sexy Only in Britain. There was just me. I felt a hot flash wash over me and chugged my soda.

"Why have you gone red?" Toby demanded.

"Shut up," I muttered, and gulped down some more diet Coke.

"So," Suzanne said, trying to be casual. "How did you all do on the papers?"

"Fair enough," Jason said, smiling, all blue eyes and charm.

"Did you read your comments?" Suzanne asked. "Jessica Ferrar is scary. She really didn't like some of the things I said in my paper." She tossed her photocopied comments into the center of the table, so we could all look down and see, in Sean's distinctive hand, a number with a circle around it. The number, based on the British grading system, which completely escaped me, was a mark just below Distinction. Suzanne had done very well.

"Congratulations," I said, and meant it. "You did really well."

She looked at me almost pityingly. "I didn't mean for you to look at the *mark*, Alex," she twittered. "I wanted you to read the *comments* . . ."

"That bitch!" I snarled. "Like I was some slathering competitive seventeen-year-old trying to beat her in the Academic Decathlon!" I was practically shouting.

"In the what?" Cristina asked.

"Never mind!" I shouted. "The point is, Suzanne is the embodiment of all that is evil!"

"This is not new," Cristina pointed out. "But here's something new. You know that bloke, David's friend, right?"

"The one who was here."

"Yes." She shrugged. "His name is John. He knows my name. I think he is interested."

I watched her face as I reached over and stole one of her cigarettes. "Are you interested?" I asked carefully.

"I don't think so," she said. "I don't know." She took a drag of her cigarette and leaned back so she could look out her window. We were in her room, which was always much messier than mine. Which I found comforting.

There was a knock on the door, followed by Melanie pushing her way in.

"I thought you'd be in here," she said. She wandered over and seated herself on the wide windowsill. "Well? What are you talking about?"

"That Suzanne," Cristina said.

"Suzanne is boring," I said. "We were talking about John."

Melanie grinned. "John," she said. She looked at me. "He quite likes Cristina. He was practically following her around today, like a sweet little puppy."

"He was not!" Cristina protested. But she was fighting off a smile.

"He was," Melanie said. "And she was cool and distant and mysterious, and only smiled at him once, from a distance, as she was leaving. He was smitten."

"You tease," I scolded her.

"I cannot be a tease," Cristina said dryly. "I have already surrendered the prize."

"That's not the point," I said dismissively. "He was pretty cute, as I recall."

"He's very cute," Melanie agreed.

"None of this is the point," Cristina said softly.

"I know," I said. Melanie and I exchanged a look. "But maybe it's better to have a real relationship than to yearn for something that might never happen anyway."

"How can it be better?" Cristina asked quietly. "In my heart I will always know that it was never my first choice. That David with a single look . . ." She shrugged. "In any case, who cares? John will get over it."

We were all silent.

Then, "What about Suzanne?" Melanie asked.

"Nothing," I said. "I hate her."

"Did she shout at you for sleeping with Toby?"

"I did not sleep with Toby!" I shouted. I coughed. "Just to make sure that's clear."

"Technically—" Melanie began.

"And no," I continued, cutting her off. "Suzanne was everybody's best friend today. She wanted to show off her mark."

"We don't like her," Melanie said. "How was your mark?"

"Distinction," I bragged, and grinned. They both reacted with whoops of joy. Very satisfying. Maybe, I dared to think for the first time, I was in the right field after all. "Which, I'm pleased to say, is better than Suzanne's mark."

"She must not have liked that," Cristina said.

"I didn't share."

"Good choice," Melanie said, nodding. "Her sort always like to compete, but only if they think they'll win. She wouldn't have reacted well, given the fact you keep beating her."

"She sucks," I said mildly. "And I'm not trying to beat her. I'm not competing."

"This makes it worse," Cristina said. "This keeps her awake in the night."

"By the way," I said, suddenly remembering. "Did you see George today? He's turning into a wino."

"The night of John," Cristina said, "we found him lying in the entryway, asleep."

"Or unconscious," I said.

"He's very upset," Melanie said. "I was in the library, and he came to tell me. Fiona has moved on." Her eyes were bright with laughter. "George's suspicions were correct, it seems."

I scowled. "How come the Vulture has a wild and happening sex life and I'm only *accused* of having one by an unhinged drama queen?"

"You could have a sex life," Cristina sniffed. "You just ignore the possibilities."

"If you say 'Toby' one more time, I'll scream," I warned her.

"Toby, yes, but anyone," Cristina said. "You glare at any men who approach you. You dare them to take the chance of speaking to you." She waved a negligent hand. "And this is England. British men are afraid of their own shadows. They find *you* terrifying."

"That is absolute shit," I said. The two British men in my own life came to mind, and I was suddenly furious at both of them. Not to mention the jackass Physicist and his stupid housemate. British, every one of them. "I'm so sick and tired of hearing about poor, intimidated, cringing little British men. It's a complete load of passive-aggressive bullshit. Men are almost never that shy. I think testosterone forbids it. It's a fucking *act*. Claim that you're a shrinking violet and the woman can be made to feel like a marauding beast and you win. She'll be so grateful for the crumbs of your attention that you can behave however you want and she'll take it and thank you." I shook my head. "They just want everything both ways. They want to pretend they're too shy and scared to make any moves, but they also want to be able to sit in judgment of any women they decide are aggressive. *Absolute* shit. They're not shy and scared, they're manipulative, and I'm sick of it."

"I'm not sure that's a specifically British trait," Melanie mused. "Not to defend men, who, it goes without saying, are shit. But I think it might be an international male issue."

"Bloody hell, Alex," Cristina said after a small pause, almost admiringly. "Your mouth is a thing of wonder."

Twelve

"So," George said. He was hunched over a meal at the kitchen table. "Easter break."

"Yeah," I said, eyeing him. Was he drunk? Or sober and thus returned to his original personality? Because I'd be tempted to throw him an emergency beer if we were having a rerun of Horrible George.

"Any plans?" he asked.

"Maybe I'll go to church." And maybe I would sprout wings and fly myself home to New York for a weekend, you never knew.

George was frowning at me.

"Church?" he echoed. "Is that the name of a pub?"

The campus cleared out. Everyone who could went home for a while. That meant everyone I knew was gone while I sat in my room and pretended I was working on a PhD proposal. It wasn't that I particularly wanted to do a PhD. My basic philosophy boiled down to: why not? What else was I going to do? Slink back to Jay Feldstein, tail between legs? I would rather be dead, and a PhD seemed to me to be a slightly better option than death.

I didn't actually know if I wanted to do a master's, as it happened, and I wouldn't know until I wrote my dissertation. For all I knew, writing long academic papers would make me break out in hives, or I'd hate it so much I'd have to leave. Nevertheless, it was the time of year for PhD proposals. Toby had already spent hours in the library, researching. This ran counter to my plan, which was to lounge around and wait for inspiration to strike. If inspiration didn't strike, well, it was unlikely that I would want to spend three or four years of my life buried in a topic I yanked off a library shelf.

Jason called to announce that he was back for a few days, saving me from staring in despair at my application form.

"Fantastic! Brennan!" he cried by way of greeting when I picked up the phone. "Get down to the pub immediately!"

I ran out of the house, unduly excited. It was a week or two into the six-week holiday, and I was going stir crazy. The night before, I had actually considered pounding on George's door to see if he wanted to go get a drink. Reason had prevailed—he was hardly good company, being comatose most of the time—but I was still reeling from the urge.

I made it into the village in record time. I was charging along the sidewalk, head down, when I literally slammed into another person.

"Sorry," I muttered, without looking up.

"Oh, hello, Alex," Sean said. My head snapped up.

Of course.

"Oh," I said, turning bright red.

Sean, naturally, looked like something out of a magazine, all lean and hot with dark glasses and a smirk in the spring sunshine. I didn't care if he was dating ten Miss Sexy Only in Britains, he still made my palms sweat.

"In a hurry?" he asked.

"Just to get to the pub," I said. His smirk deepened. If possible, so did my blush.

Nice one, I congratulated myself. *You lush. It is one in the afternoon*.

"I'm, uh, doing my PhD proposal," I stammered. "Not in the pub. But soon. I mean I'll give it to you soon, if that's okay."

Just kill me now.

"I look forward to reading it," Sean said, politely enough, or at least without any overt contempt. "Have a nice holiday." His smirk arched into the unholy range. "Don't spend it all in the pub."

I just stared after him as he stepped around me and continued on his merry way. Sometimes I thought that the Jet Lag Dinner should have changed things between us. I suspected he was unlikely to topple head over heels in love with me spontaneously, but I thought, you know, we should be friends. Of course, I didn't generally stalk my friends. And I tended to be able to form complete sentences while in their presence. Truth be told, I was probably a pretty unappealing prospect from Sean's perspective. What guy wanted the stammering freak girl who either stared at him intensely or veered way too close to inappropriate emotion? Repeatedly? And who, for that matter, would want the sort of guy who found

Freak Girl appealing anyway? I realized that he had probably forgotten he'd even seen me the moment I disappeared from his line of sight. This failed to make me feel better.

"I am humiliated," I told Jason, slumped over the table with my head buried in my arms.

"There, there," he said. "Have a medicinal pint and the pain will ease."

"That's the problem," I moaned. "My entire life is about medicinal pints. When am I going to stop drinking and start living?"

"Not today, one can only hope," Jason said. He clanked his pint glass into mine. "Cheers." When I didn't move, he heaved a sigh. "Brennan," he said very seriously. "You have to pull yourself together. Sean Douglas is Satan in professorial form, sent to this university to plague you. You must not give in. We must all fight the good fight."

"I'm not concerned about Sean," I snapped. Which wasn't exactly a lie. My love was true. I didn't care if he thought I was a freak.

"The force is with us," Jason said serenely. "Please begin drinking."

Another week dragged by. I decided to be really tricky the day I went to drop off my PhD proposal and various other forms for Sean's perusal. Running into him again was about the last thing I thought my heart could handle. In the sense that I might collapse with cardiac arrest. So, thinking I was tremendously sly, I staked out the main entryway to the professors' wing and waited for him to leave the premises. Which he eventually did. Congratulating myself on my stealth, I ran up and shoved my papers under his office door. I was beyond self-congratulatory and moving right along into jubilant as I skipped down the stairs—and almost smashed into Jessica Ferrar, she of the steely glint about the eye and the firm belief that I was an absolute moron. The steely glint seemed particularly pronounced as she shied away from me.

"Oh," she said, pursing her lips and focusing on me. Her eyes narrowed.

"I'm so sorry," I whispered, becoming as I spoke the physical embodiment of apology. Jessica Ferrar, radical lesbian and eminent scholar, was unmoved.

"Yes," she replied in a withering tone. "Excuse me, please."

She swept around me and continued climbing the stairs.

How had she done that? I wondered in some awe. How had she managed to slice me into microscopic bits with five short words and a single glare?

I walked down the remaining flight of stairs, subdued. When was I going to learn that all attempts at stealth led directly to hideous personal embarrassment?

"I'm back," Toby announced unnecessarily when I wrenched open the front door, and only then removed his finger from the buzzer.

"Thank you," I replied, rolling my eyes. "I was a little confused that you might be somewhere else, standing here in my doorway."

"I see the holiday has really sweetened you up," he

said. "A period of personal reflection and observation that—surprise—has led only to further rudeness."

"Okay," I said. "I'm already sick of you. Please go."

"I'll phone you," he said. "We'll go out." He grinned at me. "Unless you're afraid that people will think we're dating."

I let the door slam shut without answering.

I decided not to go out for about a week, preferring to sleep, read, and cocoon myself in my cot with the covers pulled up. This led to very late nights. One day I went to bed when it was turning light and woke up when it was falling dark outside. I was completely disoriented.

The newly returned Cristina and I had a quiet dinner. She regaled me with stories of her holiday back home in Madrid.

"Where," she said wistfully, "we have a real social life."

She went out with some of her Spanish-speaking friends, and I decided to stay in again and read a book. For pleasure and not class. I pulled my last unread romance novel from my shelf and settled down for some pure escapism. Which was interrupted when I was about halfway through—and right at a really good part.

"What?!" I yelled, annoyed.

Toby swung through the door and threw himself on the end of my bed.

"Ow," I muttered, yanking my feet out from under him.

"Brennan, are you really reading that?" He sounded

scandalized. He picked up the book with his thumb and forefinger.

"I like romance novels," I snapped, snatching the book away from him. "And I'm proud of it. I came out of the closet about my reading preferences when I was still in junior high, so you know what? If you want to mock me, you can go."

"Settle down," he said, laughing at me. "Jesus. You need a drink."

"Is it inconceivable to you that I might want to go a single night of my life without a drink?" I was exasperated, but I was mostly kidding. He ignored me in any case and busied himself opening a bottle of wine and pouring us both some.

"By the way," I said archly, "don't think I haven't noticed that you always drink my alcohol and never contribute."

"Are we keeping score?" He was incredulous. "Because I think you'll find that when you get pissed out of your head in the pub, I end up paying for all the drinks."

"And since I'm usually too drunk to remember such details," I said dryly, "I can hardly argue, can I?"

He grinned. "Why no," he said. "I don't believe you can."

We chattered about all kinds of things, and put away the first bottle in good time. The second bottle went down even more smoothly. I suspected that I might be drunk when we were into a third bottle and I found myself jumping up and down on my bed, singing along—or in any case trying to sing along—to a very bad song by an even worse British boy band.

"Brennan, you nutter, come down from there before you break your bed," Toby said, but he was laughing too hard to sound very serious. He reached over and yanked me off the bed and onto the floor.

"Ouch," I said when I landed, on my feet but hard. "I think I broke my knees."

"You're mad," Toby said quietly.

He was still holding my wrists in his hands, and we were both looking down at my knees and my bare feet, poking out from the sweatpants I was wearing. I tilted my head back to look at him.

"Hey," I said in sudden wonder. "When I'm not wearing shoes you're really not short at all."

"Alex," he said, "your shoes are absurd."

Which is when he kissed me.

And then I didn't know if he kissed me or I kissed him, but everything got tangled and breathless and there was even more kissing. Toby put his hands on either side of my face and I slid my arms around his waist and the kissing went on and on. And then we were on the bed. Which is when everything got completely out of control.

This time when I woke up the next morning, we were both naked.

"Oh shit," I said, my eyes flying open.

I felt him move beside me.

"If you're going to dive across the room, tell me now," he muttered, his face in the pillow. "Last time you nearly castrated me."

"That's such a lie," I said crankily. "You exaggerate about everything."

"I can't really believe you have the gall to let that sentence exit your mouth," Toby retorted, lifting his head.

He stretched, like a cat. This left very little room in my tiny cot. I sat up and scowled at him. He turned over and looked up at me. We stared at each other for a long moment.

"Don't even pretend that you can't remember," he told me quietly. "I can see that you do."

"I remember." I glared at him. "Why would I *pretend* to have a drunken blackout?"

"Because." He shrugged. "You're a girl."

"That gives me a frightening insight into your love life," I told him.

He rolled over and then stood up. I watched him pull on his underwear and his jeans, and then he reached over and tossed me one of my T-shirts and my sweats.

"Thanks," I said.

I yanked on my clothes and tied my hair back. Toby filled two glasses of water from the tap and handed me one.

"Do you have to smoke now?" he asked, irritably.

"Yes," I retorted rudely. I lit my cigarette.

He sat down in my chair, shirtless, holding his water. We stared at each other again. I noticed that he really did have a nice body, which I also remembered from the previous night's explorations, although I shied away from those images. I also noticed that he looked like shit in the morning, which meant we probably matched. And finally I noticed that he looked very serious.

"What?" I asked, only slightly alarmed.

"The night I got back," he said, staring at his hands. "I went to the pub with Jason and Suzanne and we all got very pissed. Then Suzanne and I walked home together."

"You pig," I breathed, getting it at once.

His head came up. His eyes were dark, but clear. "I thought, why not? There'd been all that trouble, and what had I got out of it? Just a snog."

I stared at him. "I can't believe you. You slept with her?"

"It was an accident," he said.

I took a drag and then exhaled in a long stream. "You slept with her," I repeated in a cold, flat tone. I felt as if I was shaking, although my hand looked steady.

His eyes were that dark brown and were completely unreadable. Something flashed through his gaze and then was gone.

"I was going to tell you last night," he said finally. "It's why I came round."

"Fuck you," I said, very deliberately.

"Brennan—" he began, a conciliatory note in his voice.

I cut him off. "Just get out of here."

"It's not as if I planned this," Toby continued, his eyes narrow. "How was I supposed to predict that you would—"

"Just shut up!" I stubbed out my cigarette in the ashtray the way I wanted to stub it out on his face. "Not only am I forced to consider the fact that I had *Suzanne's* sloppy seconds, but the fact you care much more about getting laid than about our friendship, you fucking *pig*—" I sucked in a breath, realized I was shouting, thought, *Good,* and carried on. "I hope you enjoyed yourself, because she's going to keep you on a very short leash and I'm about three seconds away from throwing you out my window. Get out." He didn't move, he just stared at me. "*Get out!*" I screamed.

At that, he did, closing the door quietly behind him.

And then, just like that, the third term started up and we were smack in the middle of another paper crunch. I barely had time to register that the new term had started before the madness descended, and this time my housemates were also in on the panic. Their summer exams were coming up and they were all forced to undertake massive studying—what the Brits called "revising."

I wasn't a big fan of examinations. I had never really recovered from those Introduction to Western Art classes I'd taken in college, where I was forced to flip through stacks and stacks of university prints in order to tell the difference between flying buttresses. I stared at Cristina's and Melanie's exam schedule in horror. How did you even approach studying for eight separate exams over the course of ten days? I knew that I had once managed it, perhaps on a smaller scale and with papers instead of exams, but it was all unimaginable to me now.

I avoided Toby. I avoided speaking to him, beyond certain class moments in which I employed an icy civility, and I avoided thinking about him, because no one could write a paper with an exploded head. On the occasions that I forgot to avoid thinking about what had happened, the rage nearly knocked me over. So I worked pretty hard to stop thinking about it. I avoided Suzanne entirely. I sat in my room and drove myself quietly insane—and sometimes not so quietly. Melanie shut herself away in her room and could only be seen at mealtimes. Cristina veered between intense periods of studying and desperate demands that we go out and drown our inability to concentrate. We ended up most nights in our kitchen, drunk, and vowing to arise the next morning filled with motivation and purpose.

I wrote a thousand words on the literary significance of anorexia. Then another thousand about postcolonialism. Then another eight hundred or so on who-knows-what, before screaming in inchoate rage at my ceiling, which didn't really help.

"Oh my God," Jason said over the phone, ignoring my surly greeting. "Have you checked your email?"

"No."

"Check it right now."

"I'm actually writing a paper, Jason, in case you've been busy the last few weeks picking lint out of your—"

"Just check it," he ordered, and put the phone down.

So I did, but even the vague expectation of *something* didn't prepare me for the sight of the name *Sean Douglas* in my inbox. I shrieked. And then sternly reminded myself that if Jason had received the same email, it was unlikely to be a little e-letter of love. More's the pity.

Dear Fictions of Choice students:

Please let me know, via email by Friday, the topic of your dissertation in a line or two. Please also prepare the 500 word proposal mentioned in the Graduate Handbook for your first supervisory meetings.

Thanks,

Sean

I realized I was hyperventilating.

I did what I always did in moments of academic panic—I snatched up my phone to call Toby and vent.

And then put it down again, remembering.

Stupid Toby and his alley-cat morals. Now what was I supposed to do?

The library, as it turned out, was not the appropriate venue to soothe my panic. I thought that maybe getting out of my room was the right idea, and that the library would inspire me not only to work on my current paper, but to choose a dissertation topic. Maybe I would stumble across academic zeal and purpose—who knew? Confronted with masses of the studious, however, I felt distinctly ill and left almost at once.

I wandered back across the campus in the bright afternoon and brooded, something I would have been content to do for some time. "Bright" in England did not mean "sunny," after all—it meant bright clouds. The country was a brooder's paradise. But I happened to glance up and see Toby headed toward me. There was no one else on the concrete path. I didn't know which was more disconcerting: that he was there before me and unavoidable or that he was jogging.

He slowed to a walk and removed his earphones, never taking his eyes from me. Immediately, it annoyed me that he wasn't as out of breath as I would be if I even contemplated jogging.

"Alex." He murmured my name in greeting, in a tone I'd heard before. The very English, completely default polite setting he'd once used on Suzanne. I felt my teeth clench.

"Toby," I retorted. Without the default setting.

It was a long, awkward moment. I glared at him. He shifted his weight and sighed.

"Is this it, then?" he asked impatiently.

"You have an attitude?" I was flabbergasted. "Are you kidding?" I stepped around him and began walking away. Fuming.

"I don't know what you expect me to say!" he called after me.

I turned back around. "I don't know, Toby. I can't think of anything. Except maybe *an apology*?" The sarcasm burned even my ears.

"Fine," he bit out. "I'm sorry you're so wound up about what happened. I'm sorry I didn't realize that we were dating and that I owed you full disclosure of my romantic history in the six seconds I thought about it before we got together."

"Wow," I said. "That's quite an apology. Are you aware of the actual definition of the word?"

But I wasn't walking away anymore. Toby just watched my face carefully for a long moment.

"Did you get that email from Sean?" he asked.

It was an olive branch. I stared at him, and, to his credit, he held my gaze. I was still angry with him, but it turned out I didn't know how to be in England without him there to talk to. Normally I spoke to him any number of times a day, about a thousand insignificant and significant things. I hated losing that more than anything else. Well. Almost as much as the persistent image I had of him and Suzanne—

I decided to get over it—not that he deserved it. Because he had a point. We weren't dating. Would I even *want* to date him? I decided not to answer that question.

Instead, I asked lightly, "You've already researched your dissertation topic, have you? That must be why you have time for leisurely jogs about campus while the rest of us are working hard on essays and proposals."

Toby sighed. "I think you'll find that most MA degrees require a dissertation, Brennan. Surely it can't come as a surprise to you. Of course, perhaps they do things differently in America."

"Go to hell," I suggested merrily.

He was grinning at me. I made a face at him. It was as if nothing had happened. Almost.

Some feverish hours later, I was at 3,548 words. I had only to conclude something, and then write a conclusion, and then I would be done. Give or take some fine-tuning and my suspicion that the paper lacked an argument. I would have liked to think that my essay was spare and lithe because it contained the elixir of brilliance, but that would have been a terrible lie. This meant that my only remaining writing assignment for my master's course was the dissertation. I felt light-headed and reached at once for the phone.

Fifteen seconds later, Cristina was slumped in my chair, cigarette clenched in one fist.

"I wrote three more words," I said brightly.

"I hate this place," Cristina said, with only marginal bitterness.

"That leaves me with roughly two thousand more to go. It's due in three days, if I haven't mentioned that yet."

"It's the place almost more than the people. Who would not act crazy here?" Cristina sighed. "And I think I am the craziest of all."

"There are much crazier people around," I argued loyally.

"I don't understand why everything is so hard," Cristina said softly. "Or why nothing is funny any longer." She exhaled a huge cloud of smoke, and then glared at it until it disappeared.

"It's the exam and paper tension," I said. "Everyone suddenly has too much work. And besides, there aren't any new people. We've all been sick of each other for months."

"Or just of ourselves." Cristina sighed. She stood up. "I must go study. If I return, you must not let me in."

I returned my attention to my computer screen and scowled at it.

Thirteen

Jason slammed a round of drinks on the table. "Careful," I said, as the wooden-topped table reverberated.

He paid me no mind at all as he flopped down next to me. "This," he intoned, "begins the final frontier. May the dissertations begin."

We clanked our drinks together, and I wasn't the only one who looked a little bit anxious.

"I don't really want to write a dissertation," I said. "My economics housemates only have to write about ten thousand words. Of course they also have to use graphs and mathematics. And they have to take those hideous exams. So I guess it's really a toss-up."

"Illustrations!" Toby said, his eyes brightening. "We can use them, right?"

"Only as a supplement," Jason said in repressive tones.

"Thank you, Jason," Toby said witheringly. "I thought I'd write my entire master's thesis using *only* illustrations."

"You could always test that theory," I said encouragingly. "The picture being worth a thousand words theory."

"I don't know which one of you is the least amusing," Toby said. "Right now it's a dead tie."

I treated him to a mocking grin, and received the British two-finger salute in return. I had been right about Suzanne's short leash, but had underestimated Toby. He had all the makings of a first-class prick. He'd told Suzanne that things could continue between them, but he wanted no one else to know. She had interpreted that to mean that he didn't wish to arouse my jealousy, which, naturally, had greatly pleased her. She now took great pains to hang out with us, so she could feel smug and superior and so she could eye Toby with triumph when she thought no one was paying attention. Toby, of course, did exactly as he had always done, only now with sex on tap and without having to declare himself in any kind of public way. I gave him the American single-finger salute.

"I'm only going to say this once," Jason interrupted sternly. We looked at him. He smiled. "My paper was absolute shite."

We clanked glasses again. It was just the three of us, whiling away a late spring afternoon. We'd all met up in the library, supposedly throwing ourselves into our dissertation research. We'd adjourned for lunch and had never gone back. It was sunny, and we were sitting outside in the pub garden—which was not in the least garden-like, but a concrete patio with picnic tables.

"You two are a terrible influence on me." I sighed. "I had very serious research plans for today."

Jason laughed. "What bollocks. I watched you take fifteen fag breaks in a single hour."

"I actually budget my time around those cigarette breaks," I said with great dignity.

We all soaked in the unexpected sunshine. That was the thing about England—it was truly gorgeous in the sun. The unfortunate side effect was that most English people felt the need to strip down at the first sight of it. Toby was actually stretched out on his side of the table, sunbathing. At least he had his clothes on. When we'd walked over from the library, we'd had to pick our way through crowds of British sunbathers, in various states of upsetting undress. Blue and purple flesh on shameless display, legs and torsos the color of thick cream, all of it slowly roasting to an angry pink in the spring sunshine. It was quite a sight to behold.

"The only problem with this position," Toby said after some minutes, "is that I have to exert so much effort to get to my pint."

Jason sighed. "That and the fact you look like an utter prat."

"Piss off," Toby suggested. But he sat up. He frowned at me. "Why do you have sunglasses, Brennan?"

"I don't really know how to answer that," I said. "Because I bought them? Because it's sunny?"

"It's not that bright," he said.

"And neither are you," I replied. "Since you're trying to get a tan."

He scowled at me. I smiled back at him.

And so on, for hours.

I woke up with a loud pounding noise careening around in my head and was completely disoriented. Then I remembered: very drunk at the pub in the afternoon, had toddled home for a nap. The pounding was at my door, not in my head. It took me whole long moments to determine that. I picked up my watch and saw that it was just a few minutes before 8 p.m. I launched myself up and flung open the door, squinting when the light from the hall hit me in the face.

Jason and Toby stood there, doing the male version of giggling. Which was still giggling, but a great deal sillier.

"You must be kidding," I said.

"Come on, Brennan," Jason ordered. "The night is young. Onward!"

"I'm not going out," I snapped.

"Not looking like that," Toby agreed.

I flipped him the finger, then flicked on my light and turned to get a glimpse of myself in the mirror.

"You're right," I said, and snickered. "I look like shit."

Toby brushed past me and settled himself on my bed, slamming down a four-pack of lager with great flourish. He stared at me.

"I brought drink," he said defiantly.

"Indeed," Jason murmured. He raised his brow at me. "Apparently someone pointed out to our Toby that he ought to contribute to our nights of revelry."

"Is alcohol all you people think about?" I asked

crossly. "I think I'm hungover from this afternoon. If not still drunk."

"You slept," Toby said, cracking open a beer. "You're fine." He thrust the beer at me.

"Sobriety is completely overrated," Jason opined, seating himself. "Why be sober? Why trouble oneself with the actual dreary world?"

"Go on then," Toby ordered me. "Get dressed. Do your girl things. We haven't got all night, Brennan. It's already eight."

"I have to take a shower," I said. They both groaned.

"No you don't," Toby said. "You're fine."

"Don't be such a girl," Jason agreed.

I stared at them. "I actually happen to *be* a girl."

"Not really," Toby said, and grinned. "Aren't you turning twenty-seven soon? I reckon that makes you an old woman."

"Get out," I responded, smiling. "Right now."

When you've been drinking all day, have a nap in the middle of it, and then start up again, you have a long period where the alcohol doesn't seem to affect you at all. If anything, you feel a little hungover. But if you keep going, you eventually reach a point where all that alcohol suddenly hits you. Hard. If you're not careful, it can take your knees out from under you.

With this in mind, having experienced that loss of knees before and to my detriment, I had decided to limit my intake. I was sipping my second pint in as many hours, while Jason and Toby roared about some British television star and practically fell out of their chairs.

"You're both idiots," I informed them when they'd righted themselves. Jason was trying to steady himself. Toby glared at me.

"That's the trouble with you, Brennan," he said. "Too much of a Yank to appreciate British humor."

"Oh my God," I groaned. "Is this going to be another conversation about how Americans can't understand *irony* and how the British just love *irony* and no one in the entire world, even the world colonized *by* the British, could possibly understand British humor?" I gestured with my cigarette. "Dunkirk spirit, God save the queen, rise of the Raj, England is cool, and the U.S. sucks?" They were both staring. I smiled. "Because I can't have that conversation again," I said. "I really can't."

"Alex," Jason said with great deliberation. "You're utterly off your head."

"Dunkirk spirit?" Toby echoed in amazement. "Do you even know what Dunkirk spirit *is*?"

"Something to do with the war effort," I sighed. "Just for the record, you are aware that World War Two ended in the nineteen forties, right? Last century, I hasten to add? And not yesterday?"

"You might want to take a care to keep your voice down," Toby retorted, with sudden fury. "As you'd be surprised how long it takes people to get over being bombed daily for years."

He and I locked eyes, and suddenly we weren't talking about the war at all, at least not World War Two. I didn't exactly know what we were talking about, but I felt temper wash through me. Toby's dark eyes were unreadable again, but I knew anger when I saw it, even if I couldn't translate the cause. I opened my mouth to light into him.

"Bombings?" Suzanne's voice washed over us from above.

Toby jerked, and I looked up. She was standing there with a smile, a drink, and several of her housemates.

"You may want to run away, Suzanne," Jason said, waving his cigarette. "There has been a great deal of alcohol and very little sense at this table for some time."

Toby smiled thinly and shot me another dark look.

I leaned back and set about ignoring him.

Wow, I thought, leaning over the sink and closer to the bathroom mirror, *I really should have taken that shower.* I looked far past my sell-by date. The fluorescent lighting wasn't doing wonders for my skin tone, either. Who had ever decided that fluorescent lights belonged in bathrooms?

"I thought I saw you come in here," Suzanne said brightly, appearing in the doorway behind me. I glanced at her through the mirror. Her hair gleamed, red and shiny.

"And you were right," I replied. Lightly. I straightened and smiled. Politely.

"Can I ask you something?" she asked.

"Of course," I said, rather than *you just did,* which was my impulse.

"Are you and Toby in a fight?" Her green eyes were narrowed and fixed on mine.

I washed my hands and turned slowly. "Not that I'm aware of," I said slowly. "Why do you ask?"

"Because there seems to be a lot of tension between you two," she pointed out. As if maybe I'd missed the surliness and the fact that we weren't really speaking? *Thanks, Suzanne.*

"I don't know what to tell you," I said lightly. Then, all *I Know Him So Well:* "Toby can be pretty moody."

Was that deliberate? Just to see her frown? To make her wonder? I wasn't too proud to admit that it was, and that it worked. I was sick of her.

I was sick of him too, when it came to that, I reflected. I stepped around her without another word and headed out of the bathroom.

Back at the table. Suzanne watched Toby closely, sitting as much in his lap as she could without actually leaving her own chair. *Excellent way to keep that secret,* I thought sourly. *No one will ever know the truth.* Stupid girl. Toby, meanwhile, had taken a turn into surliness and was slumped back in his chair, one small step away from outright sulking. Jason was holding court and entertaining Suzanne's housemates, many of whom, I couldn't help but notice, were giving me some version of the hairy eyeball. Suzanne's minions, I presumed. I was watching with mild interest. When Suzanne's narrow gaze slid away from Toby and over to rest on me, with a dangerous light I recognized, I decided it was past time to call it a night. A very long, very odd, very bad night, and it was barely ten o'clock.

"I'm off," I announced.

"Why?" Toby demanded.

"Because I want to go," I said, not looking his way.

I waved at Jason and headed for the door. Toby caught up with me just outside. He pulled me to the side of the entrance and glowered at me. We were eye to eye with my four-inch heels on, and I was pleased I didn't have to look up at him.

"You're just rushing off? Without wondering whether or not you're ruining anyone else's night?" He was outraged. I scowled at him.

"What the hell do you care if I want to go home?" I demanded. "Go hang out with your secret girlfriend. I'm going to sleep. This entire evening has been exhausting."

"You only ever think of yourself, don't you, Alex?" His voice had turned cold. I gaped at him.

"What does that mean? I just want to go home, Toby. How that's even your *concern*—"

"You can do whatever you like, can't you? Never thinking about anyone else."

"I'm sorry," I hissed at him, in that British way that meant I wasn't sorry at all. "Is this *you* I'm supposed to be thinking about? What would you like me to think about you?"

"This isn't about me," he snapped.

"Then what are you so angry about?" I demanded. "Why are you in my face? Why don't you run back inside and snuggle up with Suzanne?"

His fists actually clenched at his sides. I had never seen that look on his face before.

"At least she cares about someone besides herself," he

said coldly. I laughed one of those really mean and obnoxious laughs.

"Sure," I said, in a nasty little voice. "She cares. But which one of us does she care about? Having you or hurting me?"

He opened his mouth as if the breath had been taken from him. I felt a sudden shame course through me. Another long moment passed as we stared at each other.

"I didn't mean that," I whispered.

"Alex," he said, very quietly. "I—"

"Toby?" Suzanne appeared in the pub doorway. She looked back and forth between us. "Alex? What are you guys doing out here?"

"I'm going home," I said tightly. To Suzanne, still holding Toby's gaze.

Toby glanced at Suzanne and then back at me. His mouth moved, but he didn't speak. His eyes were dark and troubled and I didn't want to care.

"Are you okay, Alex?" Suzanne asked, a little bit sharply.

"I'm just going home," I bit out, and bolted.

"You sound exhausted," Michael said. "And really weird."

"I'm sort of drunk," I said. "I'm actually way beyond drunk."

"Uh-huh," Michael said.

"I'm in that bizarre in-between place. I think I may be simultaneously drunk and hungover."

"How pleasant for you," Michael said. "Aren't you

turning twenty-seven in a matter of days? Just under two weeks? I'm just asking."

"Are you questioning my qualifications for adulthood?" I asked, grinning. "I'm deeply offended."

"You're lucky there are no tests and licenses."

"Because you think you'd pass with flying colors?" I scoffed. "Please."

"What you fail to understand, Alex," Michael said with great dignity, "is that I am perfectly content within my arrested development. You're the one who worries over the transition to adulthood. I couldn't care less."

"That's food for thought," I said, and yawned. "But I have to pass out now."

Once again, obnoxious pounding woke me. This time I knew it was the door, but there was an echo in my head that warned of impending dehydration and headache. I peered at my watch and nearly burst into tears. Two-thirty in the morning. I'd been asleep for about four hours. I felt like shit.

"What, in the name of God?" I snarled, yanking open my door.

Suzanne.

"We need to talk," she said urgently.

I rubbed at my face.

I noticed evidence of tears on Suzanne's face and in her swollen eyes. I reflected that it was two-thirty and I was cranky and tired. I reflected upon the fact that when I'd been awake and in the pub, I'd been sick of this shit. And now, rousted from bed in the middle of the night? I was finished.

"No," I said.

"What do you mean?"

"I mean, no. It's the middle of the night. I've been asleep for hours. You're going to have to wait until tomorrow." I slammed the door in her face, kind of enjoying her wide-mouthed look of surprise.

I crawled back into bed and pulled the covers over my head.

Outside my door, I heard blessed silence. Then the front door slammed. I was congratulating myself on putting my foot down when I heard feet tramping up the stairs. Voices started up, voices I told myself that I didn't recognize. Directly on the other side of my door.

A few moments went by. Then my phone rang.

"What is going on?" It was Cristina, sounding wired and annoyed. They were no doubt interrupting her studying.

"I really don't know," I snapped. "Suzanne just appeared at my door and now there are people carrying on in the hall. All I want to do is sleep." I heard her phone clank down on her desk and then, through the phone and through the walls, heard her door whine as she opened it a flight above me.

"I think it is Toby," she told me when she returned to the phone. "I can see his head. Would you like me to tell them to leave?"

I really would. But I was angry. "That's okay," I muttered. "I'm all over it."

I swung back out of bed and stalked across the room.

"Hey!" I shouted, pulling open the door.

Toby and Suzanne froze in mid-fight.

"Alex," Toby began.

"Get the hell out of my house," I snapped. "Now."

"But—"

"Just go," I said. "I don't even know how you got in."

"I hate you!" Suzanne shrieked suddenly. It wasn't clear who she was talking to, as her eyes were unfocused. I heard Cristina, somewhere above us, shout something in angry Spanish.

"You are disturbing my housemates," I said coldly, glaring at her.

Suzanne turned and tore down the stairs. We heard the door slam.

"You can go too," I told Toby. "I can't believe you would bring your bullshit into my house in the middle of the night. What is wrong with you? What could you possibly be thinking?"

He looked at me. It was a long look. "I don't know," he said.

"Neither do I," I said, but with slightly less venom. "Can I go back to sleep now? Or are you going to cause more trouble?"

"She came over here," he said. "I tried to stop her."

"Fine," I said.

"I'll go," he said. "There was a huge scene. She said—"

"I don't care what she said!" I snapped at him, venom reborn. "I don't care about anything but myself, remember?"

Toby stared at me.

Another long moment, and then he turned and went.

I stalked back to my bed and punched my pillow, then lay down and yanked the covers up around me. And was furious to discover that suddenly, I was wide awake.

Fourteen

I threw myself with frightening intensity into my dissertation. I became Academic Girl. I scowled at texts and blinked my way through articles and pounded out line after line on my computer. I was officially accepted into the university's PhD program, thanks to the proposal I hardly remembered cobbling together. I accepted that news with a definite lack of enthusiasm. *Okay*, I thought. *But what do I know about research papers?* The only way to learn was to keep working obsessively on the one in front of me.

Things kept happening, of course, but not to me. It was a relief. One fine night, Cristina's John got incredibly drunk and declared his feelings for her. Outside her window at about two in the morning. Cristina was unimpressed. And it was David the Physicist who eventually came to collect poor John and drag him off home, not without a searing moment of eye contact through Cristina's window.

"Which was almost too much," Cristina moaned. "Why does he have this power over me?"

John woke the next morning with the expected hangover combined with deep shame, and naturally felt too embarrassed to talk to Cristina. He further felt that the best expression of his embarrassment was to be hideously rude to her whenever he ran into her thereafter. Best way to hide the humiliation.

"He is a complete tosser!" Cristina shouted.

"In his defense," I murmured philosophically, "that's pretty much the way I operate."

Cristina only eyed me, and filched a new cigarette.

I spent a lot of quality time shuffling around my house like an old woman, in my pajamas and my ratty flannel shirt, which doubled as a kind of grunge-era bathrobe, and sometimes pretended I wasn't there when anyone knocked on my door. I would peer through my little spy hole, hold my breath, and wait for them to go away. *This is not necessarily my real life*, I told myself. *And the sooner I finish this thing, the sooner I can decide what my real life really is*.

Toby went home for a while to study, I discovered via Jason, who went to take a holiday with his girlfriend in Spain. Sometimes I went out, but only with my housemates. I turned twenty-seven quietly, and celebrated with a girls' night out. The school year had ended for the undergraduates, and they'd left the campus and small village deserted. All that remained was the tiny graduate community. I had realized with a single glance around me that I recognized every single person in the campus pubs and around campus, for better or worse. Anonymity was completely out of the question with no heaving undergraduate masses to hide in. We took my birthday to the city center.

"I thought that was you."

All three of us twisted around at the sound of a posh British voice. And there he was, with a broad smile across his face and his eyes still dark and intense.

"David," Cristina said, in an odd voice. She forced a smile, as Melanie and I exchanged a look that was heavy on raised eyebrows. Neither David nor Cristina noticed.

"How are you?" Cristina asked, drifting up and onto her feet. David barely spared Melanie or me a glance. He and Cristina began talking, and it was as if the room fell away from the two of them.

I sucked in a breath. "How wonderfully romantic," I whispered.

"Indeed," Melanie agreed in a similar tone.

We watched them for a moment. If I could see Cristina's heart in her eyes, I thought, what did David see? Did he care?

Cristina smiled at us, kind of dreamily, and collected her things. Melanie and I watched quietly.

"Happy birthday," Cristina said.

"Please," I offered, "make my wish your own."

Melanie and I stayed in the pub until closing, and then cracked ourselves up on the bus ride back to campus. As we walked back across the fields in the cool night together, I felt the strangest sense of release. As if I could just let myself go into the dark that was still slightly blue around the edges. It took a long time for the days to end in the English summer. They clung to the sky well into the night.

We decided to toast my birthday with more wine, and sat in the kitchen near the windows. Melanie was telling me stories of exam breakdowns and bringing me up to speed on the many salacious rumors in the economics community. I was nibbling on the stale Oreos that had come in the last care package, courtesy of my mother, who apparently thought I ate nothing but junk food. Correctly, as it happened. Suddenly the kitchen door was tossed open, and George came rushing in.

"Don't tell her I'm here!" he told us. And then, quite improbably, dove into the broom closet.

Melanie and I stared at each other.

Seconds later, we both jumped as someone came up and pounded on the window. Someone who was Fiona the Vulture. Melanie and I both attempted to hide our varying expressions of distaste. Melanie was much better at it.

"All right?" Melanie chirped through the open window.

"Have you seen George?" Fiona asked, with no attempt whatsoever at politeness.

"Not tonight," I lied happily. Fiona had gotten no less vulture-ish in the time since I'd last seen her. If anything, separation from George had made the beak on her all the more pronounced. This close, I noticed that her eyes weren't actually beady as I'd assumed, but a surprisingly lovely shade of blue. I guessed it was some kind of genetic consolation prize for the nose.

"This is rubbish!" Fiona cried, thumping the window

with the palm of her hand. I lit a fresh cigarette and eyed her through the smoke. Melanie was smiling encouragingly. "George and I need to talk," Fiona informed us. "It's crucially important!"

"We'll let him know," I said gently. "Should he turn up."

Fiona dismissed us with a sneer and turned her back, hands on her hips as she considered her next move. Melanie and I looked at each other and fought back the laughter. Which was when George, hearing the silence, decided to emerge from the broom closet.

"Thank you," he said, too loudly.

"George!" Melanie hissed, waving her hands in an effort to make him go back inside the closet. "No!"

But it was too late. Fiona reattached herself to the window. Melanie and I were forced to listen to a graphic description of her feelings, most of which involved the Vulture Libido and a revolting series of images. We stared at each other and somehow kept from screaming—with laughter or with pain, and it was a fine line.

"I could never trust you again," George finally told Fiona, in ringing tones. "You destroyed what we had."

He swept from the kitchen, head held high. Fiona stayed at the window for another moment before her face crumpled and she raced away into the darkness.

Melanie and I sat there for a beat of silence.

"Well, bless," she said softly, topping up our glasses. "That was better than *Coronation Street*."

A few days later I set out for the library, deciding I might as well enjoy the summer, such as it was. While not what I'd call hot, it was warm and often sunny. Downright pleasant, after nearly a year of rain. I set out along the fields and the footpath and thought about the year. I felt as if I were some kind of spineless creature oozing along the path to adulthood, constantly stopping to vent my incredible jealousy of all the creatures I saw around me, passing me with their effortless and unearned vertebrae and their ability to see the horizon way up ahead of us.

"Brennan."

Toby stood before me on the footpath. Speaking of spineless creatures.

"Toby," I said warily, in a kind of greeting. We hadn't seen each other in a long time. It was all temper and tantrums and too much left unsaid.

"Are we speaking?" he asked. "Or are you still having *issues*." Emphasis on the last word to proclaim the silly American-ness of the term. I narrowed my eyes.

"I wasn't the one having issues," I told him. "You might recall that you were the one talking about World War Two and then suddenly having a totally different conversation about God knows what. Not to mention that whole drama in my house in the wee hours of the night."

Toby's lips twitched. "I don't know what you're talking about. You've been creeping around and hiding in your room. Like a four-year-old."

"I was concentrating on my work," I said loftily. "I realize the master's dissertation might be of no consequence to you, but I'm actually interested in doing well."

"You might have been working," Toby conceded,

though his dark eyes were watchful. "But I knocked on your door loads of times. And I could hear you on the other side. You were looking out the spy hole."

"You're imagining things," I said. "And what are you even talking about? You were at your parents' house."

"Only for a week," he said.

We looked at each other for a long moment. Something was easier between us. Something had changed, or at least shifted.

"Where are you going?" he asked lightly.

"The library," I said. "Probably. First I was going to the department to check my mailbox."

"Don't bother," he said, with a grin. "There's nothing in it. Come on." He nodded his head back the way I'd come. Toward the village. "We'll get some lunch. I'll relate all the gossip about what's been happening in my life since your troubling transformation into an academic. It can be your shout, since you claim to bear no ill will."

"You know what, Toby?" I said, grinning at him. "I think I might have actually missed you."

"I know," he said with a sigh. "It's my curse."

I finally made it to the library later that week, having been sucked into pints and pubs and the usual silliness. I stalked around the stacks with the immediate bad mood that seemed to accompany every trip I made to the place. I busied myself with a few half-assed searches for relevant articles, but couldn't work up any of the necessary enthusiasm research required. The obsessive concentration had waned. The few articles the library actually possessed failed to keep my interest for more than a few moments. I found myself staring out the window instead, and it wasn't as if the vista across the concrete university was anything to get lost in. I was fighting a losing battle. This was always the way. I'd discovered that I had to budget enough library time to spend up to a week wasting time before suddenly having a burst of inspiration and industry. Today was clearly one of those filler days.

I trudged back downstairs and deposited my interlibrary loan requests in the appropriate box. Earlier in the year I'd been outraged at how little the university library had in the way of recent scholarship. The Eighteenth Century, Renaissance, and Medieval students had resources coming out of their ears, whereas we Modern School schlumps had to order our research from elsewhere. Earlier in the year I'd had an entire tantrum on the subject, much to Cristina's amusement. Today I just tossed in my requests with a minor roll of the eyes. I'd given up on the tantrums. What was the point? Possibly this meant I was beaten. I didn't care about that either.

What I found I did care about, however, was the look of absolute hatred that I got from Suzanne as I opened my mouth to say hello when I saw her approaching the library. I blinked.

"What was that?" I asked, shocked.

"You know what," she snapped at me. "You know exactly what."

She treated me to another green-tinted death glare, and then pushed her way through the doors. I stood there like an idiot for a moment, and then lit my cigarette. Thoughtfully.

Toby hadn't mentioned Suzanne at all, which I'd assumed was because even he knew better than to raise that subject in my presence. Repression in the interest of peace between us was the name of the game. The list of things we didn't talk about grew longer all the time. Suzanne. Sex. Definitely sex. I got angry even thinking about how I wasn't thinking about it.

I adjusted my bag on my shoulder and prepared to set off for home and discuss the whole thing with Cristina. I had only taken a few steps, however, when I heard my name—snapped out with a whole lot of venom. I swiveled back around.

"Yes, Suzanne?" I asked warily.

"I was just going to let it go," she said. Across the distance and to the avid interest of the other smokers. "But you know what? I can't let you get away with the things you do to the people you pretend to befriend." She squared her shoulders and tossed her head, sticking out her chin. Gearing up for battle, in other words.

I made no effort whatsoever to contain my expression. Which, if it was as closely tied to my thoughts as I suspected, should have been a particularly obnoxious blend of annoyance and irritation.

Suzanne drifted a few steps closer.

"I can finally see who you are," she told me. "And you know what?" Her face twisted. "You're nothing. You're small and mean and disgusting."

Okay. I'm not too proud to admit that hurt.

"Thank you," I managed to say. "I really appreciate that."

Suzanne was even closer now. "I'm just getting started," she snapped.

I had the sinking sensation that she really wasn't kidding.

"I thought *we* were friends," she told me. "I thought you cared about me. I never thought that you would turn out to be as manipulative and devious as you are. You could have just told me, Alex. I asked you a thousand times. But it was obviously more important for you to play your little games."

"I think I'm getting the main idea," I said. "If you have a problem with Toby, why don't you take it up with him? Why drag me into it?"

"Drag you into it?" She laughed wildly. "When weren't you in it?"

"This has never had anything to do with me!" I exclaimed. "If anyone put me in it, it was you!"

"You're pathetic," she told me. "I should have known it was all an act! You just inflict your insecurities on anyone stupid enough to let you near. Well, you don't fool me anymore."

I blinked. For once in my life, I had nothing to say.

Suzanne rocked back on her heels and regarded me with her eyes glittering and her mouth twisted into a smirk.

"What?" she taunted. "No snide comeback?"

That was her mistake.

"Is this what you do, Suzanne?" I asked quietly. I flicked my cigarette to the ground and watched it bounce in my peripheral vision. Sadly, not onto Suzanne's flammable shoes. "Sidle in next to people just so you can tear them down?"

"I know what friendship is, Alex," she began.

"Really?" I watched her as I cut her off. "Because let me tell you what it isn't. It isn't dropping your most intimate secrets all over people you hardly know, and then deciding they have an obligation to you because you chose to bare your soul. Without ever being asked. Anything you don't like about your situation, you brought upon yourself."

"You're a piece of work, Alex," Suzanne scoffed. She shook her head, and then her eyes turned mean. "You're toxic."

The irony of being called toxic by the human equivalent of Chernobyl was not lost on me. I almost laughed.

"I hope that means that you'll finally stay the hell away from me?"

"Oh, very nice," she said. "Very mature."

"What did you think I would say to this, Suzanne?" I asked, incredulous. "Did you think I would beg for your forgiveness, or your friendship? You know what?" I met her glare with one of my own. I was on a roll. "I think the only reason you even wanted Toby was because you thought he wanted me. You'd be something along the lines of a single white female if you weren't so bad at it."

Suzanne smirked. "You wouldn't be so smug if you knew what our relationship really—"

"Don't be even more of an idiot," I interrupted, very

coldly. "Of course I know. Did you really think he wouldn't tell me?" I almost smiled when her expression changed. I adjusted my bag on my shoulder. "I'm not going to stand here and trade insults with you, Suzanne," I said. "Certainly not about Toby. Who is actually my friend, and who doesn't sneak around having sex with me on the sly because he's too embarrassed to admit it in public."

A direct hit. She stiffened, and an ugly flush washed down her neck. But she didn't crumble. "Oh, really?" she sneered, with ten times the usual venom. "Because I got the impression that's exactly what he did to you."

Sucker-punched.

But I rolled with it. I didn't even blink.

I would assess the damage later. I would analyze the fact that my stomach had fallen six feet and the fact that Toby had actually told Suzanne about what happened between us. That treacherous little shit. But first:

"Um, no," I drawled, as if amused. "It wasn't *Toby* who wanted to keep it private." I turned on my heel and began walking away. Just casually enough to indicate a complete lack of emotional response, if anyone was looking for one.

"You think you've won, don't you?" Suzanne said to my back, bitterly. I turned back to look at her.

"This isn't a competition, Suzanne, no matter how much you want it to be."

"I hate you," she hissed.

"Good," I said quietly. "I think that's the only honest thing you've ever said to me."

• • •

"In front of the library!" Cristina said with disgust. And not for the first time.

"In front of the library," I confirmed. Also not for the first time.

"That girl," Cristina said darkly. "She is like a kind of virus. She must be stopped."

"Who cares?" I asked. "Suzanne is unlikely to be dropping by anymore. All things considered, I couldn't be happier."

Cristina only rolled her eyes and stared out the bus window. We were going into the city again, to escape the claustrophobic atmosphere on campus. Cristina wanted to sit and have a coffee. I just wanted to be somewhere other than campus.

The bus let us out inside the city walls, and we walked up the street until we reached Cristina's favorite café. In celebration of summer, there were tables set out on the sidewalk. We took one toward the back so we could keep our eyes peeled and our backs to the wall.

"So," Cristina said, when we each had coffee in front of us and a new cigarette in hand. "We are not doing very well, are we? As far as the heart goes."

"I thought you were," I said. "After your night with David the Physicist."

Cristina made a wry face. "Nights with David the Physicist are upsetting," she said. "And unconnected." She sighed, took a drag, exhaled. "There is talking, about a thousand things. Laughter. Even some kissing. And then nothing. Nothing *inspires* him, if you see what I mean."

"I'm not sure I do."

She shrugged. "Nothing impacts him, I don't think. His head, maybe his heart, these things are involved in the moment. I believe they are. But then the moment is over and he never thinks of it again. Or chooses not to care."

I slumped back in my seat. "He cares," I said. "I mean, I've seen him. When he looks at you, it's like no one else exists."

"And when he looks away," Cristina said quietly, "it is as if I don't exist." She toyed with her cigarette. "I don't think he means to be cruel. I think he might think he is being kind instead." She smiled. "After all, he cannot control what I feel. What the things he does make me feel. Or the things he does not do."

"I greatly dislike him," I said.

"I wish I did." Cristina sighed. "But what would be the point? He is like a storm. You don't like or dislike something of nature, you just try to survive it and hope for the best. Right?"

"I don't think he's a force of nature," I countered. "I think he's just a coward. There's no way he likes anyone more than he likes you."

"Maybe not," Cristina agreed. "But that doesn't mean that everything automatically leads to a happy ending. I don't think there will be any happy ending with David the Physicist, Alex. I think there will maybe be one or two other nights I will have to survive, and then he will disappear because he's a coward or because he just will, and I will cry some more and smoke some more and never know why." She shrugged. "But there are worse things."

"Like what?" I stared at her. "Dental surgery?" She laughed.

We relaxed in the sun, and in the heady feeling that we'd escaped campus and all the intricate complexities of the graduate community. Strangers sat at the tables around us, strangers passed by on the street, and we were two anonymous girls sitting at a coffee house. I felt the tension easing away from me.

"I don't know why," I told Cristina. "But I'm actually relieved that I had that showdown with Suzanne. I feel like it's been coming since last fall."

"Yes, but I wish you could have torn her into little pieces," Cristina grumbled. "She is the one with problems. You were much nicer to her than I would have been."

"It's not like I was really very nice," I said. "In fact, I probably wasn't ever very nice to her."

"She is a maniac," Cristina said flatly. "Not reporting her to the health services is being nice, as far as I'm concerned." She glared at me. "Don't start thinking that anything she said was true. It wasn't."

"Maybe it was," I said. "Maybe I was playing games. I never wanted her and Toby to get together, you know. She was right about that. It bothered me."

"Because Toby is your friend and this girl is insane!" Cristina said. She smiled. "As the most obvious reason, anyway."

I sighed. "Please don't start."

"I just think that you are going to have to deal with Toby sooner or later," she said, with a meaningful look. "I think you know it too."

• • •

"All right?" Toby called through the window.

I turned from the stove and wandered over to him, stating the incredibly obvious through the window opening: "I'm cooking dinner."

"Anything edible?"

"Ha-ha." I considered him for a minute.

"What?"

"Nothing." I shook a cigarette out of my pack and lit it. My spaghetti could boil untended. It was unlikely to be anything but disappointing anyway, given the miserable set of ingredients I'd compiled.

"Fancy a pint later?" Toby was watching me closely, with that strange look in his eyes again. The one I couldn't read.

"Maybe," I hedged. "I want to finish this incredibly boring article, though. I might just fall asleep."

"I'm not sure I can allow that sort of studiousness," he said mildly, smiling. "It contrasts unfavorably with my own laziness."

I blew out a stream of smoke and leaned my hip against the windowsill. "I had some words with Suzanne," I said, with no inflection. Toby searched my face and then his own expression closed up.

"Did you? About what?"

"The basic theme was my evil," I said. "She recently concluded that I'm the root of all that hurts her. As well as being immature, conniving, and so on." I smiled slightly. "You wouldn't know what spurred that on, would you?"

"No," Toby retorted. He scowled. "Did she say I did?"

"She said a lot of things, Toby," I murmured. "Are you and she still—"

"No," he said, kind of fiercely. "That was never really a constant thing anyway. A shag here and there. Nothing particularly intense."

"But I'm betting she didn't share that view of it," I said dryly.

Toby looked away for a minute. It was after eight and the sky was still blue. He looked strange and suddenly unfamiliar standing there. He ran a hand through his dirty-blond hair, which I noticed was getting a little bit shaggy, then smiled wryly. His head swung back around and his eyes met mine.

"If you remember," he said. "I did warn you. Ages ago."

"Warn me?"

"I told you that I treat every woman I come across like shit. I never pretended otherwise, did I?"

"You told me," I agreed. "But what do I care?"

"That's a very good point, Brennan," he said. He laughed a little bit, though he sounded uncomfortable rather than amused. "What do you care?"

"What I don't understand—" But I stopped. I wanted to kill him for telling that little psycho about something I'd shared with no one. No one on either side of the Atlantic. But for some reason, I didn't say anything.

"Is what?" he asked, with a kind of weary hostility.

"Is anything," I said. "Why she's so crazy." I frowned. "Any of it."

The air between us seemed to stretch taut. I had the

strangest sensation that Toby was different somehow. It was something in the way he stood there.

"I don't know," he said finally. He looked away again. "I really don't know."

Fifteen

The racket started up just before midnight. Someone was shouting, in a strange singsong rhythm that was so annoying I went over to the window and stared out, prepared to vent a little of my pent-up aggression.

"Oh my God," I told Cristina over the phone. "Get down here right now. Bring Melanie."

They arrived in a rush, and joined me at the window. All three of us crammed up against my windowsill and stared in wonder at the scene below.

Fiona the Vulture, clutching a bottle of something in one hand and taking restorative nips every few seconds, was singing. At the top of her lungs. Up at George's window.

Well. "Singing" might have been overstating the case. She was very drunk, and very tone deaf.

"I think this is one of those situations where the thought is what counts," I murmured.

"This is all very embarrassing," Melanie whispered. Delighted.

"*And through it all, he offers me protection*," Fiona sang. "*A lotta love and affection . . .*"

"I don't know how I feel about the use of Robbie Williams for the seduction of George," I said.

"Everyone in the United Kingdom has seduced or been seduced to Robbie Williams," Cristina said. "It is the natural choice for a serenade!" She made a face. "Even a Vulture serenade."

"Do you suppose this is *their song*?" I wondered. "Because I'm a little bit skeeved if so."

"You have no soul," Cristina admonished me. "George is the Vulture's troll angel. What could be sweeter?"

Around the courtyard, people were hanging out their windows and watching the performance. Fiona kept right on going, plowing through another verse. George, I could see if I leaned out really far and craned my head, appeared to be cowering behind his curtains.

"Now she's beginning at the beginning again," Melanie pointed out. She stared at us in sudden horror. "Do you suppose she plans to keep singing this song until George cracks? What if it goes on all night?"

"What if she keeps skipping around in the verses?" Cristina asked. "It's much worse."

But something else started to happen.

Everyone was joining in.

People were singing loudly, from window to window. Cristina, Melanie, and I exchanged looks, and then shrugged. Why not? We slung our arms around one another, tilted our heads back, and started belting out the words. It was impossible to live for any stretch of time in England and *not* know the words.

Singing loudly and badly, I looked over and saw Toby

standing at his window across the way. He was leaning out, resting his head on his arms, and I could see his mouth curve slightly when he saw me.

The song got louder. Fiona nearly toppled herself at one point, but kept on singing. George appeared from behind his curtains. Toby and I stared at each other from across the courtyard and across all the voices.

Fiona finished with her arms flung out, overbalancing herself and staggering to regain her footing as some mild applause floated down from the houses.

"I want you back, George!" she shouted up at George's window. "I've missed you!"

There were catcalls and whistles. "Come on, George!" someone yelled. "Give it a go!"

"I missed you too," George finally admitted in a sudden shout. "I missed you too!"

"Romeo!" Cristina cried with great drama.

"Wherefore art thou, sweet Vulture?" Melanie replied in the same overblown tone.

George threw down his keys. Fiona scooped them up and started for the front door, unsteadily. I could hear George rushing out of his room and down the stairs to greet his prodigal girlfriend. Cristina and Melanie were laughing so hard they had to sit down on my bed.

But Toby and I stood there for another long moment, just staring at each other with all that dark and noise in between.

August plodded along. Sometimes it was actually hot. Or, anyway, stuffy in the little Fairfax Court rooms. I produced a first draft of my dissertation, which I hated and which I set about editing according to comments my supervisor, whom I had yet to meet face-to-face, provided in a long letter. A very long letter, mailed from her summer digs in the south of France. We mostly communicated by email, by which I mean we barely communicated at all.

"Well?" Michael asked one day.

"Well what?"

"When are you coming home?" He made an impatient noise. "It's disgustingly humid here, and the city is awful and reeks of urine and body odor and garbage. Everything is sweaty and Manhattan is deserted. It's summer. Aren't you homesick?"

"I don't know," I said. "Maybe I'll stay here."

"Whatever for?" Michael sniffed. "And can your liver really withstand more time in the land of the lushes?"

"A valid point," I said. "But what am I going to do if I come home?"

"What do people normally do with English MAs?" Michael asked. "Teach, right? Just think, you could bend young minds to your will. You could jump on chairs and inspire little Ethan Hawkes with poetry and eccentricity. What could be more fun?"

"Yeah," I said. "Or I could turn into one of the specters who taught in my high school. They were monsters, all of whom had a moment of joy sometime in the sixties, turned immediately bitter thereafter, and made it their life's work to crush the spirit out of any teenagers they encountered."

"Where exactly did you go to high school?" Michael asked dryly. "Sunnydale?"

"I'm just saying that teaching is good in theory, but it seems like no one ever remembers that it's an actual job requiring actual skills. As if it's all about the three-month vacation every year, and getting out of work at three every day." I sighed. "How can this year already be over? I was supposed to have everything all figured out by now."

The fact was, I realized when I hung up, I didn't have anything figured out. I hadn't thought beyond this year. What came next? What did I *want* to come next? Why did it seem that I just careened along, made random decisions, and then dealt with the fallout while continuing to careen? Wasn't I supposed to start *planning* things at age twenty-seven? And if that was all beyond me, shouldn't I stop pretending that I had the slightest idea what I was doing and ask someone else for help—someone, for example, who had spent quality time as an adult and might therefore be expected to have some opinions on how to go about becoming one? I didn't know too many of those, it was true. There was one, though, who had been making noises about my lack of foresight pretty much since I'd turned thirteen. If I'd learned anything this year, it was that just because someone was fighting with you and you didn't agree with them, that didn't make them completely wrong. I took a deep breath and called home.

"Hi, Dad!" I said, very brightly, when he picked up the phone.

It was exactly 9 a.m. in New York. The great thing about the five-hour time difference was that I could confuse people into thinking I actually got up in the morning because I called them in *their* morning.

"Good morning, Alexandra," my father replied dryly. "To what do I owe this honor? I was under the impression that you were dodging calls from home."

I rolled my eyes, but forced myself to smile so that I would sound upbeat and chipper. A well-known telemarketer's ploy that actually worked.

"Well," I said. "I've been spending a lot of time in the library." This was a big lie. I smiled winningly at the wall. "So I've been there, mostly."

"I suppose I can't complain about that," my father said. It sounded as if maybe he wanted to complain anyway, but was holding back.

"Anyway," I said, squeezing my eyes shut in anticipation of the horror that was about to come, that I was about to unleash upon myself. "I wanted to ask your advice, Dad."

There was a pause.

"My advice?" my father echoed, in a strange tone.

"Uh, yeah," I said. I charged ahead. "See, I've been accepted into the PhD program here, which is good, I guess. But I need to decide if doing a PhD is really what I want to do. If I should—or even *could*—stay in England for a few more years. Or if I should come home now. So I . . . wondered what you thought about it. What . . . um . . . you think I should do."

I realized I was a little red in the face. I had made it a strict policy years ago to avoid leaving myself open to attack, and here I was doing the human equivalent of rolling over and exposing my belly. Also I realized that I had no idea what Captain Corporate America was going to say about the very idea of further academic irrelevance. So what he actually did say took me completely by surprise.

"Well," he said a little gruffly. He paused again. "Do you know, Alex," he said in a voice I'd never heard before, "I think this might be the first time you've ever asked for my advice. On anything."

"How weird," I said to Melanie. "Maybe my entire tense relationship with my father is because my perspective has been all skewed. Is that possible?"

"Why not?" Melanie asked. She was making herself a sandwich, and shrugged. "Relationships are odd, aren't they?"

"I mean, he's definitely had his moments," I said, fiddling with my cigarette. "But today it suddenly became entirely possible that I'd been approaching him in this defensive way . . . It was really weird."

"I know what you mean," Melanie said. "I have the same sort of relationship with my mother." She made a face. "It took me a long time to work out that she mainly reacts to what's said to her, and I can therefore predict her responses. I think it's part of accepting them as people and all that."

"It kind of made me feel bad for him," I said. "And for me, for that matter."

Long after Melanie returned to her studies, I sat on my own in the kitchen and stared out at the sunshine. My father had asked for some time to consider, and although I still had no idea what my future held, I had the strangest feeling in my gut. Almost like regret.

Maybe, it occurred to me, my very solid, very matter-of-fact father just hadn't known what to do with me any more than I'd known what to do with him. My mother presented her façade of serenity to the whole world, and in fact I'd only ever seen her upset a handful of times in my life. Everyone in my family was either very calm or very good at pretending to be calm. And so I'd developed this hard shell, let no one too close, and deflected everything with the sarcasm and the wiseass remarks. Perhaps the contentious relationship I had with my father was almost entirely due to the way I approached him. Because I was too afraid to let anyone near me. I was too afraid to let people inside, too afraid that if I really risked myself, I wouldn't survive the eventual ending.

Could you really create whole relationships in your head? Could you force people into roles they never meant to play? Just by treating them in one way or another? I thought about my relationship with Evan, for example. He was just a guy. He wasn't evil or even malicious, he'd just liked me. And I'd hated him for it. I'd made him an impetus for change, and scoffed about how little he knew me, but how well did I actually know him? He was supposed to be my *real man*. But I had never seen anything except his failure to play that role to my specifications.

And Sean Douglas. God, yes, he was beautiful. He was sexy and aloof and brilliant. And epic. And completely untouchable. Not just because he was my teacher, but because he had zero interest. And yet the idea of him allowed me all kinds of emotions I could indulge in without any fear that they'd truly impact my life. Because it was really easy to prostrate yourself to love when you knew it would never work out. You weren't really risking anything.

The truth of that took my breath away for a moment.

I thought about Suzanne's accusation of emotional unavailability, and I thought about Suzanne herself. I didn't like her, and I was glad that our relationship seemed over, but what the hell had I been doing?

Sure—she was unhinged, but I'd encouraged her. I'd mocked her and moaned about her and suffered through her, but I'd never had the guts to just ask her to stop, had I? I'd known exactly what kind of person she was within hours of meeting her—within minutes, come to that—but I'd never avoided her. So if anyone was to blame for what had happened, it was probably me.

Was I really so arrogant that something in me had enjoyed her doomed attempts to get close to me? Because while I'd known all along that she was never going to get there, she hadn't known that. Removing the romantic and sexual element, had I really treated her any differently than Toby had?

I'd called him a pig, and worse. I'd told him to tell her, straight up and to the point, and I'd thought he was an immature shit for avoiding it. So what did that make me? Was I any less guilty because I'd behaved much the same way?

"I think I'm a friendship terrorist," I moaned to Melanie.

"I don't," she replied. "It's not up to you to explain to

the world why they can't act in all the nasty ways they do act."

"No," I agreed, "but it is up to me to tell the people in my life what I do and do not find to be acceptable behavior, right?"

"I think you're talking yourself into guilt," Melanie countered gently. "Anyone with a brain—so you see I'm excluding that Suzanne creature—should have been able to realize from the way you responded that you were not interested in her. She didn't want to know. *She's* the friendship terrorist. She picks a target, bombards it, and then moves on when the damage is too intense."

"I don't know," I said. "I'm not sure it's that simple. I think there's a gray area. I think I'm sinking in the gray area."

Melanie was quiet for a moment, and pulled her legs up beneath her chin to better settle into the chair.

"What is that noise?" she asked, an appalled look on her face. I was sitting at my desk, and therefore right next to the wall I shared with George. The wall through which the noise came.

"Oh," I said innocently. "Are you referring to that thumping, squeaking sound?"

"Oh no."

"Oh yes," I said, grinning. "That would be George and the Vulture, celebrating their reunion. It's been going on for weeks. He apparently wasn't kidding when he said their relationship was based on sex."

Melanie was silent for a very long moment.

She sucked in a noisy breath. "I think I may be ill. Excuse me."

• • •

My head was a little bit too full, and I couldn't seem to let go of the notion that I'd managed—without even realizing it—to completely determine the outcome of all these various relationships, which had caused me so much grief. Did I even know how to have a real relationship? Or was I condemned to love only the potential I saw, only the people I created in my own mind and sketched over the faces of the real people around me?

I had been trying to wean myself off nightly Sean stalkings, but I decided I needed a fix. Maybe I needed to confirm his status in my life. Or be done with it altogether.

I waited for dark and made my way over to the bushes, which were starting to feel a bit too comfortable. Sean's lights were on, and he was tucked in his kitchen with Miss Sexy Only in Britain, eating a meal where he and I once ate a meal, when I was jet-lagged enough to think that meant more than kindness.

I studied the woman from my stalker's vantage point. I would never understand why women with mullet-like hairdos were considered attractive in this country, but so it was. It was like listening to middle-class English boys sing along to gangsta rap—an out-of-body experience, but ultimately sort of sweet.

The British liked beauty they could touch. No magazine goddesses for them—they liked their celebrities to look like normal people, people you might see strolling down the street. They didn't go in for the practically alien life-forms of Hollywood, all that golden glow and stardusted chic. Mullets were probably just par for that same course. Women were allowed to carry weight, to look as if they actually consumed food on a daily basis. I supposed that all of that was healthy and better for the rest of us. But in truth I couldn't understand it. If anyone on the street could be famous, if almost everyone was considered attractive, surely that meant my own obscurity was even more upsetting. At least at home I wasn't even involved in the competition.

Sean, I noticed, stared at Miss Sexy Only in Britain as if he'd never seen a woman before. As if she were the only one alive. They laughed. Their hands touched across the table. There was no sign of the smirk, or that mocking glow in his wonderful eyes. Despite the fact that I felt Sean deserved a celestial creature—or me—it was hard not to be a little bit moved by their obvious delight in each other. And I found myself thinking that actually I didn't even know him at all. He was a complete mystery to me, all images of Heathcliff and smart remarks, because he was all wrapped up in his professor persona and I, as a student, could never get beyond that. The personality I accorded him in my more lurid fantasies had nothing to do with who Sean Douglas really was. I couldn't even begin to know him. I'd never even started.

I took a last long look at the two of them, cocooned in the light and their preoccupation with each other. I realized I was saying goodbye, and that made me smile. Maybe I was growing up after all, against my will.

I got to my feet and skulked back around the corner of the house, which involved a complicated little duck-and-cover routine to get me by the living room window.

I was moving pretty quickly, and checking over my shoulder, and maybe that's why I didn't notice anyone else was around until I smashed into him.

I managed not to scream, though I jumped back. I thought, *Thank God, it can't possibly be Sean—*

But it was worse.

It was Toby.

Sixteen

"What the hell are you doing?" I demanded.

Because it's always better to start from strength.

"What am *I* doing?" Toby asked. His face was in the shadows, but I could still see the gleam of fury in his dark eyes.

"Don't you know any better than to sneak up on women in the dark?" I snapped. I started walking, trying to put distance between us and Sean's house. "Don't you know that's how people end up accidentally getting themselves hurt or reported to the authorities?"

"If anyone's likely to get reported to the authorities," Toby said in a frigid tone, "it's really not me."

"Meaning it's me?" I glared at him. "Why? Because I have the temerity to walk home alone?" I rolled my eyes. "You're right. Lock me up."

"Are you really going to pretend that you weren't just hiding in the bushes outside our lecturer's house?" His voice was an unpleasant mix of incredulous and furious. He grabbed my elbow and jerked me to a stop. "Is that the plan, Alex? Because I saw you."

"You were following me?" I was incensed. "What gives you the right to follow me around?"

"You're some kind of voyeur? A Peeping Tom? Is this how you get your kicks?"

"I don't have to answer to you," I snapped. "And get your fucking hands off me."

"With pleasure," Toby snarled, releasing me. "I can't believe that I just saw what I just saw. Are you a *complete* nutter, Alex? Quite apart from the fact that it's appalling to *spy* on someone else, how exactly do you think Sean would react if he was ever to know that you spend your spare time crouched down in his shrubbery? Staring into his windows? Like a stalker?"

The word "stalker" sounded far less amusing in his mouth than in my head. And also a bit sick.

"I'm not planning to tell him," I said tightly. "And I really don't want to have this conversation with you. It's none of your concern what I do with my spare time."

"Of course not," Toby sneered. "It's no one's concern but yours. Alex Brennan, self-contained and self-sufficient unit, touched by nothing and no one."

"I don't know what that means, and I don't care what that means!" I yelled at him.

I felt the kick of my temper. One small flare and it ignited, ripping through me like a tidal wave. I expressed it by hauling off and punching him in his stomach. Hard.

He yelped. "What the—"

"How *could* you?" I shouted at him. "How could you tell that psychotic little bitch that we slept together? What were you *thinking*?"

His mouth fell open.

"She asked me directly," he said after a beat, one hand across the place where my punch had landed. My hand throbbed. I was alive with a trembling, shaking emotion I couldn't identify. I clenched my hand into a fist and ignored the throbbing.

"So you just *told* her? Without even asking me if that was information I wanted to share?" I stared at him for a moment, then backed away. "I can't believe you. I can't believe you would—"

"I couldn't *lie*," he said, anger kindling again in his voice.

I gaped at him. "Of course you could lie! What are you, twelve years old? What possible good could ever come from telling her something like that?"

"Listen," he said hotly. "I'm sorry if it's so repulsive to you. But I don't lie. Not even to Suzanne. Not even to protect you."

"Whatever," I snapped. "I'm done. I'm done with all of this shit. Fuck Suzanne and fuck you—the two of you deserve each other!"

I turned then, and took off toward my house, so angry I could hardly see the path in front of me.

"Alex—damn it—"

I heard him yell after me, but I kept going. I could feel his eyes burning into my back. But I didn't turn around.

And this time, Toby didn't follow me. Not then, and not later. He didn't turn up at my door and he didn't call.

So I told myself I didn't care.

• • •

I took it out on my dissertation chapters. I slapped postcolonial theory around, and delivered some serious ass-kicking to imperial social orders. Or anyway I tried to. I was vehement. I was tough. Strangely, manhandling texts only made me feel worse.

Cristina and I decided to take out our dissertation aggression on our bodies. We decided we would buff and tone and thereby make sure we were really hot if we failed our degree courses and were forced to take to the streets to make a living. This involved a single overenthusiastic trip to the gym. Cristina cycled like a crazy person, and I experimented with the machines like I was trying out for the Linda Hamilton *Terminator 2* award.

We spent the evening lying on Cristina's floor in agony, while Melanie poured restorative whiskey down our throats. Cristina and I then decided that our bodies would have to take care of themselves.

My supervisor emailed me with further corrections and notes on my work. I moved away from the chapters—which I had printed out into a little pile and stared at every day—and applied myself to the introduction and conclusion. The introduction was generally held to be easy enough, once you'd written everything else and knew exactly what you were introducing. I thought this was kind of amazing. It had never occurred to me that the reason all those introductions I'd read over the years were so right on was because the author had already written the rest of the book. I'd just presumed that everyone else had a much better idea about where they were headed. Or had a much stronger grip on the wheel.

The conclusion, however, presented different problems. It didn't have to be as long, but it did have to wrap things up satisfactorily. That sounded a whole lot easier than it felt when I sat down and glared at the screen in front of me and the words failed to come. I wasn't exactly sure what I thought that my dissertation was really about, despite the work I'd put into it. I certainly didn't have any conclusions to draw about it.

"Okay," Robin said briskly. "Enough about you." She took a breath, and I could hear that she was beaming ear to ear. "I think Zack is going to propose."

I had thought we all knew that Zack was going to propose, on schedule, this summer. But that was not the correct response.

I screamed, and descended into serious girlie-ness.

"There's no ring yet," Michael said. "But it's only a matter of time. Particularly given the fact that Zack called me and has enlisted my aid. We will lose Robin to the married side and that will be that, but at least the ring will be fabulous. Do you think she'll let me appear at her wedding in drag? Just so you and I can match?"

"I think she most emphatically will not," I said. "I can't talk to you, I'm trying to conclude."

"Conclude what?"

"That's a very good question, Michael." I sighed. "I really don't know. Something. Anything. I get the feeling that everybody else *just knows*. Everyone knows where they should end up, or at least where they should go. But me? I have all these words and a big vocabulary and no freaking clue."

"I love it when you go all metaphorical," Michael said. "Go on. Give me more."

I was stalking along the footpath, scowl at the ready, glaring at the ground as I stamped my way toward campus on the millionth printer run. I heard the approaching group, but very deliberately kept my eyes trained earthward. They could freaking move out of my way. Which of course they didn't, and I had to jump onto the grassy side of the path to avoid being mowed down.

I muttered under my breath, and then noticed that Suzanne was one of the group. She fixed her green death glare on me, which caused me to roll my eyes practically into the back of my head. Suzanne rocked to a stop, with her hands on her hips. I saw her buddies—her housemates—stop in a loose little group a few steps behind her. Were we about to rumble? I wondered with some amusement. Were they planning to *kick my ass*?

"What?" I asked rudely, and took the opportunity to light a cigarette.

"I don't appreciate you telling Toby what went on between the two of us," she said.

I had to stare at her for a long moment while I processed that. Because yes, she really said it.

"Are you out of your fucking mind?" I asked, almost laughing.

"You know what, Alex, you're—"

"No," I said, cutting her off. "I don't want to hear it. Why don't you go back to your house with your buddies here and think really hard about why that's probably the most ridiculous thing you've ever said to me."

Suzanne blinked her green eyes at me, those blank and yet somehow cunning eyes. One of her housemates said her name, but she just stared at me. Then suddenly her face changed.

"I just heard from this private school in Delaware," she said neutrally. "I'm being hired as an English teacher for their high school! Isn't that great? I'm leaving next week, so I have to have my dissertation in early."

It was my turn to stare. And then I did what I should have done months before: I turned on my heel and walked away as fast as I could without actually running.

I was storming out of the computer room on campus, clutching my latest crap effort at a conclusion. I was in a really foul mood, and it was only partially related to Suzanne and her evident madness. I mean, what could you do about a redheaded fruitcake like Suzanne except stay out of her way? Why engage? It had only taken me a year to reach *that* conclusion.

"Oh," I said, when I looked up.

"Alex," Toby said in his default tone.

"Guess who just had a psychotic episode on the footpath?" I decided to follow our usual script and ignore any lingering tension. But Toby just glared at me.

"I can't imagine I'm likely to care," he said, in that same tone.

"We're in a fight?" I asked, amazed.

"You hit me," he snapped.

"You deserved it!" I snapped right back. "And apparently you had even more to say to Suzanne."

"Can I go now?" Toby asked, his dark eyes furious.

"You can go to hell for all I care," I told him, and stalked away from him.

Directly into Sean.

"Hello, Alex," Sean said.

I looked over my shoulder and saw Toby. And, more to the point, the look on Toby's face. Sean greeted him and Toby muttered out a reply.

"Um," I said. "Hi, Sean . . ."

"Can I have a word?" Sean asked. Toby looked disgusted and slammed into the computer room. I turned back and looked up into Sean's fantastic hazel eyes.

"Of course," I said weakly.

We sat in his office.

"So," Sean said. "You've yet to accept the offer of a position in our doctoral program."

I'd had a brief moment there where I believed he was going to politely ask me to refrain from staking out his house.

"Oh!" I said, relieved, and then got ahold of myself. "I'm not really sure what I want to do."

"Ah," Sean said, and looked down at his hands.

"What does that mean?" I asked.

"You remind me of myself," he said. He smiled, a real smile, and I just stared, transfixed.

"I *do?*" I asked, in a tone that was a bit too strident. I modified it. "I mean, really?"

"I think I told you once that I ended up in academics by default," Sean said calmly, that unholy amusement all over his face. "The truth is, many academics are the same. Conventional employment doesn't appeal, and one has a certain aptitude." He shrugged. "It's not the end of the world to find yourself uncertain."

"There's uncertain," I told him. "And then there's completely lost."

"I think you exaggerate," he said. "You're quite talented, Alex, as I think you know. I don't know what life awaits you back in New York. But I would like to encourage you to remain here, if I can. I don't think you'd ever regret the doctorate."

"I'm not sure yet if I regret the master's," I said flippantly.

I realized that I felt differently around him than I normally did. He was the same smirk and mockery, hazel eyes and that gorgeous face, but my stomach wasn't clenched in agony.

I'm not afraid of him anymore, I realized. It was like the sun coming out from behind a cloud. Seriously. I blinked in the sudden light of the realization.

"I've offered to oversee your doctoral project," he said. "I think the project requires some narrowing of focus, but is otherwise very interesting." He cocked his head to the side and considered me. "Is there anything I can say to convince you?"

That you love me, want me, need me? That you've just

now realized that you can't live without me? That you've kicked Miss Sexy Only in Britain to the curb and are about to toss yourself prostrate at my feet?

But I didn't really mean it.

I smiled. I had that feeling again—that those eyes of his looked way too deep and could see exactly what was inside my head.

"Well," I said, "I'm not sure. You could look into the future and tell me what I'm supposed to do with it all."

"Alex," Sean said, smiling. "Only you know that. And even if you choose the wrong thing, only you can ever be the judge of it. It's like performing in a play and missing your lines. The audience only knows if you stop still and flounder about. If you simply keep going and stay in character, no one is ever the wiser."

"I'm pretty sure adulthood is all about knowing the lines," I said.

His eyes gleamed with that liquid gold, and the flash of his smile was still pretty amazing. Fear or no fear.

"On the contrary," he told me. "Adulthood is knowing that a fully realized character is always more important than the lines."

"Okay, Dad," I said. "Are you ready? What do you think?"

"I don't have a tremendous amount to say," my father said. "I think that if you want to go on and get the PhD, you should. If you want to stay in England, I'm happy to support it."

"Really?" I asked. I must have sounded particularly disbelieving.

"Your mother and I have every confidence in you," my father said.

I grinned, basking in the glow of parental support and understanding. Then my father had to keep on going, bringing us right back to more familiar ground.

"I have less confidence that you'll ever manage to repay me on a professor's salary, but that shouldn't dictate your choices," he said. "You should concentrate on your professional advancement and let me worry about your increasing debt."

I rolled my eyes. And what exactly had I expected? A Very Special Bonding Moment? This was still my father. Greater understanding of our relationship didn't mean he would suddenly transform into somebody else.

"Well, okay," I said.

"You just let us know what your decision is," my father said. "Although, Alex, I think that if you do plan to return home now, you should have a good brainstorming session about the kinds of opportunities you'll be able to find. Have you thought about the fact that it won't be possible to find a teaching position this late in the summer? You should be realistic—"

I tuned out, and began easing my palm over the receiver.

Dissertation word count: 19,064.

Pages: around 60.

Level of achievement: while not Nobel Prize material, it was not entirely crap, either. Though the assorted professors who would be forced to mark it might quibble with that assessment.

The final due date was the day after tomorrow. Meaning all footnote issues and grammar checks had to be completed and the entire thing copied and bound.

I believed that I had, for the most part and barring a few small details, completed my master's dissertation.

I leaned back in my chair, looked around the room, and waited for some sense of great accomplishment, or even joy. I thought, *I am awash in anticlimax*.

My still unseen and unmet supervisor emailed her response from Cannes.

"*Good work*," she wrote. "*Having finished, you can now relax. Your degree is assured and thus what remains is your level of pleasure in what you've produced.*"

Oh yeah, I thought belatedly. *Pleasure*. Pleasure was the reason for all this? There was a thought. I swiveled around in my chair and viewed the culmination of a year's work. My neat pile of dissertation copies and, beyond that, the horror of my little cell. I had a tube of potato chips and a box of grapefruit juice, empty cigarette packs and drained diet Coke cans, liters of mineral water and ashes drifting across all surfaces. Piles upon piles of dirty clothes, papers and books and shoes in precarious jumbles across the floor, stacks of CDs and used crockery, and a bed last made sometime in July. A single bed, an airless room, and the riot of my possessions.

I tried to remember work I'd taken pride or pleasure in, but nothing came to mind. My memories of my undergraduate thesis were vague. It was all the drama of the process, my inability to deal with my college years ending, and the thrill of procrastination beyond all believable limits. My undergraduate thesis had not been a big success.

All my work between then and now was pointless at best. Motions and other legal documents for Jay Feldstein. Someone else's idea of work, never mine—tasks to complete that had no bearing on me.

This dissertation, however, was supposed to be the pinnacle of my year. My greatest feat. So why did I feel like tossing it out the window and starting over from scratch? Or maybe not starting at all. Maybe doing something else entirely. The Peace Corps, for example. Or moving out to Seattle the way I'd always meant to during my grunge phase.

"Alexandra," I admonished myself suddenly. "I believe you're terrified."

The bindery was located around the back of the library. Inside, strange little men in aprons moved gracefully between long tables piled high with all sorts of manuscripts. Next to all the pounds and pounds of paper, my puny sixty-page dissertation just looked a little sad. Like the geeky kid picked last for gym class games. I handed the man my blood, sweat, and tears—and watched him toss it carelessly on a different table. So much for the sort of divine respect I had accorded the thing myself. The man told me, in a forbiddingly thick accent I mostly had to guess at, to pick the thing up after ten the following morning.

Almost entirely finished.

• • •

"This is what happened," Robin said, her voice scratchy with joy and excitement. "We were walking back from dinner, and he said he always wanted to check out those fountains by the Met, you know?"

"Oh my God—" I breathed.

"And so we sat on the steps of the Metropolitan Museum of Art and he said—" She stopped to let out a little excited laugh. "He said if he could, he would give me the city and all the lights and everything in all the museums, but really all he had to give me was his love, for a lifetime, for as long as we both lived."

"He really said that?"

"He really did," Robin said. "And then he said, 'Oh, and I'd like to give you this,' and he whipped out this box. Which I knew was a ring, and I freaked. And I couldn't speak. And he said he loved me and he wanted to marry me and have my babies. So would I marry him."

"And you said yes. Did you actually *say* yes?"

"First I screamed," Robin said. "Then I cried. And much later, like hours later, we both remembered that I hadn't actually said yes. So then I did."

"Wow," I breathed. "You're *engaged*. Do you feel different? Is it like a state of being?"

"It feels right," Robin said simply. Then she laughed. "It feels *great*."

"Okay," I said, settling back against my wall. "Describe the ring. In minute and exhaustive detail, so I can visualize it on my finger."

• • •

"Hi," I said. "You are speaking to someone who just completed a master's dissertation."

"Whoopee," Michael said. "Do I have to be more excited now than I was three hours ago when you first told me?"

"No, but I just kind of enjoy saying that."

"When are you handing it in?" he asked.

"Tomorrow."

"Are you scared?"

"Scared to hand it in?" I laughed. "I can't wait. I've been waiting for this moment since I arrived in this country. I never thought I could write the damn thing, much less finish it. Much less actually hand it in. Can you believe that I actually did this? My ultimate grade is totally irrelevant. The major thing is that I *did* this. I picked up and moved here and knew no one and had this whole year and really *did* this."

"You're terrified," Michael said in a flat tone.

"Well," I said. "It's a big thing. And what am I going to do next?"

"Whatever you want," Michael said at once. "That's the point, right? You can do whatever you want."

"Yeah," I said. "I guess I can."

I lay in the cradle of my little bed and let the afternoon flow over and around me. I felt adrift. Not in a bad way. I let my mind drift too. I thought of nothing and of everything. I thought about the tumult of Manhattan, the noise and the dirt and the effort it took to live there.

I remembered the difficulty, the disconnection. The turning off, the tuning out, to avoid the reality of so many lives and histories thickening the air like heat. It was impossible to do more than wade through it all—a sort of dog paddle through humanity, keeping your head back and your hair dry. Thinking, *Maybe no one is really happy here*. Or thinking nothing at all.

I thought, *You think too much*.

I thought about nights under the stars or in the rain. I thought of my beloved friends at home, and my new ones here. The ones I'd made it through the madness with. I thought that even though it seemed chaotic and all over the place, it had been a good year. I was changing the way I thought about my father. Everyone around me was growing up. Robin was a fiancée. I was soon to be possessed of an MA. Adulthood was right here. It was happening. Even to me.

I thought, *Being here has been a really good thing, after all. A necessary thing*.

Here it was always quiet. Here there was always space for thought. Maybe too much space, and we filled it up with drink and intrigue. Here we had the wind and the rain to take the place of New York's millions. Here we lay each in our single beds and dreamed of other things.

I thought about Suzanne, and how silly all of that had been, and how easy it was to focus on someone else's madness. I thought about Sean, and how choosing to obsess about him had been such a convenient place to put things I didn't really want to deal with, like all those messy emotions. Emotions scared me. I was better with words.

And then, finally, I thought about Toby. I realized that I had been trying not to think about him at all, for about a year now, and I thought about that. I thought about the way his eyes crinkled up when he laughed and the way he sometimes looked at me. I thought about the way he lounged and the way he walked. I thought about the first time he kissed me and that look he sometimes got that always reminded me of it. I thought about the night we slept together and then, a little breathlessly, the night we *slept together*. I thought about what a stubborn, irritating, full-of-himself—

And then it hit me.

Like a speeding train to the side of the head.

"Oh my God," I breathed.

The courtyard had never seemed so vast.

One of Toby's housemates let me into the house, and I climbed the stairs to his room slowly. I knocked on his door.

I heard him call a slightly annoyed "Come in," and when I did, he was wearing his glasses and looking pretty rough. That hair of his in little dirty-blond spikes and stubble along his jaw. He swiveled around in his desk chair and fixed me with a frigid glare, made more effective with the glasses.

He'd never looked better to me.

"Hey," I said.

"I can't imagine what you want," he said in that arctic voice.

"I don't actually know what I want," I said, sitting down on the end of his bed.

"That," Toby snarled, "has been blindingly obvious for some time."

Seventeen

I really don't like fighting with you," I said. I slumped with my back against the wall and settled my gaze on him. I ventured a smile, which he ignored. "So go on then. Get it out, whatever it is, and let's get it over with."

His eyes narrowed. "You think you can just swan in here and everything will be fine?"

"I don't actually understand what you're so worked up about." I shrugged dismissively. "So you caught me being a complete psycho. It wasn't your window. No bunnies were boiled in your kitchen. Why should you care?"

"That isn't the issue," Toby snapped. "As if I care about your schoolgirl's crush on Sean Douglas."

"Oh, I can see how much you don't care," I murmured.

He yanked his glasses from his face and winged them across the desk. They bounced off the wall, but somehow didn't break. The whole thing was violent enough to wipe the smirk off of my face.

"I just think you should think about how your behavior might be perceived," he said angrily.

"So you know I have a crush on Sean Douglas and that I resort to acting like a freak." I shrugged. "Is that really news? Let's talk about your behavior. You told Suzanne that we slept together, and then, after I told you how much that upset me—"

"After you thumped me!"

"—you went and had yet another discussion with her. Why? What game are you playing, Toby?"

"I told her to leave you alone," he said. "Her issue is with me, and I asked her to confine her bile to me. If you like, I'll be happy to nip round and tell her she can let loose on you."

"She's already loose on me," I said. "Did you really think she'd back off just because you asked her to? She's not entirely sane, Toby."

He stared at me for a moment. "Fair enough," he said at length. "I just . . ." He sighed suddenly, and shook his head. "I can't figure you out, Alex."

"You don't have to figure me out," I said lightly. "But why are you so furious with me? I didn't actually do anything to you."

"No," he said. He stood and shoved his hands into his pockets. "It's more what you don't do. You're the only girl I know who I can talk to. And who I also fancy. Usually it's one or the other." He glared at me. "And you don't give a toss, do you?"

"Well—"

"After that first night with Suzanne," he said in a low voice, cutting me off, "she clung and she demanded . . . proclamations. Which I'm not unused to, actually."

I rolled my eyes. "You big stud."

"That's not the point," he snapped. "The point is that you are the anti-Suzanne."

"I certainly hope so," I snorted. I could see his frown. "Toby, come on," I said. "What is this? Would you be happier if I'd clung to your trouser leg wailing, 'Please don't leave me'?"

"No," he said, disgruntled. Which meant: maybe.

"Then what?" I searched his face. "You think we should be together?"

He held my gaze, his eyes dark and unreadable.

"What if I did?"

I smiled. "Then I'd politely decline," I said. "And I think you know why."

"Enlighten me," he said stiffly. He had a strangely vulnerable look about his face. I felt a rush of tenderness.

"You don't want a girlfriend," I told him. "And you know it. And even if you did, I don't want you as a boyfriend. At least not now. Maybe when you're about thirty-five."

He looked away briefly, then returned his gaze to mine.

"Thirty-five?" he repeated, but I could see laughter creeping into his eyes. "You think eleven years will sort me out?"

"I think you won't even start being sorted until you're at least thirty," I said, giving him a look. "And that might be overly optimistic as it is."

I got up and hoisted myself up onto his high windowsill.

"Don't smoke in here," he said immediately, but without any heat.

"You'll survive," I retorted, and lit a cigarette. He let out a long-suffering sigh.

"You know I'm right," I said, still in a light tone. "You told me yourself, repeatedly. You treat women like shit. Here I am your *friend* and you sold me out to Suzanne. And not to make her feel better, but to make her feel worse. You can't be trusted, you have the morals of an alley cat, and you're proud of it. You're a nightmare."

"Like you're not a nightmare yourself," he said, but his grin was back. I was so pleased to see it I grinned myself.

"I'm great," I told him.

"You're a complete nightmare," he contradicted me.

"You're probably right," I said. "My life seems to be a little bit complicated."

He came over and leaned a hip against the windowsill, so I was looking directly down into his face. Those marvelous dark eyes and his grin, the one that was just for me.

"You make your life complicated," he said gently. "You enjoy it."

"Probably," I agreed. "Maybe I should stop drinking."

"We should all stop drinking," Toby said, and smiled. "But not in the middle of writing a dissertation. That could be dangerous."

I looked down at my cigarette. "And I should definitely quit smoking," I said. "But I'm not really mentally or emotionally prepared to take on that project yet." I looked at him. "We're okay?"

"That depends on your definition," he said. He reached over and pulled on the end of my ponytail. "We're quite a pair, Brennan," he said, his grin beginning again in the corners of his mouth. "You'd do well to cling to my trouser leg, because I've a suspicion we match."

"You should be so lucky as to be my match," I told him, but I was teasing and his eyes were warm. "And there will be no trouser leg clinging."

"We can argue about it later, as I think you'll eat those words." He stretched, and then flashed me a cheeky grin. "A man has other, more pressing needs."

"Did you really say that?" I asked, rolling my eyes. I finished my cigarette and flicked it out into the courtyard, then slid down from the windowsill and faced him.

"And what if you start a fire?" Toby demanded. "Did you ever think of that?"

"What makes you think I care if Fairfax Court burns to the ground?" I asked.

I was wearing flat shoes, which meant I had to angle my head back to look him in the eye. Suddenly, there was something in Toby's dark gaze that made my stomach perform a backflip or two. This, I could read.

And I thought, *Why not?*

And then: *What am I waiting for?*

"So while we wait for me to reach thirty-five," Toby said slowly, smiling, "I think it would be best if you monitored my progress closely."

I tilted my head and looked at him. He slid his fingers into mine and tugged me closer.

"Very closely," he murmured.

"I think that's an excellent plan," I said. I smiled. "But I don't want you getting too . . . *clingy*. And there won't be any *proclamations*, either. Think you can handle that?"

"Think you can?" Toby countered, grinning.

But he didn't give me a chance to answer.

In the end, I walked very slowly from the bindery to the English department office. I held my three bound dissertation copies tight to my chest and looked neither left nor right. Once at the office, I signed my name on the appropriate sheet and slid the copies to the secretary. She smiled. I may or may not have returned the smile. I turned and walked back out.

And that was it. I was finished.

I wandered, dazed, down the stairs.

"Hail, Brennan! Well met!"

I looked up, saw Jason's impish grin, and smiled.

"I did it," I said.

"I saw you ascend the final steps," he told me. He sketched a bow. "A thousand congratulations, Brennan, MA."

"And you," I said, laughing.

"And now, the world! Life!" Jason exclaimed. "The air is sweeter with the scent of our success!"

We walked out into the college's courtyard, where I'd once seen Sean storm by in all of his grandeur. There was sun up there somewhere, trying gamely to break through the clouds. We both tipped our heads back and got facefuls of the gray.

"You both look complete prats," Toby drawled.

He was coming toward us from the opposite direction.

"Excellent!" Jason cried. "The merry band reunited! To the pub!" He paused. "Although I'll have to meet you there, as I have a last meeting with His Highness Sean Douglas, King of the Unintelligible. I want you both with pints in your hands. I'll be there in twenty minutes." He charged away.

"Are you finished? All handed in and signed away?" Toby asked. I nodded. "Your mad housemate accosted me on the way here."

"Which one?" I asked.

His eyes crinkled in the corners. "Cristina," he said. "She's headed down to the pub herself."

"We're finished, Toby," I said. "Can you believe it?"

We looked at each other, and then around at the courtyard.

"Too bad the college is so appallingly ugly," Toby said. "It spoils the moment."

We fell into step together, headed in the direction of the pub. I thought about all the different things I'd done, or could do. I thought, *I'm already on this path, which is half the battle*. And it wasn't such a bad path, either.

"Well?" Toby asked as we drew near the pub.

"Well what?"

"Have you decided?" He rolled his eyes when I stared at him. "What next? Are you going back to America? Don't we have to move out of university accommodation soon? Don't you have to make up your mind?"

"Don't be such a drama queen," I said, grinning. "I'm

staying here. Cristina and I are going to rent a place. If you're very lucky and on good behavior, we might invite you round." And as I said the words, something clicked inside me, as if in agreement. *Why not?* And again: *What am I waiting for?*

"Really," he said, looking at me with his dark eyes gleaming.

"Really," I said.

"I have to tell you, Brennan," Toby said with a smile, "I'm not entirely certain the country can stand it."

"I'll look forward to hearing you whinge about it at my deportation hearing," I told him.

"Brennan." Toby heaved a long-suffering sigh, but he was grinning. "Just shut up and kiss me."

"Are you sure this is edible?" I asked, poking the food in front of me with a fork. Melanie snickered. Cristina fixed me with a glare.

"It is not only edible, you had better start eating it," she snapped. Then grinned. "This way we will all get sick if I am wrong. As a shared experience."

"I think it's wonderful," Melanie said loyally, forking in a big bite. "Alex is just jealous as all she ever cooks is pasta."

"Hey," I said. "I'm the pasta *queen*."

"You are the drama queen," Cristina retorted. "Don't confuse the two."

"My mother sent us Nutter Butters," I told Melanie in an exaggerated whisper. "So at least we have dessert."

We had lit all the candles and were having a last supper. In the morning, the ultraefficient Melanie, having handed in her dissertation early two weeks ago, would take off for the big city. There was a flat ready and waiting in London, and she already had a job sorted.

"You two must visit," she said, over Cristina's rather extended rant on the subject of American snack foods.

"You have to visit us in Casa Fun," I said. "No shared kitchen, no Fairfax Court . . ."

"Heaven!" Cristina declared, recovering herself.

I took a bite of Cristina's attempt at a paella. It was surprisingly tasty, but of course that didn't mean that food poisoning wasn't lurking around ready to strike later. I was cautious.

"Thank God you're staying," Cristina told me. "We will watch the telly and eat like normal human beings all the time."

"And I've seen so little of the country," I said. "I need to stay and explore."

"And really why *not* stay?" Melanie mused. "England has its claws in you now. How could you live without all the rain, the cold, the gray? The English countryside's numerous plagues. Foot-and-mouth, mad cow, and let's not forget the train derailments and race riots. What's not to love?"

"Thanks for that," Cristina said. "I am now even more excited to chain myself to three more years in this place." She sighed. "Why do I think I want a doctorate, anyway?"

"I didn't realize you did," I said dryly. "I thought you were staying in the country in a desperate last bid for David the Physicist— Ouch!"

I rubbed my shin where Cristina's booted foot had connected. Hard.

"Now, now," Melanie said serenely. "None of that please, children. Alex, if you can't play nicely, someone might have to mention the fact that we know *you've* been sleeping with Toby."

I didn't even try to pretend. Which was a good idea as the bright red flush was betraying me anyway.

"Huh," I said. "You know about that? I was meaning to tell you."

But first, I thought, I had been hoarding it to myself.

"We weren't actually sure," Cristina said with great satisfaction. "Now we are sure."

"Whatever," I said. I grinned at them. "It's all very casual."

"Cristina," Melanie said, "isn't Toby staying on at university to do a doctorate?"

"I believe he is, Melanie," Cristina replied. They wore matching smirks.

Any retort I might have made—and I might not have made any—was cut off by the kitchen door slamming open. George appeared, with a thunderous look across his Richie Cunningham face.

We stared at him. He stared at us, and then arranged his face into something more stoic. Which was pretty strange to watch, as "stoic" on George required some interpretation.

The outside door slammed shut, and we all swiveled around to stare out the window. Where, sure enough, the figure of the Vulture strode by. She stopped, wheeled around, and stormed back. Even though I watched her wind up to do it, I still jumped a little bit when she pounded a fist into the window.

"Damn you, George!" she shouted.

This was like a tennis match—we all turned back to George.

"I've made my decision," George said, in ringing tones.

A look back toward the Vulture showed her face screwed up in what I chose to interpret as despair, though it was mostly just frightening.

"You'll regret it! You will regret losing *me*!" she promised him. And then she turned on her heel and stomped off into the night.

We looked back to George. His chin was trembling, but his head was held high.

"I won't regret it," he announced. "After all this time, I think the spell is broken. I just can't trust her. I can't allow myself to sink into the oblivion of her body—"

"*Okay!*" I interrupted before I had to vomit. "And just for the record, it took you long enough to decide that the sinking into oblivion wasn't the way to go. We share a wall, you know."

Cristina thrust the bottle of wine at him, forestalling any response he might have made.

"Please," she said. Urgently. "Drink."

George let his eyes sweep across the three of us. Our overly full wineglasses and our ashtrays. The pot of Cristina's paella and our plates filled with bright yellow rice. He glared at me and then at each of the others in turn.

"My head is finally clear," he said, with great drama.

"You can see clearly now the rain is gone?" I offered, trying to be helpful. Well, not really. Melanie and Cristina gave me a quelling glare in tandem, and I lit a cigarette and tried to look quietly attentive.

"I don't know what I've been trying to do," George said.

"Oh God," I said under my breath. "Here comes the philosophy." Okay, maybe not as much under my breath as over it.

"*But,*" George said, glaring at me again, "it's obvious that a clear head leads nowhere good." He offered a slight smile. It made his urchin-meets-cowboy outfit almost cute. "I'll get a glass."

We sat around the table in the pub and stared at one another.

"I can't believe Melanie is gone," Cristina said mournfully. "The year is ended truly now."

"And oh what a year it's been," I said ruefully.

"It's been a perfectly good year," Toby said. He was in his usual position in the corner, with his head propped up against the wall. But his legs touched mine beneath the table.

"Agreed," said Jason. "And what is a year save an arbitrary collection of moments?"

"There were moments indeed," Cristina said.

She reached over and poked George in the stomach. Then again, hard. He propped open an eye and regarded her blearily through the effects of ten pints.

"What?" he asked.

"What was your best moment all year?" Cristina demanded.

"Ugh," I said. "I actually heard some of his best moments in the making, Cristina. I'm not sure anyone needs a replay. My poor ears have hardly had the chance to recover as it is."

"My best moment was the moment I laid eyes upon my Fiona," George announced, unsurprisingly, and returned to his unconscious state.

"It was not my best moment," Cristina said, "but a memorable moment was when this one"—she nodded at George's slumped form—"made that ridiculous statement in the kitchen. You know the one, Alex."

"Oh yeah," I said, laughing. "'I only go out drinking when I want to pick up women.'" I gazed over at George. "How the mighty babe magnets have fallen."

"That was the first time Melanie, Alex, and I had a meeting of the minds," Cristina said. "Wasn't it?"

"It was," I agreed.

We all raised our glasses and toasted Melanie and her departure. We'd helped her pack up her car and had waved her off. Cristina and I hadn't known what to do when she'd gone. We'd stood there in the car park for far too long afterward, until the rain picked up and we'd had to run indoors.

"What about you?" I asked Toby.

"The year's not over yet," he said with a lazy grin. "I'd hate to be premature."

"Alex would also hate it," Cristina said under her

breath and snorted into her pint. Toby didn't hear her, as he was too busy channeling the music from the jukebox. I glared at Cristina.

"Hey," I said, "isn't that the Physicist over there?"

"Very funny," Cristina said. But she looked. Then she smiled at me. "I couldn't resist."

"You can't let those science types confuse you with their hypothesis this and theory that," Jason advised. "He's not worthy of you."

"Hang on," Toby said. "Cristina, is that dodgy bloke with the dark hair still following you around? You need to sort him right out."

Cristina beamed. "I love you both," she told them. She looked at me. "Did you hear that? Is David following *me*?" She sighed happily. "This is now my favorite moment of the year."

Later, we were staggering back across the fields, Toby trying to keep George vertical. Jason had abandoned the cause and staggered off to locate a taxi.

"I'm tempted to leave him at the side of the road," Toby bit out, puffing with the effort and the laughter. He leered at me. "You could lend us a hand, Brennan, if you're not too busy doing fuck-all."

I stuck my tongue out at him and tilted my head back to look at the stars.

"Hello!" Cristina shouted at the night sky. She had had too many tequila shots and was doing a little performance art along the fields. "Hello, England! We have survived a year here!"

I shoved my hands into my pockets and watched

them—the fools and the drunks that God was supposed to watch over with special interest, the ones I knew so well in so many surprising ways.

I was one of them, I thought, and grinned.

www.bohmphoto.com

About the Author

MEGAN CRANE spent the last five years at university in England, working on her master's and PhD in literature. She has since followed the sun to California and now lives in Los Angeles. You can find out more about her at www.megancrane.com.